George W. Darby

Incidents and Adventures in Rebeldom

Libby, Belle-Isle, Salisbury / by Geo. W. Darby

George W. Darby

Incidents and Adventures in Rebeldom
Libby, Belle-Isle, Salisbury / by Geo. W. Darby

ISBN/EAN: 9783337409715

Printed in Europe, USA, Canada, Australia, Japan

Cover: Foto ©Andreas Hilbeck / pixelio.de

More available books at **www.hansebooks.com**

INCIDENTS AND ADVENTURES

... IN ...

REBELDOM

LIBBY, BELLE-ISLE, SALISBURY.

By GEO. W. DARBY.

DRAWINGS BY J. W. RAWSTHORNE.

PRESS OF RAWSTHORNE ENGRAVING & PRINTING COMPANY,

PITTSBURG, PA., 1899.

DEDICATION.

To all soldiers who defended the Union from "sixty-one" to "sixty-five" when "The bloody hand of Treason sought its overthrow." To the memory of the noble dead on many bloody fields and to those heroic martyrs who "Suffered death before dishonor" in the prison hells of the South, this work is respectfully inscribed by the author.

"THE SPECTER OF THE REBEL PRISON HELL."

PREFACE.

As the events herein narrated are true and veracious facts no apology or excuse is necessary for their publication. Let the work be judged according to its merits or demerits. I believe that the criticism on McClelland's conduct is fully justified by the evidence produced. Enthusiastic and unreasoning hero worshippers of whom I was one of the most radical had erected Gen. George B. McClelland upon a high pedestal of fame, loyalty and patriotism and were enthusiastically paying devotion to the shrine they had so unthinkingly erected. And yet they were unknowingly paying homage to the most secret, wily and specious traitor that this century has produced. He laid siege to Yorktown when its ramparts were defended by wooden guns manned by a corporal's guard of rebels. He camped in the swamps of the Chickahominy for three months while twenty thousand of his soldiers died of disease, and never made an effort to take Richmond. During all this time he was howling for more men, when he well knew he had plenty of men and that the government had no more men to spare him. The battle of Malvern Hill afterward conclusively demonstrated that there never was a time during the entire campaign when his army could not have defeated the rebel army and taken Richmond. Lee's army being defeated he ordered a retreat on Richmond and McClelland's victorious army was ordered by him to retreat on Harrison's Landing, and thus were the victor and vanquished fleeing from each other at the same time. On Lee being informed of McClelland's retreat he returned and occupied the battle ground. All of McClelland's delays were purposely made by him to avoid striking a death blow at the rebellion before the rebels were fully prepared to successfully resist it. I have no motive or desire to malign the dead but the facts as set forth in this work are made to correct the false praise and flattery so lavishly bestowed upon this miserably incompetent general by historians and hero-worshippers ; to vindicate the bravery and devotion of the noble old Army of the Potomac, and that coming generations may know the actual truth and execrate him as his baseness and treachery so richly merit.   This work has been compiled from the vivid recollections of the events as they occurred during the civil war, and now after the lapse of thirty-four years the memory of them seems as fresh and green as though they had occurred but yesterday.   I appreciate fully this grand era of brotherhood and goodfellowship now so happily arrived at between the two sections of our re-united country and therefore beg indulgence from the reader for any seemingly too vigorous language which may occur within this work, but truth impels me to say that the cruelties perpetrated upon the defenceless prisoners of war fully justify its use.

THE AUTHOR.

CONTENTS.

CHAPTER I.

The Coming Struggle.

There come scenes and incidents into almost every human life, which so electrify the whole being, mental, moral and physical, that the impress of them is never effaced ; and so it happened, on a beautiful spring morning in the month of April, 1861. The hurly-burly of the exciting presidential campaign of 1860—when that wonderful westerner, Abraham Lincoln, had been chosen chief executive—had subsided, and the calm which succeeds the storm had come, and notwithstanding that there was to be heard, now and then, the rumbling of complaint from the southland, which fell upon the ear of the law-abiding, peace-loving citizens of the north, like the diapason of the dying thunders when the summer shower is overpast. But alas ! there was to be a fearful awakening from the supposed security, which it was thought had been secured to the nation in the election by constitutional methods, of a president who, according to usage, should preside over the destinies of the country for the term of four years next succeeding. But the institution of slavery, of which the immortal John Wesley said "it is the sum of all villainies," had so ingrained itself into the web and woof of southern thought and action, that the people of that section had come to regard it as inseparable from their happiness and prosperity. Indeed they professed to believe, and so declared to the world, that they proposed to build a Republic, the chief corner stone of which should be the institution of human slavery, and with that fearful heresy, which had grown with their growth, and strengthened with their strength, fastened upon them, until it had become their nemesis to lure them on to certain destruction.

They trained their guns upon historic Fort Sumter, and when, at high noon of that calm and lovely April day in 1861, the lanier of that cannon was pulled, its brazen throat brayed out the challenge of rebellion, and its reverberations were heard around the civilized world ; and the cause of human freedom everywhere stood breathless with amazement, and although the cheeks of patriots blanched, and trembling seized their frames, it was not the blanching of fear, nor the tremor of cowardice. Oh ! no, it was rather a prescience of the fearful sacrifice which they so clearly saw must be made in blood and treasure, to vindicate before the world the inspired teachings of the Declaration of Independence that all men are inherently possessed of certain inalienable rights, among which are life, liberty and the pursuit of happiness. So we say armed rebellion had thrown down the gauge of battle and thus were we of the north not only put upon our mettle as patriots, but our position was well defined. We contended no longer for an abstract dogma, or capricious whim, but for the salvation of our country, and its beneficent institutions.

As the reverberations of Ruffin's cannon went sounding through the land, waking the country from profound peace to the realities of civil war, (the first shot was fired upon Sumter by Edward Ruffin of Virginia), the whole nation, but yesterday wrapped in the habiliments of a profound peace, now flew to arms and the dread alarms of war waked the echoes on hill and dale, and from the rock-ribbed coast of New England, to the golden horn of the Pacific, preparation for the on-coming struggle was the all-absorbing order of the day. Old men upon whom advancing age had laid the heavy tribute of decrepitude, forgot their years and rushed to arms, and the youth of the land, in the first blush of young manhood, flocked to the rendezvous, and offered themselves willing sacrifices upon their country's altar, to serve and to die if need be in order that armed rebellion should be crushed out and Old Glory made again to shake her starry folds in every breeze that springs from mountain top or billows crest over every foot of soil, made sacred by the blood of our fathers, in freedom's cause.

With patriotic motives burning high within me, I with

many thousands of my country's sons, donned the blue of a soldier boy with a faint conception of the hardship, danger and exposure we were to endure, but with a rugged and unfaltering determination to sustain our beloved country in its struggle with the cohorts of rebellion to the bitter end. I was nineteen years old, strong and vigorous, and my comrades were all young and hearty men, and with unquenchable patriotism those who survived the first three years of service with few exceptions re-enlisted for another three year term. Part of the time we were attached to the First Corps under McDowell, but the most of our service was in the Fifth Corps of the Army of the Potomac of which the Pennsylvania Reserves composed the Third Division.

On April 22d, 1861, the writer enlisted in Captain S. D. Oliphant's company which was organized at Uniontown, Pa., for the three months' service. On our arrival at Pittsburgh, Pa., we found the quota for the three months' men already filled, so we at once re-enlisted for three years, or during the war. I pause here to say that the company (Oliphant's) was known as the Fayette Guards, and in proof of the kind of material of which it was composed will add a list of the names of the men who were promoted from it into the three years' organization by which we were absorbed :

S. D. Oliphant promoted to lieutenant colonel.

T. B. Gardner promoted to major.

S. B. Ramsey promoted to first lieutenant.

H. H. Patterson promoted to second lieutenant and adjutant.

W. Searight promoted to captain.

H. C. Dawson promoted to captain.

H. H. Macquilton promoted to second lieutenant.

J. W. Sturgis promoted to second lieutenant.

We were temporarily quartered on board the river steamer Marengo, which lay at the foot of Market street, and were drilled in a public hall at the corner of Market and Water streets. We were boarded at the Girard House, on Smithfield street. This hotel was at the time kept by a gen-

tleman by the name of Fell. We were afterwards removed
to Camp Wilkins. (the old fair grounds), which we occupied
for some length of time, in common with Colonel McLain's
Erie Regiment. This Erie Regiment had been uniformed
in suits of gray consisting of jacket and pants, and they soon
became worn and ragged, and all appeals for clothing had
been refused. One genius among them whose pants had
been entirely worn away at the seat, determined to appeal to
the public which he did in the following original manner. It
was the custom for crowds of visitors to come to camp on
Sunday and the Erie man having painted the words "The last
resort" in big black letters on a large shingle, attached a cord
to it and hanging it over the seat of his pants, went parading
around camp among the visitors. This novel walking adver-
tisement of their necessities soon brought the desired clothing, and I think they were mustered as the Eighty-Third
P. V.

Here we received our assignment as Company G,
Eighth P. R. V. C., Colonel Geo. S. Hayes commanding.
Soon after we were sent to Camp Wright which was located
on the Allegheny River above Pittsburgh.

After a short sojourn here we received marching orders ;
accordingly we were marched to Pittsburgh, where, after
passing that most trying ordeal of leavetaking of the loved
ones left behind, we took the cars on Liberty street and
headed for the seat of war. This was on the 21st day of
July, the day of the first battle of Bull Run. The tidings
from the bloody field were flashing northward over the mag-
netic wires, and the news was not of a reassuring character ;
excitement ran high, and any man, or woman, who that day
wore a smile, was looked upon with grave suspicion, and
in order to put a check upon the exuberance of expression
of any sympathizer with the cause of the Confederacy, there
were hempen nooses decorating all the lamp-posts along
Liberty and Penn avenues. But we sped on, and without
incident worthy of note arrived at Harrisburg, Pa., where
we were hastily armed with old Harper's Ferry muskets.

These muskets will be remembered by the old soldiers as the gun that the boys of '61 used to say, "The fellow who stood at the butt end was in more danger than the one who was shot at." We were supplied with a few rounds each of fixed ammunition, in order that we might be ready to fight our way through Baltimore in case we should be attacked as some of the New England troops had been a few days previously, but fortunately no opposition was offered.

We remained for a few days in the outskirts of the city of Baltimore and then moved on to the capital of the nation, and encamped at Meridian Hill, where we were formally transferred from the state to the United States service, for the term of three years or during the war, said transfer being made on the 29th day of July, 1861.

The first fatal shooting accident in the regiment occurred while in camp at Meridian Hill. Our muskets had been loaded with buck and ball in anticipation of an attack from the rebel element while passing through Baltimore, and it became necessary to extract these charges. To do this a ball screw is attached to the end of the ramrod and inserted in the muzzle of the gun, screwed into the bullet and the charge withdrawn by pulling out the ramrod. A man in Company B neglected to remove the cap from the nipple of his gun and in pulling out his ramrod the cock of his piece caught on a small pine tree at the butt of the musket, discharging it. The charge, ramrod and all struck him in the pit of the stomach and passing obliquely through his body came out at the back of his neck. I was standing nearby and ran to his assistance but he was dead when I reached him. Our next move brought us to a place called Tennelly Town where we proceeded to construct a formidable fortification known as Fort Pennsylvania, and some ten miles distant at the great falls of the Potomac, our command was inducted into the mysteries of picket duty.

I had forgotten to mention that the arrival of our command and other troops from Baltimore, at Washington, was highly opportune, as the Secessionists of both these cities had become aggressive and threatening to the safety of the capital ; this danger to Washington was greatly enhanced by the recent defeat of the Union forces at Bull Run. The arrival of this well organized division had the effect of restoring confidence, and assured for the time-being, the safety of the capital. The wisdom and foresight of Governor Curtin and the legislature of the state in organizing and equipping the Pennsylvania Volunteer Reserve Corps, and holding them in readiness for an emergency, was now fully vindicated. After the danger which had menaced the city had subsided our command crossed the Chain Bridge, and built at Camp Pierpont, on the south side of the Potomac River, our winter quarters. It was while we were in camp here that the Battle of Drainsville was fought and won ; this occurred on the 20th of December, 1861, and was the first victory recorded for the Army of the Potomac.

The prisoners captured here were Alabamians and they were the first rebels I had seen in armed rebellion against the authority of the United States. While at Pierpont M. P. Miller of my company became insane from reading yellow back novels of the Claude Duvall species. Commodore Jones, of South Sea Exploring Expedition fame, owned a mansion nearby and Miller having secured a long, rusty old-fashioned navy cutlass there, belted it around him and returning to camp at dress parade, took position in rear of Colonel Hayes and with his rusty blade imitated all the movements of the colonel. Afterwards he took to the woods and running to the Potomac plunged in. He was saved from drowning and removed to the Insane Hospital at Washington, where he died.

Grim-visaged War, horrible in all its aspects, nevertheless finds some mitigation in the character and disposition of those who make up the rank and file of its legions. Every company in all our vast army probably had one or more individuals, who, by their pranks and idiosyncrasies made even the life of the soldier on the march and in the field tolerable, by injecting something of the ludicrous into the most serious and disheartening circumstances. Well, Company D, of the Eighth Reserves, had one of the aforesaid geniuses in the person of one, Bud Gaskell. This man Gaskell numbered among his varied accomplishments a mysterious power over the reptile family, and as a matter of fact he could and did handle snakes with perfect impunity. Bud was a fine specimen of physical manhood, in short he was an active athlete, and hence his practical jokes were usually endured by his victims with more complacency than would otherwise have been the case. While our command lay at Tennelly Town and Pierpont, Bud in some manner secured two snakes of fair dimensions which he carried constantly about his person ; sometimes they were secreted in the sleeves of his blouse, sometimes in his hat, and revolting as it may seem, I have seen him with his pets in his mouth. Colonel Hayes, of the Eighth, was a special victim of Bud's pranks, and although he frequently expiated his fun by a sojourn in the guardhouse, he was insuppressible. The colonel being a man of nervous temperament, naturally hated the sight of a snake, yet Bud would approach him, extending his paw for a shake with a genial "how do' do, Colonel," when down would come one of Bud's snakes into the colonel's hand, then of course it would become necessary for the redoubtable Bud to adjourn for the time being. I once saw this fellow approach the colonel with a snake coiled within his mouth, its head protruding from between his lips, its tongue darting out, and in order to secure the officer's attention, he says "Granny ! let me kiss you." On this occasion the colonel was the first to beat a retreat. There being abundance of timber in the vicinity of our camp, we had constructed cabins of a very comfortable character, from the trunks of these trees. Each one of said cabins was embellished with a huge stick chimney, daubed within and without with mud to render them fire proof, yet it not infrequently happened that the mud dried, and crumbled off, leaving the sticks exposed to the blaze. So one day as the colonel stood talking near his quarters with Captain Connor, he discovered the chimney of his cabin to be on fire. He called to his negro man to bring a bucket of water, and extinguish the flame ; the negro seized a bucket of water and climbed nimbly up the corner of the building, followed closely by the ubiquitous Gaskell, who seemed so very anxious to be of service in the emergency that his motive was not questioned, but alas ! just as the negro dashed the water into the chimney, Gaskell feigned a slip of the foot and falling against the poor darky, sent him, bucket and all, crashing down the chimney into the hot ashes on the hearth below. There was a wild yell from within the cabin, and instantly there sped through the door, covered, wool, face and clothing, with ashes, the negro, who made good time to a creek nearby, into which he plunged, thus saving himself from serious consequences from his burning clothing. Meanwhile Gaskell, to give color of accident to the matter, suffered himself to roll off the roof to the ground, whence he gathered himself up, and with distorted face and limbs, and groanings which would almost move the heart of a stepmother, he limped off to his tent as though the burden of the disaster had fallen upon him. The colonel looked on in amazement and turning suddenly to Captain Connor, he said "Captain where in h——.did you get that —— —— fool."

Gaskell, like many another soldier, was possessed of a weakness for stimulants which sometimes got the better of him. Shortly after the episode with the darky, myself with several others, among whom was Gaskell, were detailed for camp guard duty, and as we were falling into line I observed that Gaskell was counting the files from the head of the column and he finally fell in as No. 23. This number being designated as Headquarter guard, of course brought the redoubtable Gaskell's beat in front of the colonel's tent, and as battalion drill was to be held that day in a field about one mile distant from the camp, our hero no doubt thought he saw an opportunity for a speculation of which he proposed to make use. Accordingly as soon as the troops had proceeded to the drill ground Gaskell entered the tent and confiscated the colonel's whisky bottle, and proceeded at once to convert its contents to his own use. The colonel, on his return to camp, being desirous of a little something to strengthen and stimulate the inner man, proceeded to where he had left his bottle, but he looked in vain for it. He probably mistrusted what had become of it, for, coming out of his tent, he beheld Gaskell staggering up and down his beat, holding his gun to its place on his shoulder with both hands. As is usual on such occasions, there were standing about a large lot of comrades waiting to see the fun. But the colonel, not wishing to have it generally known among the boys that he was given to the use of whisky as a beverage, restrained his wrath for a short time, but it appeared that the longer he watched Gaskell, who was evidently drunk on his whisky, the madder he became, so when he could restrain his ire no longer he shouted out, "Gaskell ! you d——m scoundrel and thief, you stole my catsup." Whereupon Gaskell cocked his eye upon him, with a comical leer as he said, spelling the words and pronouncing them in a drawling tone, "C-a-t-s-u-p, catsup, but it wasn't that ! it was r-o-t-g-u-t, rotgut ;" but that sort of orthography was too much for the colonel, so he roared, "go to your tent, sir ! you wooden-headed thief, you ; I will allow no such scoundrel as you are to stand guard at my tent." So Gaskell staggered off to his quarters singing, "When Johnny comes marching home again," and probably as the colonel did not care to have it bruited abroad that he kept whisky in his quarters, that was the last of that matter, but poor Gaskell never had the chance of standing guard over the colonel's tent again. But woe to the peddlers who frequented the camp when Gaskell was off duty. Many a camp peddler's heels flew up, tripped by him, while their wares were scattered broadcast, to be gathered in by the hungry boys, who were ever ready to profit by Gaskell's tricks.

At Tennelly Town our camp was located on a hill side, and one day a man drove in with a covered wagon, in which he had a barrel of ice cream, which he was vending at ten cents per saucer, and Gaskell was very anxious for some of that cream, but he was short the ten cents, but here again his wits stood him in good stead ; he secured his game by deftly removing a linch-pin from the hinder axle, and giving the horse a cut with a brush, over went the wagon, out tumbled the barrel, and starting to roll down the hill was arrested in its mad career by the ever present Gaskell, who dived into the contents of that barrel clear up to his middle, and came up smiling with his arms folded low across his breast, and a pyramid of ice cream resting upon them,

GASKELL AND THE ICE CREAM.

which towered high above his head, and thus he made for his quarters, eating as he ran, and shedding ice cream at every jump.

Gaskell's favorite trick was to spring astride a horse behind a mounted orderly or citizen, with his snakes up his sleeves, and reaching his hands in front of the rider's face the squirming reptiles under his very nose would so affright him that he would fall from his horse into the dusty road and Gaskell after riding a short distance would slip back over the animal's rump and hanging on to his tail would reach forward his feet and lock them around the hind legs of the horse and bring him to a stop, and then dropping lightly to the ground, scamper off to avoid any unpleasant consequences.

At the Battle of Fredericksburg our command was so nearly annihilated that it was ordered back to Alexandria, Va., to be recruited and re-organized. During this time we did patrol duty in that city. The government had established a contraband camp at that point in which was kept several thousand negroes ; it also happened that Nixson's circus had gone into winter quarters there, and Gaskell, true to his instincts managed to steal a clown's fantastic suit which was decorated with horns, fringes and bells. One evening he dressed himself in this outfit and put in a sudden appearance in the negro camp performing acrobatic feats. The terrified negroes thinking the devil himself had dropped down among them, men, women and children fled precipitately through the street, scattering in every direction. Gaskell, for this trick, was confined for a time in the slave pen. The negroes were employed by the government to perform labor on the fortifications, and many of them were so frightened that they never returned to their work again.

CHAPTER II.

THE COLONEL EXCITED.

I will now relate two incidents which occurred at Tennelly Town and Pierpont showing the excitable nature of Colonel Geo. S. Hayes. Post guard No. 8 was stationed immediately in the rear of the colonel's tent. The guards had been instructed, in case it became necessary, for them to leave their beats during their turn on duty to call the corporal of the guard to take their place during their temporary absence. So late in the night the guard near the colonel's tent raised the cry "Corporal of the guard post No. 8." The cry was repeated by the next guard and so on until it reached No. 1 which was at the headquarters of the guards. The corporal failing to respond, the guard continued repeating the cry. The colonel jumped out of his bunk, and hastily buckling on his sword, rushed up to the guard house, where he found a man soundly sleeping on the ground. Roughly shaking him he demanded if he were the corporal of the guard. "No, sir," quickly came the answer, "I am the sergeant of the guard." "Well then," says the colonel, "where in h—— is the corporal of the guard?" "He's out calling the relief sir," said the sergeant. "Come with me quick," said the colonel, "there is something seriously wrong at post No. 8." So they hurriedly made their way to the guard and the colonel excitedly said to him, "sentry, what is the matter with you? What are you raising all this hullabaloo about?" "Why," said the sentry, "I want a drink!" "Drink! H—— and d——," says the colonel, "are you going to arouse the whole Army of the Potomac whenever you want a drink? Sergeant arrest that man and place him in the guard house. I'll learn you to want a drink while on duty," and the colonel walked off to his tent, while the sentry was marched off to the guardhouse.

Another striking and ludicrous example of the colonel's

excitable nature occurred at Camp Pierpont. The colonel
had the regiment out drilling on a gently sloping hillside
and gave the command to fire by file from right to left.
Now the colonel was mounted on a horse that would not
stand fire and at the first crack of a gun he turned tail and
fled, notwithstanding the strenuous exertions of the colonel
to hold him, but each additional shot lent wings to his flight
and he carried the colonel over the hill and out of sight.
Meanwhile the firing proceeded and finally the head and
shoulders of the colonel could be seen above the brow of the
hill excitedly swinging his sword and yelling, "Cease firing !
Cease firing," accompanied by numerous cuss words to add
emphasis to his orders. But the men were enjoying the situation and could not hear his orders, and whenever they fired
a new volley the head and shoulders of the colonel would
suddenly disappear again. They finally ceased their fire and
allowed the raging colonel to approach, who instantly
ordered the regiment to camp, threatening to buck and gag
the first man that fired off his gun on the way back.

I shall not attempt a discription of the many battles in
which we participated, only in so far as may be necessary to
the explanation of incidents properly coming within the
province of a work of this nature.

On learning that the enemy had evacuated Manassas,
the reserves broke camp at Pierpont on March 10th, 1862,
and marched for that point. This march, owing to the in-
clemency of the weather, was the hardest, most exhausting
and fatiguing that the reserves ever experienced during
their term of service and was caused by the stupid blundering
of some one high in authority.

This senseless and worse than useless march was made
from our camp at Pierpont during one of the most terrific
storms of sleet and rain which it was ever my misfortune to
encounter, and to add to the aggravation of the situation,
when we had almost reached Manassas, our objective point,
here came the order to countermarch on Alexandria, and on
reaching that point during a heavy snow fall we were loaded

upon platform cars, and sent back to Bull Run. This experience was simply awful ; it was a regular Burnside stick-in-the-mud with additional horrors. The roads throughout this section of the country had been transformed into rivers of mud, axle deep, and rain and sleet continued in ceaseless down-pour night and day. Men, completely exhausted, fell out of rank, and dropping down in the fence corners, died of fatigue and exhaustion. I remember one night while on our return march we halted in a piece of woodland, completely fagged out, the down-pour continuing ; the ground was reeking with water, so that lying down was impractical, so setting to work we felled a hickory tree and building a fire against it, I sat down before it with my cap drawn over my eyes, and immediately fell asleep. On awakening I found the leathern frontis entirely burned from my cap. On resuming the march, it being impossible to follow the roads on account of the depth of the mud, we were obliged to take to the fields and woods, and as the paths formed by the advance became impassable, those in the rear would be obliged to start a new one and thus we struggled on.

Upon reaching Alexandria we were started back to the place whence we came. Now if there was ever an intelligible reason assigned for these blundering, quixotic movements, which cost the Republic vast sums of money, and the sacrifice of many precious lives, I have never heard of it. On reaching Bull Run and finding that the railroad bridge had been destroyed, a foot-way was constructed across the stream and we continued our march to Manassas. At that point several of my comrades and myself were fortunate enough to secure a hut which the rebels had occupied and failed to destroy when they left. We gathered a lot of wood and soon had a fire started within, which dried out the shanty and enabled us to spend a night in comfort, secure against the raging of the elements.

The next morning upon going to the site of the railroad station I saw several old locomotives which the rebels had left for the scrap pile, all of which were very badly damaged ; amongst them was one named "Farquier," that being the name of the county in which Manassas is located. We moved back a short distance from the railroad and went into temporary camp. In the meantime, the elements seemed to have spent their fury and the weather had become warm and pleasant. During our stay here some of our soldier boys entered a car, which lay at the station freighted with hospital stores, and proceeded to confiscate some of said goods, but unfortunately for them among the things which they stole was some wine, and of course they proceeded to fill up on this product of the vine, but, alas ! it proved to be wine of antimony, and the result was that they paid the penalty of their escapade with their lives.

After a brief stay at Manassas, we marched away for Catlet Station, taking the railroad bed ; and as the weather was now very hot, walking on the cross ties was exceedingly tiresome and the men suffered almost as greatly from the heat on this march as they had from cold on the march of a few days previous, and it was somewhat amusing to see them shed their overcoats and blankets and on coming up with an engine which a repair gang had standing near where they were repairing the track, the boys threw blankets and overcoats upon it, until it was so completely covered up that one could scarcely tell what it was. On reaching Catlet Station, we left the railroad track and taking the county road marched for Fredericksburg, but upon reaching Falmouth went into camp in a piece of pine woods in the rear of that place. The market at Falmouth was well supplied with fish of the herring variety, also with peanuts galore. This latter commodity could be purchased at five cents per peck, but as they were raw we were obliged to do the roasting act ourselves. Occasionally some of the boys who had a little remaining money would go to Falmouth and applying at a private house would secure an extra meal of herring and bacon. It had become customary among the boys in speaking of pork and crackers, to call it hard tack and sow-belly, and it had been so long thus designated that these useful articles of army diet were scarcely known by any other name. One day Sergeant Stewart, of Company G, went to Falmouth and induced a lady of the place to get him up a dinner of herring and bacon, so sitting down to the table he proceeded to dispatch his meal, which seemed to fit his appetite to a charm, when out of compliment to his hostess' skill as a cook he thoughtlessly remarked, "Madam, this is the best sow-belly I ever tackled." The lady, greatly surprised, said "What did you say, sir ?" Stewart, greatly embarrassed and blushing, said, "Oh ! Ah ! Excuse me, I mean to say really I think this the best bacon I have ever tasted," and while that was the best he could do under the circumstances, he did not regain his wonted composure until he was well out of that house.

The bridges had all been destroyed by the rebels, but the Yankees constructed a temporary one of canal boats until they could rebuild the railroad bridge, after which we crossed over and took possession of Fredericksburg, going into camp in the rear of the city on the heights. While we were here in camp the arsenal at Fredericksburg was accidentally blown up, supposedly by the dropping of a shell from the hand of a guard, and strange to say he was the only person killed by the explosion. There were a large number of army muskets stored in the building, which were hurled high in the air, and on coming down bayonets first, were to be seen sticking upright in the roofs of the houses. In a neglected cemetery near our camp lie the mortal remains of the mother of the first president of the United States of America, and as I stood by the neglected grave of the mother of America's great chieftain, and saw the marble shaft which had evidently been designed to perpetuate her illustrious name, lying prone upon the ground, pitted by bullet marks from rebel guns, I could but think what a sad commentary upon human greatness as exemplified in this rebel respect for the mother of the Father of the Country. While in camp at Falmouth we were dispatched on an expedition to the Eagle

Gold mines to block the United States ford over the Rappahannock River to prevent the crossing of rebel cavalry.

At this place G Company of the Eighth Regiment lost its first man killed by the enemy ; his name was Jared Beach. He was shot and instantly killed by a rebel farmer. This cowardly murder of Beach was similar to that of the noble Elsworth at Alexandria, Va., but unfortunately this murder was not avenged, as the murderer made good his escape. Beach was knocking at the door when the rebel who had seen him approach the house, leveled his gun, and firing through the door, the shot took effect in Beach's stomach and was fatal. This murderer's family should have been conducted to the confederate lines, and his house and farm buildings burned to the ground. But our officers at this time strove to avoid anything that might irritate our misguided southern brethren whom they hoped to coax back into the Union by soft words and gentle deeds, which as the sequel shows, was a mistaken policy, but it does seem strange how long it took our authorities to find out and realize the fact that they were dealing with desperate traitors in rebellion, who would be satisfied with no compromise, and nothing short of the complete success of their scheme of secession, and a total separation from the sisterhood of states. Virginia was at this time infested, and in fact all during the war, by a horde of natives, who were robbers and murderers by night, but who posed by day as quiet and inoffensive farmers. At night they would rendezvous at a convenient point, and under Mosby or some other guerrilla leader, start out on murdering and plundering expeditions. These wanton villians ought all to have been punished with death, and their property destroyed from the outset as fast as it fell into our hands.

While we were lying in the vicinity of Fredericksburg, Va., our camp was thronged by contrabands of both sexes, and many laughable incidents occurred, a few of which I will narrate. One day a gray-headed, venerable-appearing old darky came into camp accompanied by two of his daughters, strapping wenches they were too ; these he wished to hire

out to the soldiers to do housework. After joking the old
chap for a while some soldier procured a cracker box and
mounting the old negro upon it, soon had him preaching
for dear life to a very mixed congregation ; but his devotion
was to be severely tried for when with closed eyes he knelt
in prayer, some one would throw a penny on the box and instantly his eyes would fly open and he would make a frantic
grab for the coin, before some other darky laid hold upon it.
The next minute the soldiers would have the old preacher
patting the juba and singing while the other darkies danced.
They would swing the wenches in a bewildering manner,
kicking up the dust, in singular contrast with the late devotional exercises. They accompanied their dance with hand
clapping, and a monotonous song as follows :

De gals an' de boys went a huckleberry huntin'
           Fo' sho', fo' sho'.
An' out dar in de woods da seed suffin',
           Jes' so, jes' so.
I'se gwine home to tell my mammy.
           Fo' sho', fo' sho'.
O Lord, mammy I seed sum' fin,
           Jes' so, jes' so.
Doan' yo' see dem niggers all a comin',
           Fo' sho', fo' sho'.
Dey gwine out fo' a possum huntin'.
           Jes' so, jes' so.
Dey kotched a possum but he don got away.
           Fo' sho', fo' sho'.
Niggers doan' eat no possum to-day.
           Jes' so, jes' so.

And with much more of the same kind until the dancers
were obliged to desist from sheer exhaustion. Among our
darkies was one who was continually laughing. He would
laugh at anything, and everything ; if you spoke to him he
laughed, if you cursed him, he laughed, as if the joke were
on you. On one occasion Comrade Jerry Jones picked up
an empty gun and pointing it at him said, "Now laugh, you
black rascal, and laugh hearty, or I will blow your brains out."
The darky, though badly frightened and dodging from side

to side to keep out of range of the threatening gun, his peals
of laughter rang out, until they woke the echoes, and one
would have thought his very soul convulsed with the mer-
riest emotions. But alas for poor Jerry ! He was wounded
badly in the hip at the Battle of Gaines' Mill, and in consequence honorably discharged from the service, but after remaining at home and measurably recovering from the effects
of his wound, he was seized with a longing to be with his
comrades in the field. Accordingly he re-enlisted and joined
his old company and served through that most arduous campaign from Culpepper to Petersburg, and while so many of
the best and most hardy of our soldiery succumbed to the
hardships of this campaign, Jerry passed through unscathed
only to be taken prisoner at the Yellow Tavern and sent a
prisoner to Saulisbury to suffer death by slow starvation in
that prison hell. "Peace to your ashes, brave, genial, generous Jerry. A fellow of infinite jest, of most excellent fancy."

On leaving Fredericksburg for the Peninsula we were
marched to a point on the Rappahannock, some eight miles
below the city, to a landing where a vessel awaited us.

We were accompanied by a fine brass band, in which
the regiment took great pride. Upon boarding the ship,
the band struck up a lively air, soon the banks of the river
swarmed with darkies who could not resist the inspiriting
strains, and a lively dance among them was the natural result. The young negroes up to the age of sixteen or seven-
teen, of both sexes, were gowned in a single garment of tow
cloth, constructed in the form of an ordinary night shirt and
I say to you that there were more shirt skirts fluttering in
the wind that day than on the clothes line of a thrifty house-
wife, after a two weeks' washing. It was a most ludicrous
scene and the boys cheered them on to redoubled exertion
until the boat sailed away.

Among the contrabands was a boy, of about fifteen
years of age, whom my messmates concluded would answer
our purpose as a cook. Accordingly he was selected and installed as cook and general utility man. His name was Rich-

mond Crutchfield and he proved to be quite an original and a highly imitative darky. We dubbed him Coon. He said he was a " 'Ligious nigger," but his " 'ligion" soon evaporated under camp influences as was witnessed by his profanity, for he soon learned to swear like a marine, and what was worse he seemed to think that cumulative profanity would be the most useful to him, so as fast as he acquired an oath he just hitched it onto one which he was already master of and then he simply swore them all off in a string.

One day, as a flock of turkey-buzzards happened to be

SQUAWK.

flying over our camp, I said, "Coon did ever you shoot a buzzard ?" 'No sar," says he, "I nebber did, but one of dem 'fernal tings spewed on me onct, sho !" "Why, how did that happen ?" I asked. "Well, I'll des tell you," said Coon. "One of ole masser Crutchfield's mules, he dun gone an died. An he war layin' in de fiel' an I go dar to fotch de cows, and dar two ole buzzards was des a pickin' away at dat ole mule's haid, an' I frowed a stone at em an' da flewed up des plum ober mi haid, an' one ob dem he jes fotch a squawk, an' he spewed a whole hat full spat down on mi haid, dats wat he did honey." "Why didn't you shoot him ?" asked one of the boys, as soon as he could get his breath for laughing at Coon's comic account of the transaction ; "Shoot him," says Coon, with a string of oaths that would have stopped a pirate ship, in mid ocean, "Shoot him ! how I gwine to shoot him when I dun aint got no gun."

Company C also had a negro boy, about Coon's age, who had the biggest opening under his nose, ever seen in a human face, and to set it off to the highest advantage, it was decorated with a pair of lips which resembled a couple of mahogany logs, lying on opposite sides of a swamp ditch. At the stern command of one of the mess, "Show us Manassas-gap," down would go his chin, until it touched his breast, and such a yawning cavern as would instantly appear would have a tendency to paralyze the average boarding-house manager. And the ivory which would be displayed would have caused an African tusk dealer to have turned green with envy. On account of his ability to perform this act we named him Manassas. There was existing, between this darky and Coon, a deep-seated hatred. One day Coon undertook to drive a shoat away from about the tent, saying, to the pig, "Go 'long out ob dis, 'fore I knock de bow knot outen yo' tail." Just then Manassas put in an appearance, saying, "Wha yo' dun struck dat pig fo'." Coon rushed up to him saying,"I dun struck 'im, yo' black rascal, I dun struck 'im." "G'way fom me, nigah, fo' I done snatch all de har outen yo' black head," said Manassas. "Whar'll I hit yo'." exclaimed Coon, shaking his ham-like fist over Manassas' head,"Gor-a-mighty Jerusalem, whar'll I hit you ? I don kick up de trash wid yo' in a minute." And no doubt a lively scrimmage would have re-sulted had not Gaskell come onto

MANASSAS-GAP.

the scene, but a sight of that magician was enough, away
scooted both the belligerents, in opposite directions, and we
saw nothing more of Coon until next day. The negroes were
so afraid of Gaskell, believing as they did, that he was the
devil, they would often go to the woods to sleep, and Coon
would not always get back in time to get our breakfast, so one
day I brought Gaskell around and he shook hands with Coon
and told him that he was a good nigger, and that he never
hurt good niggers, so thereafter Coon thought it safe to stay
in camp and accompanied us throughout the Peninsular and
Maryland campaigns.

We were landed at the White House, on the Pamunkey
River, and then marched to Mechanicsville and took position
on the right of General McClelland's army within sight of
Richmond, the capital of the Confederacy. On the 26th of
June 1862, the Battle of Mechanicsville was fought, in which
the Pennsylvania Reserves only were engaged on the Union
side. Back of the lines on Beaver Dam Creek, was a considerable strip of timber, and at the first volley the negro contingent took to the woods. The rebel artillery opened upon us,
but their aim was high, their shots passing harmlessly
over our heads ; their shells exploding in the woods,
scattered the negroes in every direction. Coon had been
made custodian of Lieutenant Macquilton's fiddle, and two
haversacks filled with rations. Next morning Coon put in
his appearance minus fiddle or haversacks and in consequence the mess had nothing for breakfast. I took it upon
myself to take him to task for the loss of the aforesaid articles
when the following conversation ensued : "Coon where
are the haversacks ?" "I dun frode em away." "Why did
you throw them away ?" "Gor Amighty, Mr. Darby, nigger
couldn't run fas' 'nuf an' tote dem ar habbersacks." "Well,
why didn't you hide ?" "I did get nudder nigger to hide
me under a house, but hadn't been dar morn' minnit fo' 'long
com one of dem shells an' it says 'Wha is yo' ? Wha is yo' '
ker bang, boom, zip. Good G——Mr. Darby, den I had to
git outen dat mighty quick, an' I was runnin' as fas' as I

could an' 'long cum nudder of dem ar shells, an' he say 'ketch-im, ketch-im' swiss-boom-whiz-z-z-z-z. Lord, Massa Darby, nigger had no bizzness roun' dar. What de pots an' de kittles was a bustin' an' a-tarin' up de groun', fus on dis side, den on dat side. No sar, niggar can't stan' no sich fiten' like dat, no sir. I codn't spar de time, or I'd frode away mi shoes."

While the loss of our grub was a serious one, for we were mighty hungry after a hard battle and a night of fasting, the comical way in which Coon puckered his mouth, and by sucking in and expelling the air, gave a perfect imitation of the sounds produced by the different sized shot and shells, in their passage through the air, was so laughable that we forgave him for losing the grub.

One summer day, as we were doing guard duty at Burke Station along the line of the Orange and Alexandria railroad, hearing the peculiar song of a grasshopper on the opposite side of the roadbed, I called Coon's attention to the singing of the grasshopper, as I wished to hear the quaint remarks which he would make upon the subject. I said, "Coon ! What is that noise over there ?" "Dat am a hoppergrass. Masser Darby," said Coon. "Well," said I, "Go and catch it for me !" "Oh, Masser Darby ! Gin I dun get ober dar, he dun fly." "Now Coon," said I, "You can't make me believe any such stuff as that. You say he is a hoppergrass, now. but if you go over after him he will be a dun-fly. Now I never heard of such a thing as a grasshopper turning into a dun-fly." "Oh ! I doan mean dat, Marser Darby," said Coon, "I des mean that he dun flew ; he dun gwine away, he dun git out ob dat ar place fo' I dun get dar." "O, I understand you now," said I, "you mean that he will fly away before you could reach him." "Now you is shoutin', honey !" exclaimed Coon, "dat am perzackly what dis niggar am tryin' to depress on yo' mine." It was this strange vernacular of the negro, and his attempts to use words, of which he had not the remotest notion as to significance, that made him a constant source of amusement to the northern soldier.

Coon was a philosopher, too, in his way, and entertained radical and peculiar views upon the subject of emancipation. He was the only negro I ever met, who was opposed to the slaves being freed ; he delivered himself upon this important topic, after this manner: "Yo' see, Marser Darby, it 'ud nebber do to make de darkies free. Now ob cose, dar am some good niggers, who will wuk, an' dar am lots of lazy niggers, dat am wuffless an' won't wuk, and dem lazy niggers, dey dest goin' ter steal all dat de good niggers make ! No sar, Marser Darby, hit won't do, niggers doan wuk, when da ain't got no masser." And so far as I ever learned, Coon never changed his views upon the great national policy of Emancipation.

On our command's being sent to Alexandria, Coon, having developed great aptitude for learning, we clubbed together and offered to send him North to school, but he respectfully declined our generous offer. He was afraid of the cold of our climate, and chose rather to remain in the South. Soon after this, in the vicissitudes of camp life, Coon became separated from us, and as I learned, entered the government service as a teamster, and that was the last I ever knew of poor, comic Coon.

CHAPTER III.

Gaines' Mills and Savage Station.

As we marched away from our camp on Beaver Dam Creek, a rebel regiment formed on the opposite bank of the narrow stream and stacked arms, neither side firing a shot. On the 27th of June the Fifth Army Corps opened the Battle of Gaines' Mills, and through some blundering mistake our colonel, George S. Hayes, was served with an order intended for Colonel Alexander Hayes, and we were detached from the division, moved to the right and relieved Duryea's Zouaves, and the Second Regulars of Syke's Division. The Zouaves were hotly engaged when we arrived and many of them had been killed and wounded. Under a heavy fire of artillery, which killed some of our men, the regiment formed line of battle in rear of the Zouaves and charging forward beyond their lines drove the rebels into a thick pine woods. We encountered here a murderous fire which caused our line to halt. My musket had become foul and I dropped to the ground on one knee and was ramming away at the cartridge with both hands to get the load down when I felt something spattering over my face and left side, and on turning round I discovered that my comrade, George Proud's head had been dashed to pieces and his brain and fragments of his skull had been scattered over me. William Kendall, another comrade next me, was also killed while I was ramming at the cartridge, which I did not succeed in getting down. In the meantime the regiment had been withdrawn and had marched away without my knowledge, as will be related hereafter. Our company loss in this battle was seven killed and thirteen wounded.

Immediately after the battle we crossel the Chickahominy River, on whose banks the battle was fought, and went into camp at Savage Station. I must be permitted here to

digress to say a few words upon a subject which puzzled, at
the time, many soldiers, commissioned, non-commissioned
and privates ; that is, this: Why our division, armed as it was
with old useless Harper's Ferry muskets, was marched right
by thousands of stands of the new Springfield rifles, with
ample fixed ammunititon for them, and forced to face the
very flower of the well-armed and equipped Confederate
Army, with those almost worthless weapons in our hands.
And the mystery does not grow less under the light of subsequent information upon the subject, for it is shown by the
records of the war department that unusual effort had been
put forth by the department, in view of the impending battle,
to get these new arms into the hands of General Geo. B. Mc-
Clelland, in order that the old Harper's Ferry muskets, with
which many of his men were armed, might be replaced with
an arm which would be of some practical use.   But as I have
before intimated we were marched by those new and efficient
arms to be hurled against our country's foe, in deadly conflict, with our facilities for doing that foe harm minimized.
This may seem a harsh criticism of General McClelland, but
in view of the fact that those arms, together with large quantities of army supplies, were allowed to fall into the rebels'
hands, without a proper effort to prevent it, seems to justify
the stricture.

Savage Station had been made a depot of supply as well
as White House Landing, and large quantities of army supplies had been concentrated at this point.   The railroad
bridge over the Chickahominy, a few miles away, having
been destroyed, a loaded train of cars standing at the station
had an engine attached to it.   The throttle was opened and
the engine and train sped onward and plunged over the bank
into the black, slimy ooze of the Chickahominy.   There had
been collected at White House and Savage Station about
four million dollars worth of army stores, and after the aban-
donment of those places, these supplies fell into the hands of
the rebels, as well as some three thousand sick and wounded.
Although we had fought two battles and had been without

rest or sleep, and almost without food for two days, McCall's Division was selected to guard the Reserve Artillery train ; and with our regiments distributed among the batteries of that organization, we marched off in darkness and rain over a narrow, muddy road for White Oak Swamp. As the army was converging at this point there was congestion, confusion and delay in getting the immense trains over the one bridge, and the arrival of our seven miles of batteries and wagons did not tend to lessen it any. We safely crossed, however, while the gallant Sumner held the enemy at bay and parked the artillery on the high ground bordering the swamp. A striking instance of McClelland's secret sympathy with the rebel cause and attempted treachery to the Union occurred on this march. Near midnight, in the rain and black darkness, an officer rode up to General McCall and told him he must turn back as he was on the wrong road.

The general replied that he was on the right road and would continue his march forward. About an hour later the officer again appeared and informed McCall that it was General McClelland's positive orders that he counter-march his division and train to another road and allow other troops to occupy the road he was on. McCall again refused to obey the order and proceeded on his way. Now a coun-termarch of six miles at this time on a narrow road in dark-ness, mud and rain was clearly useless and uncalled for, and was simply a device of the traitorous general to allow the capture of the Reserve Artillery by the enemy. And that this view of McClelland's duplicity is not an unjust one was amply confirmed the next day. On meeting McClelland at his campfire surrounded by his general officers the next day, he took McCall aside and secretly informed him that he wished to reach the James River without fighting another battle ; and this he claimed he could do in twenty-four hours, provided he destroyed all his trains including private bag-gage. As McClelland well knew that McCall and his troops had been subjected to the greatest fatigue and hardship up to this time, he no doubt expected that McCall would gladly clear the road by destroying the trains. He had mistaken his man, however, for McCall bared his head, standing in the rain, and looking McClelland steadfastly in the eye, positively and energetically declared that he would fight over every inch of ground from there to the James river before he would destroy a single wagon. To these brave words McClelland made no reply, realizing that he had approached the wrong man, and in silence the two generals returned to the camp-fire.

About five o'clock in the afternoon we were relieved of the charge of the artillery and marched on the Quaker road for Newmarket, and on reaching this point the column took an old abandoned road not shown on the maps, for the Quaker road which was three miles farther on. After marching several miles on this old road it became impassable in the darkness and we went into camp. In the meantime Syke's and Morrell's divisions of Porter's Corps counter-marched and finding a private road passed our division in the darkness and by this means reached the Quaker road and proceeded towards the James. Porter neglected to notify our command of this movement and we were thus abandoned by our corps and commander and assumed the front the following day in the Battle of Newmarket, Glendale or Charles City Cross Roads, as it has been severally called.

The Eighth Reserves were placed in support of a New York German Battery which occupied the corner of a woods. A few hundred yards in our front was a frame farm house and to the left of the house was a dense alder patch which extended across to a woods held by the rebels. The enemy finally charged our position. At the first sight of the rebel column, although as yet they were in no danger, the coward-ly Dutchmen without firing a shot, or waiting to limber up, abandoned their guns, mounted their horses and caissons and fled precipitately from the field. Standing close by I was a witness of this disgraceful flight and yet from this incident it was reported and circulated throughout the army that the Pennsylvania Reserves had been defeated, dispersed and disorganized, which was false in every particular, as was amply proven later by General McCall on his return from Richmond, where both he and General Reynolds were taken after being captured in this battle. The charging rebels were met by counter charges from the Reserves and in the hand-to-hand struggles which ensued, numbers were killed by bayonet thrusts. In the second charge of the enemy Captain Biddle, of McCall's staff, was killed and his horse ran away, but was caught and returned by me. Colonel Hayes' horse was struck and torn to pieces by a cannon shot and the heavier portions of the animal falling upon the colonel, injured him so severely he had to retire from the service. The loss of the Reserves in this engagement was twenty-five per cent. of the number engaged ; twelve hundred being killed and wounded and four hundred captured. After nightfall we were withdrawn from the field and marched to Malvern and placed in support of the line of battle on the left. As the Reserves were not prominently engaged here, they merely being held in reserve to support any weakened point, our lossses were small and confined entirely to the enemy's artillery fire. During the night the army retired to Harrison's Landing. As the cowardly and despicable McClelland had already abandoned the field at Charles City Cross Roads before the beginning of the battle, he also abandoned Malvern without waiting to post his lines, and skulked aboard a gunboat on the James River six miles away in perfect safety, under the empty and pusillanimous plea that he wanted to direct the fire of the gunboats. This service was evidently the duty of a staff officer or an orderly and not that of the commander of a vast army about to engage in a death struggle with a powerful foe. His duty absolutely required his personal presence on the field to direct the movements of his forces and there is no excuse for the absence of the commanding general during battle except death, disability or inability to be present. Who ever heard of McClelland making a Sheridan dash for the front. His famous rides were always to the rear. He was absent at the Battle of Mechan-

icsville. I did not see him and never heard of this doughty
general being present on the field of Gaines' Mill, Savage Station or White Oak Swamp, and he was absent at Charles
City Cross Roads and Malvern Hill. And yet partisans and
hero-worshippers lauded this traitorous, incompetent and
pusillanimous general to the skies. As a further review of
McClelland's incompetency and traitorous actions will be
given hereafter, I will resume the narrative. Nothing of
note occurred at Harrison's Landing except the return of
those who had been captured in the campaign, the fruitless
expedition of the Monitor and Galena against the rebel forts
at Drury's Bluff, and a vigorous shelling our camp received
one night from the enemy on the opposite bank of the James.
This fire destroyed some tents and wounded a few men but
the gunboats soon got their range and compelled them to
hastily retire. The next day a detail crossed the river and
destroyed and cleared away everything for quite a distance
back to prevent any repetition of their gun practice. Ed-
mund Ruffin, that conspicuous traitor who had journeyed
to Charleston to earn a cheap notoriety by firing the first
shot at Sumter, lived here and all his property was totally
destroyed. And thus, partially at least, was this blatant
rebel repaid for firing the shot that plunged a happy country
into a fratricidal war.

CHAPTER IV.

SOLDIER PASTIMES.

Owing to Gaskell's suppleness and agility he was the most pronounced and successful trickster, practical joker and all-round bummer in the entire command. In original invention and rapid execution of comical and mischievous tricks he was without a peer and some of them verged on the malicious, while others were so decidedly unclean and revolting they will not bear repetition in print. In this latter class of tricks I will say, however, I never knew Gaskell to indulge unless under the influence of liquor. Immediately after the Battle of Antietam we were encamped in an orchard near a brick farm house which stood on a hill above a very large spring at which the military balloon was inflated. As the house was supplied with water from the spring by a ram I went there one day to fill our canteens. A number of officers had ordered dinner which was being served and Gaskell wanted to take a seat at the table but was not allowed to. He then stationed himself at the head of the stairway which led up from the basement kitchen and as the girl bearing an immense steak dish filled with meat and gravy came up he tripped her, throwing her headlong, scattering meat and gravy all over the floor, then making a hasty exit, he ran to a sutler's tent and started a raid which soon cleaned out the sutler's stock. This unjustifiable act was done by Gaskell out of revenge for being denied the privilege of eating at the first table with the officers.

Along the Potomac between Washington and Alexandria there grows in the water betwixt the shore and the channel a species of sea grass with very long slippery blades. A favorite pastime of the soldiers was to go swimming and pelt each other with balls made from this grass. By reaching down the foot and twisting it around the grass enough

of it could be pulled up at once to make a ball big enough
for a twelve pounder and when a hundred or more men were
furiously "swatting" each other with these balls there was
fun galore.   Owing to their slimy, wet condition they would
strike a victim with a suggestive "biff" that would raise
peals of laughter at the unfortunate's expense.   Gaskell, who
was raised on the banks of the Monongahela, was an active
and expert swimmer and diver and therefore always took an
exciting interest in these battles and many a contestant
would take a sudden header and disappear beneath the water
by Gaskell diving and elevating his heels in the air.   After
these contests were over he replenished his stock of snakes
by diving to the bottom of the river and overturning stones
until he had secured enough for his purpose of frightening
the nervous and timid and the performance of his revolting
tricks.

After the Peninsular campaign we were shipped aboard
the large ocean steamer New Brunswick at Harrison's Landing destined for Acquia Creek.   On reaching Fortress Monroe a stop was made over a mile from shore and as the anchor
was being dropped, Gaskell seemingly tripped and plunged
headlong overboard and began making a strangling, suffocating noise in imitation of a drowning person.   His comrades who were in the secret raised the cry of "man overboard."   Instantly all was excitement aboard and the captain hurriedly ordered the launching of a boat in which he
took position in the bow ready for the rescue.   Gaskell in
the meantime had hidden behind the rudder and was watching the captain's movements closely, and when he rowed
around the bow of the vessel Gaskell's cries were always coming from the opposite side.   The captain finally concluded
to row clear around the ship and Gaskell was discovered
perched up on the rudder with an idiotic grin on his counte-
nance, chattering like a monkey.   The captain was furious
and cursed and damned like the proverbial tar, finally saying :   "You d—m—ed idiotic fool, I've a notion to leave
you there for an hour or two."   "Go to h—ll," replied Gas-

kell, "I'll be aboard before you are," and suiting the action
to the word he shinned up the rudder chains like a monkey
and was aboard, very wet, but also very happy because of the
trick he had served the captain. Before that official could
turn his boat and get aboard Gaskell had been effectually
hidden by his comrades from the wrath of the captain.

At Pierpont where we constructed log cabins in which
to pass the winter, tricks and practical joking seemed to be
the order of the day among the boys when off duty. Some
of the tricks resorted to there were not only mischievous
and reckless, but were actually dangerous, such for instance
as throwing musket cartridges which were loaded with ball
and buckshot down neighboring chimneys, endangering the
inmates of the cabin, to say nothing of the scattered fire. I
do not remember who originated this dangerous practice,
but suppose it could be charged up to Gaskell with the
chances ten to one in favor of crediting it to the right party.
He was the first man I saw at this trick and Colonel Hayes
was his victim. Shortly after a log guard house with the universal stick chimney had been built he played some trick on
the colonel which aroused the ire of that officer. He promptly arrested Gaskell and conducting him to the guard house
placed him in confinement. A sentry paced back and forth
at the door but at the back where the chimney was there was
no guard placed. As soon as the colonel's back was turned
I saw Gaskell's head pop out of the chimney and wag in a
very ominous manner at the colonel. As it was now getting
dark I got behind a tree to await developments. Soon Gaskell appeared crawling out of the chimney. Carefully
climbing down to the ground he slipped off unnoticed by
the sentry, and soon reappeared at the colonel's cabin with
ten rounds of ammunition which he slyly threw down the
colonel's chimney. He then rapidly ran to the guard house
and re-entered it by the chimney route and took a seat in
a corner and commenced to hum a ditty seemingly too innocent and peaceful to harm a fly. The colonel, who was in
the act of lighting his pipe at the fire, was liberally covered

with hot coals and ashes and snorting with rage he rushed to the guard house evidently suspicious of Gaskell, but on seeing that innocent individual looking so peaceful and contented, blurted out, "You are here are you ; you d—m—ed rascal, if you were not here I would swear it was you who threw those cartridges down my chimney." Gaskell protested against the colonel's unjust suspicions, saying, "Colonel you put me in here for nothing and how could I do it with a guard standing over me?" The colonel, after ascertaining from the sentry that Gaskell had not been absent, walked away still muttering curses. As his form melted away in the gathering darkness the head and shoulders of the innocent, persecuted Gaskell appeared above the top of the chimney and his voice in a rollicking song followed the receding colonel.

There was a Dutchman in Company B who started a barber shop to shave the bestubbled faces of his comrades and thus rake in some extra dimes. He had a sheet iron stove in his quarters, the pipe of which he passed out near the ground, and then by an elbow it was carried up about as high as a man's head. While the Dutchman was busily engaged with a customer, David Richie dropped some cartridges into the stove pipe which lodged at the elbow and after a while exploded. The stove was carried from its position and struck the Dutchman, who had his back to it, about six inches below the back, and Dutchman and stove mixed up with hair and lather went flying out the door into the company street. The air was filled with German imprecations for awhile, but as a jeering crowd soon gathered and fired cutting remarks at his mishap he soon gathered up the wreckage and retired within his cabin. In my mess was one Samuel Drumm, who is now living in Bloomington, Ill. Sam took the cartridge throwing fever bad and many cabin fires were scattered through Sam's agency. One day when Sturgiss was lying in the bunk and I was sitting beside the fire Sam was very active in his powder throwing, and after making a successful throw he would run into the cabin, take a seat on a back log which was lying in a corner by the fire, and laugh and gloat over the mischief he had accomplished. Joe and I discussed the dangerous practice and concluded that Sam ought to be cured of his powder throwing fever before he blew out somebody's eyes. Taking some cartridges I emptied their contents along the side of the back log just below where Sam always took his seat and then laid a train from this powder to a point near the fire place. We used a club for a poker and sticking this into the fire I burnt a live coal on the end of it. Presently Sam came in and took his seat immediately over the powder, laughing heartily at the way he had made some of the boys jump. Seizing the poker I gently drew it across the train of powder ; there was a flash and Sam's hilarity suddenly ended in a yell that rang throughout the camp. He snatched the cap off his head and vigorously fanned the seat of his pants as he jumped and pranced over the cabin floor like a three-year-old colt. Now there was a rip in the seat of Sam's pants, (which fact was unknown to me), and in consequence he was blistered so that it was more comfortable for him to stand than to sit, for several days. Sam blamed Sturgiss for serving him this trick and was very indignant at first but his good nature soon returned and his malady was so effectually cured that he never had a recurrence of the powder throwing fever.

Among other pastimes of the camp were card playing, boxing, jumping, throwing in a blanket and tossing the shoulder stone. At this last exercise Lieutenant Jesse B. Ramsey, of Company G, excelled the whole regiment. He was a most powerful man. I have seen him weigh out a thousand pounds of bar iron and then lift it bodily off the scale platform. Tossing in a blanket is a most ludicrous scene and always raised shouts of laughter from the onlook-ers, but the fun and hilarity in the practice is never enjoyed by the victim of the tossing. Company rows and occasional personal encounters at fisticuffs enlivened the tedium of camp life, and it is safe to say that among any given number of volunteers isolated in camp life there are enterprising individuals enough to create excitement sufficient to vary the tedious monotony of camp life.

CHAPTER V.

WARRENTON.

After the Peninsular campaign we, that is the Pennsylvania Reserves, were shipped from Harrison's Landing and disembarked at Aquia Creek, and thence marched to Fredericksburg and I think it was on this march that we met a large, fine-appearing darky who was walking rapidly toward the North. One of the boys said to him, "Hello ! Sambo ! whar's you all gwine now ?" "I'se gwine right straight Norf," answered the negro. "How far is it to Fredericksburg ?" asked the soldier. "Well, sar, ef yo's gwine erfoot I don spec its erbout twelve miles, an' if yo's er hoss back its erbout eight miles, an' if yo' goes an' gits on de kyars rite ober dar, yo's dar now." So you see Sambo's idea of distance seemed to be altogether dependent on the mode of transportation.

After resting opposite Fredericksburg a short time we marched one night for Warrenton via Rappahannock Station. Several miles above Falmouth we became entangled in a dense undergrowth of bushes. The night was very dark and the men began to murmur and swear as they stumbled along. General Meade had command and one of my comrades yelled as he picked himself up after falling over a log, "Boys I wonder where that goggle-eyed old fool is trying to take us anyhow ?" General Meade was riding beside us and heard the remark, but without saying anything he rode forward and halting the column we went into camp and waited for daylight. As Meade always wore glasses the boys had nick-named him "goggle-eyes," or "four-eyes," and although they yelled these names at him frequently he never paid the slightest attention to them.

On arriving at Warrenton we went into camp on a beautiful lawn which lay round about a fine brick residence. The

house belonged to a gentleman whose name was Forbes who
was serving at the time as quartermaster of the rebel army
under General Lee.   His family had fled upon the approach
of the Yankees, leaving everything about the premises.   Upon hearing that there was a fine library among other things in
the house, I concluded I would go in and draw a book or
two, as the rules in regard to returning them were not over
rigid, in short it being a game of catch as catch can.   But un-
awares I walked into a room where General George E. Meade
was giving some of the soldiers whom he had caught in the
act of destroying the furniture Hail Columbia with variations,
saying, "If you had the d——d rebel who owns the property
here, I would not care a d——m how soon you hung him,
but don't wantonly destroy property."   Then much to my
gratification he added, "If any of you boys want a book to
read, take it and go, but don't break up the furniture."   So
I walked into the library where the bookcases had been over-
turned and their contents scattered in wild confusion over the
floor, and proceeded to select my book.   I made choice of a
fine copy of Shakespeare, and going to the barn got a nice
pole of leaf tobacco.   I returned to camp and stemming my
tobacco, made it into a twist, which, together with my book,
I placed in my haversack.

The next morning, August 28th, 1862, we started on
the March for Manassas, and when we reached Gainesville the
Johnnies opened upon us with a battery of artillery and the
second Battle of Bull Run was on.   The column was halted
which left Companies G and B of our regiment in range of
the rebel fire, and as we stood in line I was scraped by a shell
which exploded after passing me, and killed Sergeant W. H.
Leithhead and J. M. Wells, of Company G, and one private
in Company B.   It also took an arm off of W. H. Doud, of
Company G, and a leg off of the adjutant of the regiment,
at the same time killing his horse.   My clothing, even to
my shirt, on my left side, was carried away by it as was also
my bayonet and haversack, Shakespeare, tobacco and all.   I
was painfully wounded, although not dangerously, but as we

were squarely between Lee's and Jackson's armies, we were
obliged to get out of there, double quick time.

After having my wound dressed, I applied for admit-
tance to a field hospital, but it being already overcrowded,
and being able to walk I returned to my command and Coon
was ordered by my messmates to care for me.   On the third
day of the battle, in accordance with previous arrangements.
I with Coon retired to the rear and took up my quarters in
a pine woods about two miles behind our line of battle ; this
wood was on the left wing of our forces.   In the evening as
the darky was engaged in cooking a piece of meat for our
suppers, I observed the rebels dash around the left flank of
our line on the very ground that General Fitz John Porter
had been repeatedly ordered to occupy by Major General
Pope.

Witnessing this move as I did, and taking into account that the enemy failed to make the least impression
elsewhere on our lines, I am forced to the conclusion that
Fitz John Porter was alone responsible for the loss to the
Union cause of the second Battle of Bull Run.

Coon and I narrowly escaped capture upon this occasion
by taking to the bush and then prudently retreating on
Washington.   In a few weeks I had sufficiently recovered
from my wound to resume my place in the ranks then on the
march in Maryland endeavoring to head off General Lee's
army.

One, Joseph W. Sturgiss, now a resident of the city of
Marietta, O., was my messmate at this time, and as we were
lying asleep under our blanket one morning our darky came
and taking hold of and shaking Sturgiss, said, "Git up Marser Sturgiss, de day's dun broke."   Joe stuck his head from
under the blanket and in a stern tone demanded, "Who done
broke the day ?   Just show me the man that done broke the
day !"   The darky struck an attitude of offended piety, and
proceeded to prophesy as he said, "Nebber yo' mine, Marser
Sturgiss, yo' soon foun out who dun broke de day.   Now de
fus battle yo' git inter yo's gwine ter git shot !   Den yo' fine
out who dun broke de day."

In the course of our marching we struck the National Pike at Poplar Springs, and from thence we marched on Fredericksburg. Arriving here we found General Reno hotly engaged with the Confederate forces, on the field of South Mountain.

Our division at this time being under command of General Joe Hooker, was ordered into position at the foot of the mountain and deployed into line regardless of a murderous fire from the enemy's artillery, and a charge was ordered upon the rebel line. The charging column swept grandly forward carrying everything before it and the retreat of the rebels from this field was so precipitous, and the pursuit so hot that some of the retreating enemy ran over the brink of a precipice at an abandoned stone quarry on the mountain side and were killed on the rocks below.

The negro's prediction that Sturgiss would be shot was literally fulfilled, for in the charge up the mountain side, he received a shot in the hand. Nevertheless, he captured a prisoner, who proved to be major of a South Carolina regiment, and a son of the governor of that state. Joe, after receiving the glove of the rebel major as a pledge that he and his companion would remain where they were, started in pursuit of the fleeing enemy. He had only gone a short distance, however, when the major's companion treacherously fired upon him, but missed. The rebel then started on a wild run down the mountain and David Richie, who came up at this time, took a shot at him, supposedly wounding him in the arm ; the rebel, however, made his escape. On Joe's return the major denounced the act of his companion and said he had fired without his sanction or knowledge. Joe and the major have met since the war and renwed their battle field acquaintance.

Sturgiss, although small of stature, has the heart of a giant. "Here's to you, Little Joe, faithful playfellow, generous messmate and brave comrade. May your shadow never grow less." But for Joe, I should probably have closed my career as a soldier early. It was at the battle of

Gaines Mill. My gun had become so foul that it was difficult to drive the cartridge home. I had dropped on my knee and was ramming away to get the load down, when I heard my named shouted and upon looking around I saw Sturgiss scooting for the rear, with bullets cutting the ground about him like a storm of hail. The facts were, that in the confusion of the battle, our command had been ordered to fall back, but we had not heard the order, and were banging away at the enemy. Joe had discovered the situation, and sounded the note of warning to me just in time to save me. I hesitated, upon seeing the bullets fall so thick about Joe, as to whether I should try it, but it was death to remain where I was, so I took the chance and for a marvel escaped without a scratch. The regiment by this time was out of sight, so I took the direction to the York River railroad station. Arriving there I found the boys had not reached that point, so I crossed the river on the railroad bridge and made for Savage Station, where I came up with them. They had crossed the river at Deep Bottom bridge, and gone into temporary camp at the station. I was not aware of the location of the bridge over which my comrades crossed, hence my wide detour.

The enemy's dead on South Mountain were mostly killed by shots through the head, as they were behind rocks and stone fences and could not be seen until they raised up to shoot. Our loss was very small as the rebels in shooting down the mountain fired high and the most of their missiles passed harmlessly overhead.

One of the saddest incidents it was my lot to observe on this field was that of a strapping Confederate soldier who had taken refuge from the storm of battle with ten or twelve others, behind a rock, all of whom had been killed but this one, and he had lost both eyes, and was being led off by two of my comrades to a place of safety, and what seemed remarkable was that all those that had occupied the shelter of the rock had been killed by bullets through the head.

Immediately after South Mountain we were headed for

the Field of Antietam. And on the 17th day of September, 1862, we were drawn up in line of battle in front of the historic corn field, which proved to be the theater of the awful holocaust of that battle ground. The fire at this point was so terrific that every thing was swept before it, except, here and there, a panel of fence. Here I saw a very strange sight. Some Union soldier in his excitement in loading his rifle had neglected to withdraw his ramrod, and in its flight it had struck and passed through the head of a rebel soldier and pinioned him to the fence, and there he stood stark dead.

Among the Confederate troops stationed in the corn field was the Eighth Texas. This regiment had a large silk battle flag bearing the Lone Star, and I noticed that although there was a most destructive fire from our line directed against it, it still continued to wave, but the sequel proved that the Yankee fire had become so fierce about that standard that no man could live in it, and the color bearer had driven the staff into the ground and the regiment had divided off to the right and left of it, hoping thereby to escape the missles of death which were hurled at it. The staff was literally riddled by bullets, but the flag continued to wave. At length one of the boys of the Ninth Reserves charged alone across the open space into the corn field, seized the lone star flag and bore it safely back in triumph to his company.

After the battle was over, I passed over this portion of the field and found that the carnage here had been appalling. The Eighth Texas had been practically wiped out. They had fought heroically, but there lay their dead in line, officers and men, as they had fallen,

"Their backs to the field,
Their faces to the foe."

Brave men they were ; but a fearful price they paid for their treason to the old flag.

Just back of the cornfield everything was in evidence of the destructiveness of our fire. I observed a rebel cannon which had been struck by a shot from one of our guns which had carried away its muzzle, while wrecked caissons, dead men and horses were heaped in wild confusion over the blood-stained ground. In passing a nearby house, I noticed a dog in the yard. He was in a kneeling position as if smelling at a rat hole, but upon closer examination he was found to be stone dead, having been struck by a stray bullet. A visit to the farm yard revealed that the farm stock, horses, cattle and hogs, had all shared the fate of the dog, and it was indeed pathetic to see their wide staring eyes, as though they had died in amazement at the horrid confusion about them. I noticed one horse in particular with its head turned ; with its wide eyes fixed upon its flank, where it had received the fatal wound, as if it would inquire the cause of the suffering.

On entering the barn, the floors and mows were full of dead men. The grim reaper Death had gathered his human sheaves and garnered them where once had been stored the golden grain. The stable of the barn was in the basement. There, too, stalls and mangers were filled to repletion with the bodies of men who but a few brief hours before were filled with life and its varied hopes and ambitions. Surely

> "It might have tamed a warrior's heart
> To have viewed such mockery of his art."

Just beyond lay a road through something of a cut, and in the depression of that thoroughfare the dead lay in winrows. Oh ! the carnage of that field was awful to contemplate ; look where you would the ravages of the dark-winged angel confronted you. In open field and shot-torn forest lay the mangled forms of soldiers, Federal and Confederate, mingling in that carnival of death, and the foemen of an hour ago, now fraternizing in an eternal peace.

There was standing, near the field of battle, a small church edifice, belonging to a denomination of Christian people, known as the Dunkers. This unpretentious house of God had stood in the range of the artillery and had been struck by sixteen solid shot which had gone crashing through it, leaving it little less than a total wreck, while all about it lay shot and shell, late the screeching messengers of death, now the mute and silent proofs of "Man's inhumanity to man." Here, too, was to be found a most striking illustration of the power of education and environments ; the people who were wont to worship in the church above referred to were doubtless as honest and as sincere as the Christian people of the North were, yet while those of the North believed human slavery to be the "sum of all villainies," and as such prayed God for its uprooting and banishment from the face of the earth, those of the Southland believed it to be a divine institution, and so proclaimed it to be, and prayed earnestly to the same Heavenly Father for ·its preservation, and that it might live and spread itself over all the domain of our country. But just how it could be, that men had come to believe that they had the right to ignore the Divine declaration that, "In the sweat of thy brow shalt thou eat thy bread," and to transfer to others the responsibility of doing so for them, is not so clear to us. But, sure it is, that they professed so to believe ; and they hesitated not to supplement their faith by cruelly lashing the bare backs of their slaves, thus outraging every principle of human justice, until the arbitrament of the sword seemed the court of last appeal and the blackened faces of the dead on the field of Antietam, staring vacantly in the face of high heaven, protested mutely against such unchristian savagery.

After the Battle of Antietam had been fought and won, as it was by the Federals, the rebel army was truly in a most deplorable condition, having been beaten and shattered at every point ; it was penned in a bend of the Potomac River, without bridge or other means of crossing, and the army of Lee was at the mercy of Gen. Geo. B. McClelland. But that doughty commander, who had received by common consent the nom-de-plume of the "Unready," was true to his instincts, and granted Gen. Lee a suspension of hostilities for the space of twenty-four hours, ostensibly in which to bury his dead, but really in which to lay pontoons and escape with his badly whipped and beaten army, thus bearing off the garland of victory which rightfully should have graced the Federal brow, for the battle was fairly won by the boys in blue, notwithstanding, as I do truly and sincerely believe, against the desire, and intention of our commanding general, for he. (General McClelland), in his attempt to justify his conduct, and to excuse himself for not gathering up the fruits of the victory; which his gallant army in spite of his own pusillanimous conduct, had gloriously won, said he was short of artillery ammunition, and also pleaded the losses which he had sustained in killed and wounded, both of which excuses were untrue and unfounded.   John Bierer, who was a member of my company, and is now living at Uniontown, Pa., and whose verification of the truth of this statement can be had any day, was on the day of the battle brigade wagonmaster, in charge of the reserve artillery train of ammunition and had his wagons on the ground just where they were needed, and with plenty of ammunition from first to last.

The following statements of facts quoted from a letter received by me from Comrade Bierer are in his own words and I will say that this statement exactly coincides with the facts as narrated by him to me at Antietam a few days after the battle :   "I was brigade wagonmaster at the time.   Had charge of ninety-six wagons loaded full of ammunition for musketry, rifles and cannon when we left Washington, D. C., on the 8th and Rockville on the 10th of September, 1862, for the campaign in Maryland.   Was at the foot of South Mountain on the morning of the 12th in time for the battle, with my entire train of wagons.   Unloaded two wagons to supply Meade's Division before you went up the mountain, and sent one with small and two with heavy ammunition to supply the troops on the left of the pike.   The next morning with ninety-one full and five empty or partly emptied wagons, we started about nine o'clock, moving to the left of the pike, crossed South Mountain, and on the evening of the 16th at dusk crossed Sharpsburg bridge and camped by the old mill to the left of the Williamsport pike. The next morning early 1 sent two wagons up the pike to Sumner, two crossed the bridge, turned to the left and went to supply Hooker and the reserves and four wagons were sent to Burnside. In all during the battles of South Mountain and Antietam, thirteen wagons of ammunition were unloaded, or partly so, leaving me eighty-three wagons of ammunition untouched." Now when we recollect that all the divisions of the army had trains of ammunition of their own in addition to this reserve artillery train, it is easily seen from this detailed statement of Captain Bierer that there was no lack of ammunition in the Army of the Potomac at any time during the Maryland campaign. As to McClelland's other excuses, viz. : The losses his army had sustained and his desire to enable the rebels to bury their dead. I will say that the rebels met with losses also and were not being reinforced as was McClelland's army. And as for the dead, a dead rebel could lie unburied just as long as a dead Yank. I was in line in front of the cornfield when the order to cease firing was received and I well remember the dismay and consternation it produced among the rank and file. "Why do we cease firing when we have the enemy whipped ?" and "We can drive the whole rebel army into the Potomac," and kindred ejaculations were heard on every side, but a continuation of the conflict meant the destruction of Lee's army and McClelland's only possible way to avoid this contingency and save the rebel cause with which he secretly sympathized was to order a sudden cessation of hostilities. I also met and talked with new soldiers the evening after the battle who had not had a chance to discharge a gun at the enemy that day, and I know, and thousands of other soldiers who participated in that fight know, that reinforcements were arriving in large numbers during that eventful day.

In common with the rank and file of the eastern army, up to this time, I had been an enthusiastic McClelland admirer, but the facts above stated, taken in connection with his stupid conduct of the Peninsular campaign set the seal upon General Geo. B. McClelland as the chief traitor of the century, and if any confirmation of this opinion as to his character were necessary, it was furnished by the general solicitude exhibited on the part of the rebels at Richmond, on his behalf, which I observed while a prisoner of war there.

CHAPTER VI.

Camp Scenes.

After the Battle of Antietam our command went into camp in an orchard near a brick house which stood on an elevation, and just below it, in the valley, gushed one of the largest flowing springs it was ever my good fortune to see. As Gaskell was pitching his tent in the orchard, in making the necessary excavation, he unearthed an arm, and grasping the hand as he might that of a living comrade, exclaimed, "Hello, old fellow, how do you do, how is it down there anyhow ?" and then calmly proceeded with his work. A short distance below the spring were some buildings which the rebels were occupying as hospitals. Out in the open air was an operating table, where amputating was being performed. Arms and legs by the cart load had been dissevered, some of which had been buried, and it was one of those which Gaskell had disturbed while engaged in pitching his tent.

There were large numbers of sightseers and relic hunters visiting the battle field at this time, and some gruesome sights they saw, I can assure you. As I was going to the spring for water on one occasion, the surgeon was preparing to amputate a leg, and as I halted to observe the operation, a civilian who had come to see the sights, was also standing near, and as the rebel surgeon with his sleeves rolled up, like a butcher in the shambles, displayed his shining scalpel, and with one sweeping stroke, severed the muscles to the bone, around the entire circumference of the limb. At this sight down went the civilian in a dead faint. I dashed the contents of my canteen in his face ; he revived, but with an expression of horror upon his face which I shall never forget, exclaimed, "My God, this is terrible," and hurriedly left the place. Now gentle reader I imagine hearing you say how much gentler and more kindly must have been the heart

of this civilian than that of the man Gaskell. Not so. The
one was inured to such sights, and the other was not ; that
was all the difference. Probably the man Gaskell would
have rushed to the rescue of a suffering person just as readily
and as sympathetically as the other. There seems to be an
innate disposition in the human mind to adapt itself to its environments, and to make the best of its surroundings. The
soldier knows from the nature of his calling that he will be
called upon to see and undergo sufferings which are not common to civil life, and by a merciful provision of nature or
Providence, he undergoes the transition almost imper-
ceptibly.

But it is truly remarkable into what risks and adventures
curiosity will lead the average human being. One day a
young man with his family, consisting of his wife and one
child, a bright little girl, drove onto the field, which was
thickly strewn with the debris of battle, and wishing to carry
off some memento of his visit to the scene of the recent carnage, he gathered up two or three unexploded conical shells,
not dreaming that there was danger lurking there, placed
them in his wagon and drove away. But, alas ! had not
gone far when the jostling of the vehicle over the rough
ground brought the shells into contact, and a fearful explosion followed, which resulted in the death of the three persons, and the annihilation of the team and wagon.

Upon another occasion, while standing upon the hill
side on this field, in company with comrade Dave Ritchie,
we observed a civilian trudging along with his arms full of
shells. Ritchie called to him, saying, "Say, mister, if you
knew what those things were you would not be carrying
them that way." The countryman replied, "Oh, I know
what they are," but just as he was speaking one of them fell
from his arms and went rolling down the hillside. It had
gained considerable momentum in its course when it came
in contact with a stone. It let loose with a bang that waked
the echoes. It was amusing to see with what tenderness
that fellow placed the remaining shells on the bosom of

Mother Earth, and tiptoed away from them, as if he feared his footfalls might set them off. He let no grass grow under his feet until he had put a safe distance between him and those innocent-looking elongated globes.

Soon after the episode of the shells, another of my comrades and myself concluded we would vary the monotony of camp life a little by securing a "pass" and going a fishing. We put our plan into operation and proceeded to the river bank and there, James Axton, (for that was his name), and I made ourselves as comfortable as possible under the circumstances. We had been fairly successful in persuading a number of members of the "finny tribe" to leave the watery element and join our soldier band ; this we did by hook and not by crook, of course. But what I was about to tell you was that just opposite where we were doing the fishing act stood a log cabin from which proceeded a woman on horseback and I observed that she headed her horse in the direction of where the rebel army was encamped. It awoke my suspicions, and I called Axton's attention to the fact, but he laughed at my fears, and to show that he had no misgivings as to our security from danger, pulled off his shoes and wading to a rock at some distance from shore, quietly seated himself and proceeded with his fishing. I, meantime, had gone down the river some two or three hundred yards and was also busily engaged watching for bites, when all at once biff—bang from the cabin came a volley aimed at poor Jim on the rock, and the way the bullets made the water fly around that stone was a caution, and Jim said he wouldn't have cared so much about their shooting into the water and scaring the fish but he thought they were too careless about their shooting, for some of their bullets tore holes in his clothes, and he said they might have accidentally hit him. Sharing Jim's misgivings about the carelessness of their shooting, we both beat a hasty retreat. Leaving fish, shoes and all, we climbed that river bank and took refuge in the bed of a canal the banks of which had been cut by the rebels for fear it might be of some service to the Union forces, in

case it should fall into their hands, as it did happen to do.
Well when we found ourselves secure from the fire of the
enemy in the old canal bed we concluded to keep an eye on
those Johnnies for awhile and see if we could not slip back
and secure our shoes and the fish which we had left in our
hurry to move, but we concluded, after watching for some
time, that discretion was the better part of valor, so we returned to camp, provoked enough to remember that we had
not only failed to secure the coveted mess of fish, but also
to be obliged to leave behind us our shoes.   However, next
day Axton returned for his shoes and strange to say found
them where he had left them, and brought them off in
triumph, and furthermore he had taken his "gun" with him
when he went for his shoes, and by way of revenge, he aimed
and shot at every living thing he could see roundabout that
cabin.

I must tell you something in regard to this brave, generous soldier boy, James Axton.   His history is both singular
and pathetic.   His father was a glassblower by avocation,
residing at Brownsville, Pa., where James was born.   During the year 1860, work being slack in his home town, the
elder Axton took a trip down the Mississippi River on a coal
boat, was taken sick and sent to the Marine Hospital at
Memphis, Tenn., for treatment.   The war breaking out
about the time of his recovery, he was conscripted and placed
for service in the rebel general, Van Dorn's army.   On the
other hand, Jim, true to the old flag, enlisted in the Union
army.   Jim told me how matters stood, and I asked him
what he would do in case he met his father on the field of
battle.   "Why, I would take him prisoner of course," said
Jim.   His father, after serving for nearly two years in the
rebel army, effected his escape and succeeded in making his
way to the Union lines, where he at once enlisted in the
Army of the Union.   Meanwhile Jim was taken prisoner by
the rebels, and sent to Salisbury, where after suffering from
starvation, exposure and nakedness until reduced to a mere
skeleton, and with certain death staring him in the face, he

appealed to Sergeant James Eberhart as to what he should do, (Eberhart was a member of the same company.) Axton told him that he had a mind to enlist in the rebel army, and take the chances of making his escape to our lines, for said he, "to remain here a few more weeks means death to me." The sergeant said to him, "You must do as you think best." So after deliberating upon the matter for a short time, he concluded to enlist under the Stars and Bars. "Oh, the miscreant !" I imagine I hear you exclaim. Just a moment before you pass judgment upon the man. Jim Axton was a brave and devoted soldier, enduring the hardships of the march and the camp without a murmur ; gallant in battle, scorning death on the ensanguined field, faithful on guard and picket, ever wakeful and watchful for his country's honor and safety ; all this when himself. But now starving and naked, weakened in mind and body, with no hope of escape except in the way indicated. The love of life, which is innate in every human being, comes in upon him, like a whelming flood and carries him before it : he enlists, taking the oath of allegiance to the Southern Confederacy, believing that the end justified the means ; but whether he died from the effects of his treatment at the hands of the rebels or in trying to escape from service in the Confederate army, none of his friends ever knew, but that was the last ever heard of James Axton.

It will be remembered that the Battle of Antietam was fought on the 17th of September, 1862. The fall rains coming on soon after, many of the dead were literally washed from their shallow graves, and their remains left to fester and decay, exposed to the action of the elements on the very ground which a few short months before their heroic deeds had aided to make historic ; such is the fate of war. After remaining in camp for nearly three months at Antietam our command, with others, was ordered forward to Fredericksburg, Va. We crossed the Potomac at Berlin. On arriving at Belle Plains, I had the honor of being detailed as guard at General Reynolds' headquarters. While thus engaged, I made the acquaintance of his cook, who was one of the most grotesque darkies ever met with. He was known by the name of "Ben, the Monkey Turner." The following is his history as detailed by himself. He was the slave and personal attendant of the colonel of a South Carolina regiment known as the "Monkey Turners." This command was organized at Charleston, S. C., and like many other untried warriors, had indulged in a large amount of boasting as to what they purposed doing when once they got a chance at the Yankees on the battle field. Each one of them would slay at least five of the Northern mudsills, that being the euphonious title given by the Southerners to the people of the North, and when that feat at arms was accomplished they were to return to their native city and enjoy a Christmas dinner. And, by the way, they had heard of the Pennsylvania Buck Tails, and they boasted that if they ever got a swipe at that command they would simply wipe them from off the face of the earth. Well they got the chance, for at the second Battle of Bull Run it so happened that the Monkey Turners were pitted squarely against the Buck Tails, and the Lord have mercy on their souls, for the Buck Tails, with their seven shooting Spencer rifles, almost annihilated the regiment. Ben's master was killed, and as Ben was going onto the field to try to bear off the body of the fallen officer, he chanced to meet three or four of the Monkey Turners running for dear life to the rear. Now Ben thought, those fellows are headed for Charleston for that Christmas dinner which he had heard so much talk about, so he said to them, "Is youn's all gwine back to Charleston to git yo' Christmas dinner?" One of the number stopped running long enough to say to Ben, "Shut up, you black son of a b——, we's all dead but fo'teen." Ben was taken prisoner by the Buck Tails, and General Reynolds installed him cook at headquarters, where he presided with great dignity, and proved not only to be an efficient cuisine artist, but also an unfailing source of amusement to all who came in contact with him, as he had an exhaustless fund of funny stories locked up in his black cranium, from which he was ever able and willing to draw for the entertainment of his friends.

One night, as we were lounging about the camp fire, Ben broke out laughing, and we recognized it at once as a precursor of a story, and two or three of us at the same moment exclaimed, "Well Ben, what is it ?" "Oh, I'se jes' thinkin' 'bout Brudder Pete." "Well, what is it about Brother Pete ? let us have it." "Well I'le des tell yer, Down dar ner Charleston dar was a niggar libed an we all done call him Brudder Pete case he so ligus, and so lubbin'

SNAKES.

an 'fectionate to de sisterns. We all hab bush meetins down dar ebery yar, an' Brudder Pete he dun alwas speak at dem metins an' de sisturns all tink dare ain't nobody like Brudder Pete. Arter one of des meetins I dun seed Brudder Pete snekin off trough de woods with de putist wench of de hole meetin' and I des foler em. Arter a while dey come to a log an' Brudder Pete, who was a stuttering nigga, he say, se-se-set down yer, Sis-Sis-Sister Ma-Ma-Mary mi-mi lub so Brudder Pete can talk to-to-to you.' 'Oh, no, Brudder Pete I'se feard ob snakes,' says Sister Mary, so dey jes mosey along a little furder and den dey cum to whar dar war a grapevine gro ober

a bush, and mek a nice shady place, den Brudder Pete, he
dun mek a seat 'mong the leabes, den he says, 'S-s-sit down
yer, S-S-S-Sister M-M-Mary, mi lub, dar's no s-snakes yar.'
Mary dun sot down and den Brudder Pete des tro he arms
'round Sister Mary an' he gib her a kis dat jes smak like de
cracin' ob a plate.   Den she say, 'Oh, oh, Brudder Pete dat
am so sweet,' and Brudder Pete say, 'Su-su-sweet to me Ma-
Ma-Mary, mi lub, it am mity good,' and he was jis' gwine to
gib her nudder smak wen I hollered snakes.   Good Lord if
you seed dem ar niggars git outen dar an t'ar fru dem dar
woods like 'zif de Debbil hisself is arter um, yo' would jis
kil yo' self larfin."   While it is impossible to put upon paper
the peculiar effect given to a story by the idiom of the African
race, yet it may show to the reader how the light of mirth
and laughter sought the heart of the soldier, even when his
surroundings were gloomy and forbidding.

About this time there were very stringent orders pro-
mulgated against foraging, and woe to the fellow taken in
the act.   He would be escorted to the general's headquarters and caused to stand on the head of a barrel, with the
stolen property, whatever it might be, placed upon his
shoulder, and there under guard he would be obliged to
stand for a longer or shorter time, according to the enormity
of the offense, to be guyed by his comrades.   One day one
of the boys having a longing for some veal bought a calf
from a planter and paid him for it by giving him an order on
the quartermaster, taking a receipt from the planter for the
same.   He boldly led his calf up in front of the general's
tent, and there deliberately drawing his sheath-knife, cut its
throat.   Now the general, who, as is well known was a great
stickler for strict discipline, thinking he had caught a forager, red-handed, in the overt act, called a guard, who
placed the man under arrest, but the soldier assured the general that he had purchased the calf, and in proof of his assertion, showed the planter's receipt.   Of course that settled
it, and the soldier was released.   But the fun was not yet
ended, as the next day the planter put in his appearance at

the general's tent demanding payment for his calf on the order given him by the soldier. Then there was music in the air, but it was not of a devotional nature either, but the calf was eaten, and the general could not find the soldier who had tricked him, and the case was out of court, but still furnished lots of amusement for the boys.

Cyrus Eislie was easily the most wily, crafty and successful bummer and forager in Company G, if not in the entire regiment. He would "accumulate" anything from sutler checks to mules. I have myself seen him abstract checks

SOJER FOTCH BACK DAT GOOSE.

from the drawer of the sutler's desk while the sutler was writing on top of it, and then have the unblushing gall to buy goods and pay for them with the stolen checks. On the outskirts of Fredericksburg, while Eislie was roaming around looking for something to "accumulate," he discovered near a house an old goose setting on a nest of eggs in a laudable endeavor to hatch. Sneaking up he grabbed the goose by the neck and started on a dead run for camp. Just at this time a lusty negro wench made her appearance at the door and seeing Eislie and the goose scooting across the field, stopped long enough to yell, "Massa, Massa. White man

done steal de old goose," and then started in a hot chase
after Eislie with "Massa" a close second.   The wench kept
yelling, "Sojer, sojer, fotch back dat goose; fotch back dat
goose ;   dar goes de last goose on de plantation and how's I
gwine to hatch dem aigs widout a goose."   Owing to the
resistance of the goose with its powerful wings to being
towed along in this manner. Eislie soon discovered he was
being rapidly overtaken by his pursuers and that the out-
cries of the wench had been heard by a mounted patrol who
also joined in the chase.   Eislie therefore was compelled to
release the goose and he narrowly escaped capture by jumping a nearby fence and taking to the bushes ; but it was certainly a laughable and exciting goose chase to those who
saw it.

CHAPTER VII.

The Night Before the Battle of Fredericksburg—
A Dramatic Incident.

"Time rolls his ceaseless course ; the race of yore,
Who danced our infancy upon their knee,
And told our marvelling boyhood legends store,
Of their strange ventures, happed by land or sea,
How are they blotted from the things that be !
How few, all weak, and withered of their force,
Wait on the verge of dark eternity,
Like stranded wrecks, the tide returning hoarse,
To sweep them from our sight ! Time rolls his ceaseless
course."

Who that survives of the Army of the Potomac, that
witnessed the night bombardment of Fredericksburg, can
ever forget the terrific grandeur of the sight, while our guns
were hurling the tokens of Yankee retribution upon the traitorous city, in the shape of shot and shell, where they crashed
and fell like the wrath of God on Sodam and Gomorrah.
The northern heavens were illumed by the glories of an
aurora borealis which shot its lances of purple fire, and
spread its banners of flame athwart the sky, rendering the
scene one of the most awful sublimity. It surely was a
sight which will live in the memory of all who participated in
that unavailing fight, until their dying day. To think of all
the unrequited valor, and the precious lives which were
snuffed out on that bloody field, is truly appalling ; for
never since the day when arbitrament by the sword was introduced among nations, did men behave more splendidly,
or fight more gallantly than did they. Burnside hurled his
valorous columns six successive times against the enemy's
works, when the first assault demonstrated, beyond a doubt
that the enemy's position was impregnable, and yet the holocaust went on, and thousands of patriotic lives were ruth-

lessly sacrificed to somebody's stupid blundering. And what renders it more obvious that an awful blunder in the order of the battle had been made, was the fact that while the frightful carnage was being enacted on Mary's Heights, on the right. The enemy's lines had been pierced and had the movement been properly supported, instead of a crushing defeat, Fredericksburg would have been a glorious victory for the Union army. General Meade's command carried the enemy's lines in a gallant charge under promise of timely support of General Franklin's division, but through some dereliction the promised succor was not forthcoming at the supreme moment, and the position so heroically gained, had to be abandoned. A pathetic and never to be forgotten episode occurred here. In the charge of Meade's Corps, a beloved nephew of the general had fallen, pierced by rebel bullets. His dead body was secured and placing it in front of him on his horse, and as with his precious burden he was following his decimated columns as they were forced from the field, for lack of the promised aid, he chanced to meet General Wheaton of Franklin's Corps. Meade in an agony of grief and rage at the useless sacrifice of his men, and covered with blood from his nephew's wounds, and with tears streaming from his eyes, he drew his sword to kill Wheaton for not moving his column to his support at the proper time, and was only prevented from so doing by the interference of members of his staff. What a dramatic scene. One worthy the brush of a painter, and yet in so far as I know. it has not been mentioned by any writer on the field of Fredericksburg.

The gallant Bayard of the cavalry was killed by a shell, and many company and line officers of the Reserves were also killed or wounded. Our total loss in this battle was one thousand eight hundred and forty-two men. My own company was left under the command of the fifth sergeant, and the regiment was left under the command of Captain Lemon, and in fact the ranks of the division were so depleted that the entire command was sent back to Alexandria to be recruited up and reorganized.

Every soldier who participated in the tiresome, ener-
vating and distressing march known as the "Burnside stick-
in-the-mud" will remember its hardship, exposure and suffering until his dying day. From start to finish the windows
of heaven were wide open and a cold rain incessantly, day and
night, beat upon the heads of the devoted soldiers. The
roadway was speedily converted into a quagmire in which
the wagons were buried up to their beds and the mules dropped down in their harness and suffocated in the mud. The
troops floundered along both sides of the quagmire in mud
from ankle to knee deep, their destination being the fords of
the Rappahannock, and their design, to flank the rebels out
of Fredericksburg. Owing to the severity of the weather
the movement was a complete failure. The order was coun-
termanded before the objective point was reached and the
troops were returned to their old camps. The rebels were
informed of this fiasco and on the picket jeered and taunted
our men over this miserable failure.

The screaming farce, "Burnside Stick-in-the-Mud,"
was dramatized from the original performance as given by
Burnside by Mr. Bud Gaskell, who was a participant in the
first performance. Gaskell being the originator of the play,
was also the star actor, and as he was a whole troupe in himself needed no assistance. The literary merits of this work,
I am sorry to say, were not of a high order, consisting as
they did principally of ejaculations and exclamatitons of violent disgust, interspersed frequently with a liberal variety of
cuss words that were far more expressive than elegant. His
wardrobe for a performance while not grand or expensive
was at least singular and attractive. It consisted of a battered plug hat and a ragged coat, if he could get them, if not
his uniform as a soldier was amply sufficient, as his performance was always gratis and therefore popular. With
pants rolled high above his army brogans, disclosing his
hairy calves, and clothed in his ragged coat with the battered
hat set at an acute angle on his unkempt head, he would go
floundering through and falling into imaginary mud holes,

seemingly scraping and wiping mud from his person, all the while swearing and uttering exclamations of disgust and at every step emitting a sucking sound exactly imitating the noise made by withdrawing the foot from deep mud. When to this was added his grimaces, contortions and groans it altogether made a scene that was inexpressibly ludicrous and laughable. Being on patrol duty in Alexandria one day I saw a crowd gathering at the corner of King and Henry streets and approached to see what was going on. A show-man had rented a room and had on exhibition a large Ana-conda and a blowhard posted at the door was enlarging on the wonderful sights within, something after the following manner : "Here's the greatest living Anaconda in the world, twenty-seven feet, two inches long and weighing one hundred pounds. Caught in the wilds of Central Africa by three black natives. By the kind treatment of his master he has become perfectly docile. You can stick your finger in his mouth and he will not bite you. Step this way, ladies and gentlemen, and see this great living curiosity for the small sum of ten cents." Directly Gaskell approached the showman and an animated conversation took place between the two. I found that Gaskell wanted to be admitted to perform with the big snake but the showman refused. Gas-kell remarked that he would bust up his old fraud of a show and going over to the opposite corner began to cry in mock-cry of the showman : "Here's the only living Anna Conder. She was caught running wild in the lowlands of old Virginia by three black niggers. By the kind treatment of her cap-tors she has become perfectly docile. You can kiss her black ebony lips and she will not bite you. Step this way, ladies and gentlemen and without money and without price see the great 'Burnside Stick-in-the-Mud,' after which Anna may easily be seen in the audience." He then began his per-formance as described, and in a very short time he had an immense motley crowd of whites and negroes collected around him that completely blocked both streets. The showman was left without a single patron and he finally came to Bud and gave him two dollars and a half to go away. Gaskell, after having a good time and investing a portion of his money in bug juice, returned to camp hilarious.

On reaching this city we were moved out to the east a mile or so and having been supplied with Sibley tents, established camp. These tents were more roomy, commodious and aristocratic than the little dog tents we had so long occupied and from which the boys used to stick their heads and bark like a dog from his kennel. The irrepressible Gaskell was now in his element and soon made his presence known both in city and camp. One day he came to our tent about half drunk and amused himself climbing the center pole and falling to the ground and tripping and pitching headlong over straws. Whilst engaged in his comical performances one of the numerous demi monde which infested Alexandria at that time, made her appearance in camp. Gaskell approached her and pulling his flask of whisky gave her a drink and conducting her in front of our tent induced her to sing the following local song parodied on "When Johnny comes Marching Home :"

In eighteen hundred and sixty-one.
Skewbaul. Skewbaul.
In eighteen hundred and sixty-one.
Skewbaul says I.
In eighteen hundred and sixty-one
This cruel war it was begun,
And we'll all drink stone blind, Johnny fill up the bowl sir.

We met a misfortune at Bull Run.
Skewbaul. Skewbaul.
We met a misfortune at Bull Run.
Skewbaul says I.
We met a misfortune at Bull Run
And all skeedaddled for Washington,
And we'll all drink stone blind, Johnny fill up the bowl sir.

The Marshall house it is the spot.
Skewbaul. Skewbaul.
The Marshall house it is the spot.
Skewbaul says I.
The Marshall house it is the spot
Where Colonel Ellsworth he was shot,
And we'll all drink stone blind, Johnny fill up the bowl sir.

The slave pen it's as cold as ice.
Skewbaul. Skewbaul.
The slave pen it's as cold as ice.
Skewbaul says I.
The slave pen it's as cold as ice.
Get up in the morning full of lice,
And we'll all drink stone blind, Johnny fill up the bowl sir.

I bought a rooster for fifty cents.
Skewbaul. Skewbaul.
I bought a rooster for fifty cents.
Skewbaul says I.
I bought a rooster for fifty cents
But the cockadoodle flew over the fence,
And we'll all drink stone blind, Johnny fill up the bowl sir.

After singing this doggerel ditty she stepped into a tent
and siezing a tin cup from a shelf, containing almost a half
pint of commissary whisky, she drank it down with a gulp.
Well she was simply paralyzed in a short time and the officer
of the guard had to call an ambulance and send her off to the
slave pen.   Gaskell, after tripping up a peddler and securing
some apples started in the direction of the colonel's quarters
falling many times on the way over imaginary straws and
twigs.   A mounted officer, seated on his horse was engaged
in an animated conversation with the colonel in front of his
tent when Gaskell slipped up and seating himself on the
horse's hock joints under his tail went to munching his apples amid many comical grimaces and contortions.   The
colonel and the officer were entirely unaware of the monkey

show being performed under the horse's tail until a laughing, jeering crowd had collected, when the colonel discovered him, but Gaskell scooted without waiting to hear any remarks from the colonel.

About three miles above our camp was a small lagoon, or bayou, that put into the land from the Potomac, which was much frequented by wild ducks, as were the swamps bordering the river. Several of the comrades had made ineffectual efforts to shoot them with their army rifles but the Springfield was a complete failure for duck killing and they had their trouble for their pains.

Baer, who was much given to self laudation and praise, went to the bayou early one morning, stealthily approached the shore, and seeing several ducks, fired and by accident killed one of them. He returned to camp with his prize, triumphant and greatly elated over his success, and after plucking and nicely dressing it, he placed it in a mess pan ready for cooking and then proceeded to the camp fire where a number of the comrades were congregated and began to blow about the accuracy of his aim and his expertness as a hunter. After allowing him to blow for a while one of the men said it was probably a wooden decoy duck he had shot as he had seen a number of them down there the other day. This riled Baer and he declared that all the other men who had been down there after ducks were chumps and pot-hunters that could not hit a barn door with a rifle, and therefore they were jealous of him, but he continued, "I'm going to have duck for breakfast in the morning and you fellows can stand around with watering mouths and get a smell while you see me eat it." Richie said, "Baer, if I was you I would not blow so much about that duck. Somebody might pick its bones for you before morning." "Oh," said Baer, "I'm not a bit afraid of that. I would like to see the men in this company that is smart enough to steal that duck." Richie said no more and Baer, after placing his precious mess pan at his head, went to bed and to sleep. Marching orders for the next day were issued late that night and Richie was de-

tailed to cook the meat and have it ready for issue to the
men in the morning. About midnight Richie went to the
back of Baer's tent and silently raising the canvas reached
in and abstracted the duck which was placed upon the fire,
cooked to a turn and devoured by himself and comrade.
The bones, after being trimmed, were returned to the mess
pan and it was replaced at Baer's head without disturbing
his slumbers. Baer upon discovering the loss of his duck,
raised a howl that was pitched in an altogether different tone
and tune to the song of fulsome self praise he had been singing the previous evening, but as the laugh was on him and
Richie was decidedly handy with his fists, Baer had to stand
the gibes of the entire company. On the march and for days
afterward in camp he would be greeted with such ejaculations as the following : "Who stole Baer's duck ?"   "Who
eat Baer's duck ?" and "Baer done swaller dat duck whole, I
see de fedders on his upper lip," and "Baer, wy doan yo' pick
dat duck meat outen yo' teef ?" This continual nagging became unbearable to Baer, and taking advantage of an order
issued by the war department permitting infantry to re-enlist
in the cavalry he left the company and joined that arm of
the service.

Jeremiah B. Jones and William R. Mitchell were two
comrades belonging to Company G, of the Eighth, who were
over six feet in height each. They were both naturally wag-
gish and witty and overflowing with good humor. "Jerry"
was long and rather thin of build, while "Bill" was both long
and broad. As a number of us were lounging about the
campfire one evening Bill said, "Jerry, where was you
raised ?" Jerry answered, "Up in the mountains near the
Virginia line." "Oh yes," said Bill, "I have heard of the
place ;   the whole township stands on edge and the boulders
stick out the side like the warts on a toad's back." "Where
was you raised, Bill ?" asked Jerry. "On Barren Run, near
West Newton," replied Bill. "Oh yes," says Jerry, "the kill-
deers go running over that district with a knapsack on their
backs containing eight days' rations and tears of grief and

despair falling from their eyes." "I hear," said Bill, "that stock raisers in your township have to tie the sheep together by the tails and hang them over the rocks to pick the grass out of the crevices." "There is no stock on Barren Run," replied Jerry, "as they can't raise fodder enough there to feed a sick grasshopper through the winter." "The farmers of your township," said Bill, "have to shoot the wheat under the stones with shot guns." "Well," replied Jerry, "the farmers of Barren Run have to mow with a razor and rake with a fine tooth comb." "It would no doubt be a healthy place to live in the mountains," said Bill, "if so many of your people were not injured in scraping their shins and killed by breaking their necks falling over the rocks." "Barren Run would also be a healthy place if so many of your people did not die of starvation while searching the barren fields with microscopes and field glasses to find dock and dandelion enough to make a mess of greens." "In your township," said Bill, "they always take dynamite along with the funerals to blast a hole big enough to hide the corpse in." "And in Barren Run all funerals are accompanied by a cart load of manure to throw in the grave to rot the corpse," answered Jerry. The controversy now ended amid the laughter of the hearers, with the honors about equal and the principals retired to their tents. The genial Mitchell bravely and nobly met his death on the bloody battle field at Fredericksburg, and the cheerful Jones perished in the prison hell at Salisbury. Peace to their ashes.

While our ranks were being recruited at Alexandria, small detachments from the regiment were placed along the line of the Orange and Alexandria railroad for its protection and guarding negroes and teams employed in getting out from the surrounding forests, large quantities of wood for the use of the army, and also timber to be used in the erection of blockhouses. The whole of the country in this part of Virginia was overrun by guerrillas, and they were very crafty and active, both day and night, and consequently we were obliged to exercise the utmost vigilance in guard and

picket duty, and at best they had us at a disadvantage for
they were on their native "heath," and knew perfectly every
foot of the ground, and could ride fearlessly, where we were
obliged to feel our way, but notwithstanding this fact, we
were always able to hold our own with them. Wild game
was abundant in the woods of Fairfax County at this time,
as it had not been disturbed much since the opening of hostilities, between the sections of the country ; men had been
too busy in hunting men to waste their energies on smaller
game, hence game birds, turkeys, deer, foxes, rabbits and
squirrels, had multiplied exceedingly, but the fellow who
had the hardihood to take to the woods in quest of game
was quite sure to become himself the quarry before the hunt
was ended. But the indomitable Richie one day sighted
what he supposed were two fine wild turkeys, and being a
dead shot, he maneuvered until he got within range, and firing brought one of the coveted birds to the ground, but imagine his chagrin when gathering in his prey to discover it
to be a buzzard only. He seemed to relieve his disgust for
that particular kind of game by a flow of language which
was more remarkable for energy than elegance, and his day
dream of feasting on turkey was dissipated for that time at
least. A very singular incident occurred near camp one
morning as a gang of negroes were going to their work in
the woods. They came upon a fox lying asleep under a tree,
and being confused by its sudden awakening, it dashed into
a hollow log which was lying close at hand. The negroes
clubbed it to death, brought it into camp in the evening,
cooked and feased off its carcass. I believe this the first and
only instance I ever knew of a crafty Sir Reynard being
caught napping. One of the most peculiar and distinctive
wild fruits of this section of the United States is the persimmon. They grow in great abundance in most of the Southern states, and are very toothsome, especially in the late
autumn and winter, when they fall from the trees, and become food both for man and beast. I have gathered them
from the snow under the trees, in the month of February,

and they were delicious, having passed through a candying process in their own sweet juices. They are very nutritious and the persimmon tree becomes a snare and a delusion to the rabbit, where in winter he resorts to feast upon the fallen fruit and thus he falls an easy prey to the negroes, who are well aware of his weakness for the succulent fruit. The persimmon is utilized to some extent also in the manufacture of an intoxicant known to the natives as persimmon beer. The following was the formula : The fruit is first mixed with wheat bran or middlings, dampened, made into large cakes, or pones, and baked in a Dutch oven, and when desired for use, the pones are placed in a keg or other tight vessel and cold water poured over them, and as soon as fomentation takes place, the beverage is ready for use.

At the station at which we were doing service, (I have forgotten the name, however, I think it was the first station out of Alexandria, south on the Orange railroad), we had very comfortable quarters, but as we were obliged to escort to the woods and guard the men composing the timber contingent, we were at first unable to get a warm meal at dinner, but at length we hit upon a scheme which enabled us to overcome this difficulty, and it worked like a charm. This was the device : Holes about two feet deep and sufficiently large in circumference to nicely admit a camp kettle, were dug in the clay soil, then the first thing upon arising in the morning a rousing fire was started in and over these holes, and the result would be that by the time we had our breakfasts, the holes in the ground would be hot, so we would just insert our camp kettles, (all of which were provided with metallic covers), into the holes in the ground, first having filled the kettles with beans, having a liberal chunk of pickled mess pork smothered in their midst, then we covered the kettles over, with the hot embers left from the morning fire, and on coming in at noon time, there would be our pork and beans, done to a turn, and these supplemented by hot coffee and hardtack, made a meal fit for a king. At least it would fill the aching void beneath a soldier boy's blouse.

One day while at this we were permitted to see what looked
for a time as though it might prove a fearful catastrophy, but
really ended in a laughable episode.   There was standing on
the track at the station a train of flat cars, loaded with wood
ready to pull out, when around the curve came thundering
a train from Culpepper.   This train was made up of box
cars, filled with soldiers, some of whom discovered that a rear
end collision was inevitable, and gave the alarm, and of
course every fellow was intent on saving his own life, and of
course they concluded that to jump was the only way out of
a bad scrape, and jump they did, one after another, headlong, from the car doors into the bushes which lined the
track.   In their flight through the air they resembled a
drove of giant frogs, leaping from the bank of a mill pond
into the water.   The trains collided with considerable force,
but aside from the scratches the boys received from jumping
into the bushes, no one was hurt, and all survived to laugh
over their needless alarm.   However, soon after this, some
two miles beyond our camp, the rebels succeeded in causing
a wreck which proved disastrous.   These rebels were commanded by a Johnny Bull who had recently come from England, named Rodgers, and had taken service in the rebel
army, with the rank of captain.   The command had one piece
of artillery.   This they had placed in a concealed position in
the woods, then they drew the spikes which held the rail
in position, and attached a wire to the rail, and carrying the wire to their hiding place in the bush, were ready
when the train approached to displace the rail by means of
the wire.   The train was derailed ; then they opened fire
upon the wreck and sent a shot from their cannon crashing
through the dome of the engine.   Several of the cars also
were somewhat shattered by their cannon shots, but the
"Yanks" were too many for them.   Speedily forming, they
charged into the woods, took the cannon, killed the captain
and captured or killed all his men.

   While our command was engaged in doing this guard
duty along the line of railroad, the headquarters of our regi-

ment was still at Alexandria, where we had constructed bar- . racks near the government bakery. This was the largest bakery in the world. It converted into bread five hundred barrels of flour daily. The bread was baked in sheets of six- teen loaves, each loaf weighing sixteen ounces, and one loaf of soft bread, or in lieu thereof, twelve ounces of hardtack was the daily allowance for each man, when on full rations. One hundred thousand loaves were sent daily from this bakery to Culpepper for General Grant's army, and large . gangs of negroes were constantly employed in carrying these sheets of bread and packing them in the cars, and although the distance was sixty miles to Culpepper, the bread reached them still warm from the ovens. While lying in barracks near Alexandria, a company mess was organized and our ex- cess rations were placed in a general fund with which to pur- chase extras for our tables. A negro cook was employed, and as he was an expert in piscatorial matters, and as all kinds of fish were plentiful and cheap, the baked shad and sturgeon which often graced our tables would have caused the mouth of an epicure to water. As the Yuletide drew near the bakers secured a fine lot of turkeys which were dressed and placed in the pans ready for roasting for their contemplated Christmas dinner, but "The best laid plans of mice and men gang aft aglee," and it is safe to say that the bakers dined, on that Christmas day, without turkey, as some of our wide awake boys had seen their way clear to confiscate the birds. And so it turned out that what was the bakers' loss was the soldiers' gain. But the bakers were wrothy and lodged complaint with the colonel, and he of course ordered an immediate search of the quarters. Lieutenant Ramsey, of our company, being officer of the day we were promptly in- formed that an investigation was on, also we were given to understand the dreadful consequences of being found guilty of the offense charged. But some how the officer of the day on this occasion was a trifle slow in getting around to our quarters, but he finally arrived, and made the investigation, but not a turkey bone was discovered in or about our quarters, although there was a lingering suspicion of an odor which might have been mistaken as arising from roast turkey. However, it would have been impossible to have convinced any of the boys of our mess that we did not have turkey for dinner that day.

CHAPTER VIII

DEATH OF SISLER.

While lying here the rebel hosts invaded the old Keystone state and the Reserves immediately petitioned Governor Curtin to have them sent to the defence of their native state. Two of the brigades were sent and tackled the Johnnies at Little Round Top, some of the boys fighting in sight of their homes. The other brigade was held at Washington and Alexandria for the defence of those cities in case of rebel attack. On General Grant taking command of the Army of the Potomac, the Reserves, having recouped and refilled its ranks, rejoined the army at Culpepper, and participated in all the battles of Grant's subsequent campaigns. The series of battles which followed on Grant's assuming command, have been fully described by able writers, but a few incidents of personal observation during the campaign from Culpepper to Petersburg may be of interest to the general reader.

While the death of a comrade always brought sadness to the hearts of those who survived, yet there seemed something inexpressibly sad in the death of one, who having endured the privations and hardships of the soldier life, until after the expiration of his term of enlistment, when his heart and mind were full of the joyful anticipation of the home-going. I say it seemed more distressing to see such a one fall just upon the eve as it were of his home-going, but how often it so happened, many a surviving comrade can attest. Among my messmates was one, a genial, great-hearted, brave young man whose name was John Sisler. Death had deprived him of both fatherly and motherly care ; for at a very early age he was left an orphan. He had found a home and had been carefully reared by a family near Uniontown, Pa., by the name of Parshall. At Robinson's Farm, May 8th, 1864, where the field was skirted by a dense piece of woodland, the

timber of which was principally of pine, we had improvised a
line of rifle pits from which our skirmishers would sally, ever
and anon, to feel the strength and position of the enemy.   I
had observed, not far from our rifle pits, an oak, growing
among the pines, which forked at about four or five feet from
the ground, forming two trunks.   In the rear of our position
was an old field wherein had sprung up clumps of bushes,
here and there.   On our withdrawal from our skirmish line
at the margin of the woods, a rebel sharpshooter had located

DEATH OF SISLER.

himself in a pine tree and from his perch among the branches
amused himself by picking off such officers and men as had
occasion to pass through the field.   John Sisler and David
Richie, the latter residing at Connellsville, Pa., were detailed to go out and kill him if possible.   Accordingly they
slipped over to the timber and Sisler took shelter behind the
oak tree above mentioned, and while looking through the
forks of the tree was discovered by the rebel, who fired, his
bullet striking Sisler squarely between the eyes, killing him

instantly. Richie, however, discovered where the rebel was located, and shot at him, but his gun was not of sufficient range to reach him, so he came back and reported the fact, whereupon two of the Buck Tails were dispatched with their Spencers to do the job, and they soon brought Johnnie Reb to terms by shooting him dead from his roost in the pine. We secured Sisler's body and digging a grave in the rear of our battle line, we sorrowfully laid him to rest, marking his lowly grave with a cracker box lid. Sisler was killed about two weeks after his term of enlistment had expired, but as the companies composing the regiment had entered the command at different dates, the time had been averaged, which resulted in detaining our company, to which Sisler belonged, a few days longer than we were justly entitled to serve, with the result as above stated. Sisler's body was afterward removed to the National Cemetery at Fredericksburg.

CHAPTER IX

INCIDENTS OF THE MARCH.

On the march to the North Anna River our rations had become exhausted, the commissary wagons not being able to keep up with the marching column, and consequently we suffered from hunger. Observing a farm house some two miles from the road in the edge of a wood, myself and three comrades fell out of line and proceeded to it, hoping to get some food. A middle aged man dressed in a new suit of bluish gray, and two daughters met us at the door. The girls were crying and the three were badly scared at our arrival, but we assured them we would do them no harm and they became quite friendly. One of the girls who had an incipient mustache growing on her upper lip said, "I hope you all won't hurt that tanner over thar, (pointing to a house a mile away), he's nevah been to the war and says he'll nevah go either." We accused her of being in love with the tanner and she finally acknowledged the soft impeachment and we calmed her fears, telling her we would not disturb her lover. I asked the man if he had any eatables. He said he had twenty-one mouths to feed and they had nothing but some bacon, eggs and milk. I asked him where his twenty-one mouths were and he said he had taken his niggers to Richmond for safety. He also informed me he had paid one thousand dollars for his new suit in that city and the times had become so desperate that the planters did not know what was to become of them. I told him we were out of food and if he would let us have some bacon and eggs we would pay him a fair price for the same. To this he consented and while the girls went after the eggs, myself and a comrade accompanied him to the smokehouse where he uncovered a barrel half full of bacon cured from the celebrated variety of hog known as "razorback." Selecting a ham about as big as my two hands

placed palm to palm, I gave him a dollar greenback for it and
the other boys having paid for their eggs he was so pleased
he conducted us to the milkhouse and gave us all the milk
we could drink. By this time the column had gotten quite
a distance away, but we overtook them as they were going
into camp on the North Anna. Our artillery was engaged
in a lively duel with the rebel batteries at this time, while
pontoons were being laid preparatory to crossing the river,
so our mess hustled lively to get our bacon and eggs cooked
and eaten before the battle should commence. After crossing the rebels were driven backward steadily until darkness
settled over the scene. After the desperate Battle of Spotts-
sylvania had been fought, the regiment's term of service having expired, they were marched to the rear and sent home,
while those of us who had "veteranized" were consolidated
with the Tenth Reserves. This parting between old comrades of many hard fought battles was pathetic indeed and
some were moved to tears. Our officers and comrades, our
band and beloved flag were taken away and we were left disheartened and dispirited, and several days elapsed before we
regained our wonted cheerfulness. In a few days we were
on the march for Bethesda Church, with our minds fully occupied by the dangers of the present instead of grief for the
past.

We reached Bethesda Church on May the 30th and on
this day the time of enlistment for the whole division expired,
it having been averaged to fall on this date, as some of the
regiments had been mustered into service sooner than others.
We formed line of battle behind a rail fence which ran along
side of a dense woods ; to our left was a farm house, in front
of which was planted a battery of artillery ; in our immediate front was a cleared field, in which stood two negro
cabins, and beyond the cabins the field was skirted by a heavy
pine forest which our battery at the house was vigorously
shelling. We had torn down the fence and piled up the rails,
and with picks and shovels were busily engaged in throwing
earth over them to make rifle pits, when suddenly we heard

the rebel yell. On looking to the front we saw a Virginia brigade, commanded by General Ramsey, coming at full charge out of the pine woods, and they were making for our battery double quick. We dropped our spades and grasping our rifles we poured a most deadly cross fire at close range into their ranks, while the battery rained double shotted grape and canister into them, and in less time than it takes to tell it, that rebel brigade was almost annihilated, a very few only making their escape back to the woods. As I was firing across the top of the pit, a piece of a human jaw containing five teeth struck and stuck upright in a rail just in front of me. I suppose the rebel to whom it had belonged had been hit by a cannon shot and his head dashed to pieces. A few yards in front of our position was a slight ravine in which some seven hundred of the enemy who were immediately under fire of our guns had taken refuge. We called out to them, "Johnnies come in out of the rain !" and they did not wait for a second invitation, but they came at once. One long, lank Virginian, as he stepped over our slight breastworks and saw our shovels, exclaimed, "by G—d, spades are trump this time," but he was evidently happy at the prospect of becoming a boarder at Uncle Sam's expense for a while.

After the battle the division marched away to the tune of "Home again, home again, from a foreign shore," and the organization known as the Pennsylvania Reserves passed out of existence in the full tide of battle.

Thus the veterans who had re-enlisted and the recruits who had joined us, were left on the field without colors, officers or organization, whatsoever, but we were soon afterward formed into the One Hundred and Ninetieth and One Hundred and Ninety-First P. V.

While the battle was in progress I had noticed a rebel soldier with an unusually bright canteen hanging at his side kneeling behind a stump, and being placed after the battle on a picket detail, I concluded to go and see what Johnnie was doing there. I found that he was dead ; his canteen and his body were both literally perforated with bullets. I passed on to the woods from which the rebels had charged, to find the whole intervening space thickly strewn with the dead. My beat extended from the woods to the first of the negro cabins before referred to, and mine was the last post on the line in that direction. By the time the pickets were posted darkness had set in. Oh, the pitiful cries and groans of the wounded and dying made of that night a night of horrors in very deed. But as we had been without rations all that day, when the excitement of the battle was over, nature asserted herself, and we were desperately hungry. I began to look about for something with which to satisfy hunger's demands, and directly finding a dead rebel whose haversack seemed to be reasonably well supplied, I cut it off his shoulder, opened it, and in the dark ate what I supposed to be some water-soaked hardtack, but imagine my feelings when in the morning I discovered that instead of being water-soaked, they were blood soaked, but it was then too late to correct the mistake. I was obliged to submit to the inevitable. After walking my beat for a half hour or so, the thought occurred to me that it might be well for me to explore the cabin at the end of my beat. Accordingly I approached and opened the door and walked in, to find housed there twelve rebel soldiers, one captain and eleven privates. To state that I was surprised is drawing it mild ; as a matter of fact I was badly scared. I could feel my face blanching and my hair raising, but quickly regaining confidence I exclaimed, as two of them were raising their guns to shoot, "Johnnies you are inside our lines. You are all prisoners. Everybody stack their arms in the corner," and as their captain repeated the order they sullenly obeyed without a word. I then called the corporal of the guard. While waiting for the corporal I talked with the captain who had been shot, the ball passing through the wrist just above the hand. He was a young man, about twenty-one years of age, I judged. He was fine appearing, and very gentlemanly. I asked him if his wound was painful ; he replied that it was not, and as at the time it was not bleeding, I had no appre-

hensions in regard to it, but I made him as comfortable as
I could and assured him that I would take him to the hospital
as soon as I was relieved in the morning, so that he might receive the surgical attention of which he stood in such evident
need. The eleven privates had been taken by the corporal
and his guards to a place of safe-keeping, and the captain had
the cabin all to himself, where I had left him in seeming comfort, but my surprise can be better imagined than described
when on going to the door to call my prisoner in the morning I found him cold in death. Reaction had evidently
come after the shock caused by the wound, and with it, a
hemorrhage in which his young life had ebbed away. It has
ever been a source of deep regret to me that I did not think
to guard against such an exigency by placing a tourniquet
upon his arm. The commander of this rebel brigade, (General Ramsey), was killed, falling in close proximity to the
other negro cabin, in which were taken ten or twelve rebel
prisoners also ; there was found upon the person of the
dead general, a fine gold watch, a gold mounted sword, and
other valuables, all of which were restored to his friends at
the first opportunity, I believe. After being relieved those of
us who had been on picket duty rejoined our respective commands, which had moved back a short distance from the
corpse strewn battle ground, near to a commissary, where
our hunger-puckered stomachs were soon filled out with an
abundant allowance of Uncle Sam's hardtack and "salt hoss."

This battle field was within six miles of the field at
Mechanicsville, where less than two years before the Reserves had crushingly defeated a greatly superior force of the
enemy—the end thus being near the beginning. The two
thousand of the Reserves that remained of the ten thousand
who had fought at Mechanicsville determined that the end
of the service of the division should be as glorious as its beginning. From the 1st of May our total loss in the division
was one thousand two hundred and ninety-nine officers and
men. One hundred and twenty-four officers and two thous-
and and thirty-eight men were all that remained of the

thirteen regiments composing the Reserves. One thousand seven hundred and fifty-nine men re-enlisted, leaving about twelve hundred to go home. As those who re-enlisted participated in the balance of Grant's campaign, the glorious old Reserve Corps was represented in all the battles of the Army of the Potomac from Dranesville to Appomattox.

After the Battle of Bethesda Church we were organized as the One Hundred and Ninetieth and One Hundred and Ninety-First P. V., and after General Grant had butted against the impregnable lines of the enemy at Cold Harbor, like Burnside had done at Fredericksburg, and with the same result, he flanked their position. The query naturally arises : Why did he not flank before he butted and thus save the useless sacrifice of thousands of brave, patriotic lives ? After the disaster of Cold Harbor, which was fought on the same field as was Gaines' Mill, two years previous, with the hostile armies reversed in their positions, we were moved to Seven Pines. We were formed in line of battle in a woods and were sent into action here to relieve cavalry who had been fighting dismounted, with every fourth man holding the horses. We went in with a hurrah, but the enemy seeing the infantry coming in such enthusiasm and numbers, wisely decided to withdraw, leaving us easy victors on this field. I saw after this battle a remarkable illustration of the wonderful tenacity of human life under conditions which it would be thought impossible for one to survive, even for a single moment. I came upon a rebel soldier who had received a shot in the head, the minie ball having entered the skull a little above and in front of the ear, on one side, passing obliquely through and coming out behind the ear on the opposite side. A white slouch hat lay beside him with holes through it, corresponding exactly with those in the head. A quantity of brain substance had oozed from the wound, and while standing in wonder that the man still breathed, one of our ambulances was driven up, a doctor stepped out of it, approached the wounded man, raised his head and gave him a drink of whisky. Shortly after taking the potion, the man

got upon his feet, walked to the ambulance and unaided, got
in and was driven to the hospital. Two things were, I
thought, thoroughly demonstrated in this case, viz., first,
that man can stand more and severer mutilation than
any other animal, and secondly, that commissary whisky
must possess great revivifying power, as here certainly was
the most marvelous display of vitality that I had ever observed in any living thing, unless we except the snapping
turtle, which is said to live for nine days after having its head
severed.

This was the last hostile meeting our command had with
the enemy on the right bank of the James River, and the
ground had been made historic by the battle fought there
some two years previously.

Soon after the events narrated in the previous chapter
occurred our command was ferried across the James River
and advanced on Petersburg. We encountered the first rebel line some four or five miles from that city. While they had
a strong position here, it had a fatal defect as will appear from
the following description. They had a finely manned battery planted near a well of water in the corner of a pine
woods, which had formerly been used by the people of Petersburg as a picnic ground. Several hundred yards in front of
the battery and of the woods, was a well constructed rifle
pit which was defended by South Carolina troops. About
three hundred yards in front of the rifle pit was a well defined
ravine which ran parallel with their line of battle. The sides
of the ravine were clothed with a small growth of timber
and bushes, while the space between the woods and ravine
was clear. So the ravine proved their Jonah, as we entered
lower down, out of their range, and marching up until opposite their pits, we were protected from their fire, which passed
harmlessly over our heads. Creeping up the bank until we
were on a level with the field, we used our bayonets and tin
cups in scooping out holes in the light sandy soil, which
made excellent protection, and from these "gopher-holes"
we were able to pour a continuously hot fire upon their bat-

tery and rifle pits. Soon after I had finished my little pit, a major of a Massachusetts regiment ordered me out of it, I replied that I was not in his command. He said that made no difference, that we were overlapping his line and I must get out. Dave Richie, a comrade, spoke up and addressing the officer, said, "Who are you, anyhow ?" "I am Major Doolittle, sir." "Yes," said Richie, "Doolittle, both by name and by nature ! Get out of this, d—— you, or I will shoot you !" And he got. This was my first experience under fire of explosive bullets and they did crack and snap about us in great order. When one of them came in contact with any hard substance, the result was an explosion. One of my comrades, by the name of Samuel Wilcox, was struck in the thigh by one of those bullets at this battle, which exploded on striking the bone, and the fragments tearing out in different directions made six distinct wounds, and it is supposed that he died from the effects of this wound, as we never heard from him afterwards. All day the battle raged, until darkness set in, when the firing on both sides ceased. Shortly after darkness had settled over the scene, without a general order, and as if by intuition our line got to their feet and without firing a shot, charged simultaneously the rebel works, and rushing over their pits, were among the Johnnies before they knew we were coming. We secured as prisoners the whole batch of them, not a man escaping so far as we knew. The morning following I went over to where their battery had stood on the opening of the battle, and Oh, what a sight was here ! It seemed as if the entire human and animal life which had composed its working force had been swept at one fell swoop into the vortex of death. Two of the caissons had been blown up, and among the wreckage dead men and horses, torn and dismembered, were lying thick. I thence proceeded to the well from whence had erstwhile flowed the life-giving water ; it is now choked by the stream of death. In it are the bodies of from eight to ten dead men. Turning from this scene of war's horrible carnage, we moved on to the enemy's main line of defence about Petersburg, and took possession of a line of rifle pits which had been abandoned by the rebels when our advance was made.

Here we were directly under the fire of the enemy, and as the men were worn out with fighting and marching, a ration of whisky was issued to each soldier. Being inspired with a sort of false courage, the order having been given to occupy a more advanced position in our front, which by the way was one of great danger, the detail under the influence of the stimulant recklessly exposed themselves to the rebel fire and a number of them lost their lives in consequence. There were two brothers in the detail, one of whom was killed and his body borne to the rear. The remaining brother rent the air with wailing and lamentations for awhile, then turning, shook his fist fiercely at the rebel line and called down heaven's maledictions upon the murderers of his brother. A man of Company F was here shot through the head and though unconscious he lived for several hours. While he was dying a grave was dug alongside of him into which he was laid as soon as the breath had left the body. The part of the line upon which we were was near the point at which the rebel fort was mined and afterwards blown up. But about the time the mine was commenced we were moved several miles to the left, where we encamped in the woods and constructed Fort Warren. To our right was a cleared field which was over half a mile wide, and extended clear up to the rebel line. This field was covered with a rank growth of ragweed. The woods on either side of the open space extended flush up to our rifle pits. Stretching obliquely across the field was a strip of oozy, boggy ground, terminating at a spring near the woods on the right, and still another strip of miry ground which terminated in a magnolia swamp at the corner of the woods on the left. This field as well as the woods on both sides, was swept by a terrific fire from the enemy's lines, by both artillery and infantry. It seemed whenever the Johnnies felt like burning powder, this was their objective point, and it appeared to us that they never tired, for they kept it up day and night.

The One Hundred and Ninety-First was commanded by a Colonel Carle who had served as a sergeant in the regular army. He was quite a martinet in his bearing and was greatly given to his cups. He was also overbearing and tyrannical, especially so, when drunk. One day when pretty well boozed he was ordered to relieve a Massachusetts regiment which was in the more advanced rifle pits ; in fact these pits were only a few yards from the enemy's lines. Forming his regiment and riding at the head of the column, with a canteen of whisky swinging from his shoulder, he marched us through the open field in full view of the rebels, up to the rifle pits. The enemy opened upon us a galling artillery fire, under which nine men were killed and wounded before we could reach cover in the rifle pits. Some of the company officers were so indignant at this foolhardy and criminal action on the part of the colonel that they unloosed their swords and refused to serve longer under him, but in some way he managed to pacify them and succeeded in prevailing upon them to resume their swords. One of the men in the command which we went to relieve, while engaged in laughing at seeing us trying to dodge the rebel shells, got his head above the level of the works, and a cannon shot carried the back part of his head away, leaving his features complete, which were still convulsed with laughter, as he lay there in death, like a statue of Tragedy, wearing the mask of Comedy. But for the overweening recklessness of our puerile colonel, we should have reached our objective point without the loss of a man. We could easily have done so by a slight detour, on either, hand through the woods, and that method was thereafter pursued when relieving the line. At this time our fire upon the works of the enemy was incessant, day and night. Our fixed ammunition was brought onto the field in boxes containing one thousand rounds each. The boxes were split open, and the soldier could help himself.

The opposing lines were in such close proximity on some parts of the field, that a conversation with the enemy

could be carried on in an ordinary tone of voice, and we finally arranged a truce, the conditions of which were, that in
case either side received orders to reopen hostilities, a sig-
nal shot must be fired in the air, as a fair warning to the other
side. And to the honor of both parties, be it said
this stipulation was faithfully carried out. This ar-
rangement was made between the men without the consent
or knowledge of the officers. We finally became upon so
good terms with each other that traffic sprang up between
us. The barter usually was coffee and tobacco. Of the former we frequently had superabundance, and of the latter they
usually had an excess, so the conditions of trade were favorable, and under this treaty we became quite neighborly, so
much so indeed, that sitting on top of our rifle pits, we would
read aloud from our Northern papers for Johnnie's edifi-
cation, and Johnnie would reciprocate in kind, by reading
aloud to us from the papers of his section, and to hear the
criticism that would follow the reading of an article, by those
of adverse side, would furnish lots of amusement for the
boys. It was in listening to an article read by a Johnnie,
from a Southern newspaper, that we first learned of the capture of General Stoneman, who had been raiding with his
cavalry in Northern Georgia. At the time the rebs read the
article we utterly scouted it, but sure enough in a very few
days the account was confirmed by the Northern press.

On the right of our line was a road leading to Petersburg and directly across the road was a fort or rather a strong
redoubt, which had been abandoned by our forces evidently
from a suspicion that it was being mined by the enemy. I
had an opportunity one day, and I took a look into it. The
guns had all been removed, and there were oat sacks hanging over the embrasures, but it did really bear traces of coun-
termining ; however, a fort was built near it on the opposite
side of the road. I had been posted as a vidette between the
lines for the purpose of watching the movements of the
enemy to prevent surprise. I had just been relieved by
Comrade Warman when we heard the warning shot which

was immediately followed by a volley. We were lying outside our pit, but soon rolled into it, and returned the fire.
But finally the fire slackened somewhat, when one of our fellows hallooed across to the Johnnies, "Fire away there you
d—m—ed rebels! you can't hit anybody," when they
ceased shooting in apparent disgust. Our men made a lot
of gabions, and ramming them solidly with earth, and getting behind them, rolled them up to where they purposed
building a fort, and under cover of this protection commenced digging. This being done during the night the
enemy heard them, and opened fire and vigorously shelled
them, but with little effect, and by day-break next morning
we had a stout embankment, which grew in a short time into
a strong redoubt. The lines at this point being so close to
each other, it became a favorite spot for desertions. A number of the rebels came to us here, but soon a strict watch
was instituted by both sides to prevent desertions. I never
knew of but one of our men to attempt it, and it resulted disastrously to him, as he was shot and killed just as he reached
the enemy's rifle pits. The shooting was done by one of the
Buck Tails.

After being relieved from service on this part of the line,
we returned to our old camp. Here the colonel at once proceeded to institute new regulations which consisted of everything being done by tap of drum, and as we had not been
schooled in that sort of tactics, it was very awkward business
for us, and as a consequence, mistakes were frequent. This
would exasperate the doughty colonel and he would tyran-
nically and brutally resent it. Taps were sounded for roll-
call early in the morning. Upon one occasion some of Company F's men not putting in an appearance as promptly as
Colonel Carle thought they should have done, he rushed to
their tents and kicked them out. That night several shots
were sent whizzing through his tent just over his head, and
rushing out he found a coffin at his tent door, inscribed,
"Beware," and on it the crossbones. He took the hint and
learned the lesson which it took West Pointers sometimes

so long to learn, viz., that volunteers were not regulars. However, it cured him of his brutal practices and made a pretty decent officer of him.

The next time we were sent to relieve the picket line it was to the left of where we had been before, and quite near to the magnolia swamp. A number of the Massachusetts men had been killed in this swamp and if I recollect correctly, had not yet been buried.

The rebel vidette post at this point was so close to our pit that he could hear our conversation, and it was determined that he should be crowded back further, and as it was my trick on as vidette, I was sent out to occupy his post before he came on for the night. As darkness had not yet settled down, I cautiously crawled out through the ragweed and reached the place undiscovered, and after getting my bearings a little, I began looking about me. I saw two Johnnies in bright new uniforms lying outside of their pit. My first impulse was to shoot and I drew a bead on one of them, when it occurred to me that it would be too much akin to deliberate murder, and I could not pull the trigger ; but I have often thought, that if "somebody's darling" had realized how near he was to death's door that evening, it would have caused the chills to chase each other up his spinal marrow in rapid succession. I stood my "trick," or rather I should say, crouched it, in the weeds until relieved by Comrade J. Malone, (who was afterwards captured and died of starvation at Salisbury). Soon after I was relieved the rebel vidette put in his appearance, and on seeing his post occupied, he called out, "Say, Yank ! You are on my post !" "I know it, Johnnie," said Malone, "but you can't have it any more, you are too close to our pit. Here, move back !" And he moved without further protest.

After we had completed the construction of Fort Warren we were moved still farther to the left, and being deployed we covered the line which had been previously held by the Second Corps. This corps, (the Second), had been marched to the rear of the mine, and it was their misfortune to be involved in that blundering and terribly mismanaged fiasco. Myself and a comrade by the name of Williams were placed on picket here, our station being in a strip of pine woods, and we remained on this post for sixteen days, relieving each other every four hours, day and night, our food being brought to us. This was a very lonely spot, and the mournful notes of the whipporwill at night rendered it still more distressingly lonesome. Williams was a long, lean, hungry-looking man, with an inordinate appetite. He would frequently eat his sixteen ounces of bread, meat and beans in proportion, at one meal, washing it down with a quart of strong, black coffee, and like "Oliver Twist" wish for more. He informed me that this voracious appetite was acquired in working as a boatman on the Allegheny River, and that he could easily stow away a small ham, a peck of potatoes, with bread and butter and such other garnishment as might accompany, at one sitting without the slightest inconvenience to himself. But as my rations were more than sufficient to meet my requirements, I cheerfully contributed my surplus stock, which helped to make Williams' stay in the woods more endurable, but I frequently thought that his buzz-saw appetite would wreck the oldest boarding house establishment in the realm in a brief time. From our post in the woods we had a distant view of the mine explosion in front of Petersburg, and a fearful eruption it was. It caused the earth to sway and rock as though riven by an earthquake, while an immense black balloon, a thousand feet or more in diameter, shot into the air a distance of several hundred feet, then bursting, scattered its death dealing fragments far and wide. At least five hundred rebels, with their ordnance and equipment were blown to atoms by the explosion of over ten tons of powder which had been buried beneath the fortress, and had the Federal forces, designated to charge the rebel line when the mine should explode, had they, I say, followed the orders given, that day would doubtless have seen Petersburg occupied by the Union army. But some one high in authority had grievously blundered, as had so frequently been the case on more than one important occasion before in this army. But the soldier. "Not his to reason why. Not his to make reply, but his to do, and die."

You will allow me here to say that it is my candid opinion that the history of the armies of the world will be searched in vain for a parallel for a series of blunders such as characterized the Army of the Potomac ; all chargeable to the incompetency of its commanders. As to those made by McClelland, few doubt but that they were purposely made ; an outward expression of an inward disloyalty to his country. But what is to be said of the blundering which resulted so disastrously at Fredericksburg, Chancellorsville and Cold Harbor ? To say nothing of the abortion of the mine at Petersburg. Can these failures be chargeable to any other cause than that of stupendous blundering ? Either one of which would have been avoided by the exercise of good judgment or common sense. The superior military ability with which General Lee is accredited was due largely to the blunderings of the commanders of the Army of the Potomac. General Lee made egregious mistakes also, which if they had been taken advantage of by the Union commanders, would have resulted in the utter destruction of the rebel army. Notable among his blunders was the detaching of three whole divisions from his army and sending them to the capture of Harper's Ferry, thus leaving himself with only about thirty-five thousand men, with which to oppose the ninety thousand well armed and well fed men composing Geo. B. McClelland's army. But it is evident that General Lee knew with whom he had to deal. General McClelland knew also all about the movement of Lee's forces, as the order for their disposition had fallen into his hands ; there can be no shadow of a doubt that McClelland purposely and traitorously withheld the blow which could and would have wiped Lee's army out of existence as a military organization.

The rebels had no braver men or better fighters than had the Federals, and I maintain that there never was a time, from the moment of its organization until its muster out, that the noble old Army of the Potomac could not hold its own against an equal number of Johnnies, or any other soldiers on the face of the earth.   But the fact remains that the Army of the Potomac was greatly handicapped by the incompetency of its leaders, and as a member of that army it makes my blood boil to think how the brave, patriotic men of which that grand Army of the Potomac was composed, had to rest under the suspicion of incompetency, when, in point of fact, the whole trouble was chargeable to the character of its leadership, who not only blundered themselves, but were incapable of profiting by the mistakes of the enemy against whom they were pitted.

CHAPTER X.

The Capture.

As the enemy held the Weldon railroad, we were marched to Yellow Tavern to seize and destroy the road at that point. Here on the 18th of August, 1864, we advanced upon the enemy's works under a terrific fire from their field batteries, and in the midst of a rain storm, with heaven's artillery let loose upon us, it seemed as though the wrath of God was conspiring with the fury of man, in wreaking vengeance upon our devoted heads. We drove the enemy from their position at the railroad through a piece of woods, and into their line of works, and there succeeded in holding them at bay while the railroad was being destroyed. Our position here being very exposed, every fellow was anxious for his own safety. I succeeded in scooping out a small pit, into which I crawled, but from which I was soon forced by reason of its filling with water, as the downpour of rain continued. I then secured a position behind a nearby tree. While standing behind my tree I saw through an embrasure in the fort a man who was evidently a cannoneer. I aimed, and shot ; he fell, and I am glad that that is all I know about the transaction. I do not of course know how all old soldiers feel about such matters, but while it is probable that no soldier who was in several engagements, and did his duty as a soldier, but caused the death of one or more of his fellow beings, and while he might have been, and probably was entirely justifiable in so doing, yet there is an aversion I believe in every old soldier's heart, to knowing that he killed anybody. At about this time we dispatched Comrade Springer to the rear on a double mission, as our ammunition was nearly exhausted, and we were anxious for a cup of coffee. This little unimportant incident was the beginning of the most desperate and soul-harrowing dilemma we as soldiers were

ever fated to be caught in. Springer came rushing back in
a few moments with blanched face to inform us that we were
completely surrounded, that the enemy was in our rear, and
for every man to look out for himself. On hearing this we
very naturally started back by the way we had come. I now
think if we had taken an oblique direction, to our left, we
might have flanked the rebel line and escaped, but that was
not to be for we soon encountered a line of rebel skirmishers
whom we captured and disarmed. Among our captives was
a mounted officer to whom one of our men said, as he threat-
eningly raised his gun, "Get down off that horse, you rebel
son of a b——h! or I'll blow your brains out," and the
reb dismounted without parley. "Now make off there,"
says Yank, "I'll do the riding act myself," and we started
on with our prisoners, thinking we were taking them into
our lines, when suddenly we ran into a rebel brigade which
was drawn up in line of battle. The tables were turned,
the officer so recently dismounted looked up at the man on
his horse, and said, "I guess I'll ride that horse again now !"
"I guess you will," said the man, and jumping nimbly down,
he dashed his gun against a tree, and the rest of us imitated
his example, thus making our arms useless to the enemy,
but as Comrade Mitchell struck his rifle against a tree, it exploded, and I narrowly escaped receiving its contents in my
body. The officer whom we had so unceremoniously dismounted, proved to be the rebel General Mahone, and it
was his brigade which now stood so much in our way of escape. It was a startling and remarkable fact, that this entire rebel brigade, in broad daylight, had been marched to
the rear of our lines, formed in line of battle and deployed
skirmishers without opposition or discovery ; in fact all our
line officers had been made prisoners before the rank and
file knew that the Johnnies were in the rear at all, and not a
shot had been fired until about the time we were engaged in
taking the rebel skirmishers prisoners. About that time our
batteries opened a hot fire upon us, but they fired too high to
do the rebel brigade any harm.

Human language does not contain words sufficiently expressive with which to denounce the criminal stupidity and incompetence of the officer who was responsible for this affair ; when a simple line of pickets posted on our flank would have rendered such a move impossible upon the part of the rebels, or it would at least have given warning so that the movement could have been checkmated. There were some three thousand of us captured here by the rebels and at least three-fourths of this number were purposely starved to death in the prison hells of the South. We were hurriedly hustled off to Petersburg, the rebels stealing our blankets and the hats off our heads as we were marched along. I had a fight with a Johnnie who tried to take my hat and I managed to retain it, but soon thereafter traded it off for an inferior cap, and a five dollar Confederate note. I swapped as the Yankee would say, because I realized that it would be a question of a short time when I should be obliged to give it up, as they systematically robbed us of everything valuable we possessed. As we passed through Petersburg I observed several unexploded two hundred pound shells, which I concluded had been sent in by Uncle Sam as visiting cards. The first night of our captivity we were corralled in the open air near the city. During the night a rebel came among us for the purpose of robbing us of any valuables that might still be found with us, and seeing Comrade Richie having a blanket, he attempted to steal it, but he had wakened up the wrong passenger, for Richie jumped to his feet and promptly knocked the rebel down. Upon regaining his feet the infuriated rebel rushed off for his gun, and returning threatened to kill all the d—m—d Yankees in the camp, but a rebel officer hearing the rumpus, came up at this juncture, and ordered the cowardly cur off the grounds. The following morning we were shipped to Richmond by rail. On arriving there we were confined in a large brick building, known as Pemberton. It stood on Cary street, above, and nearly opposite Libby Prison.

While confined in this building John McClosky, who is

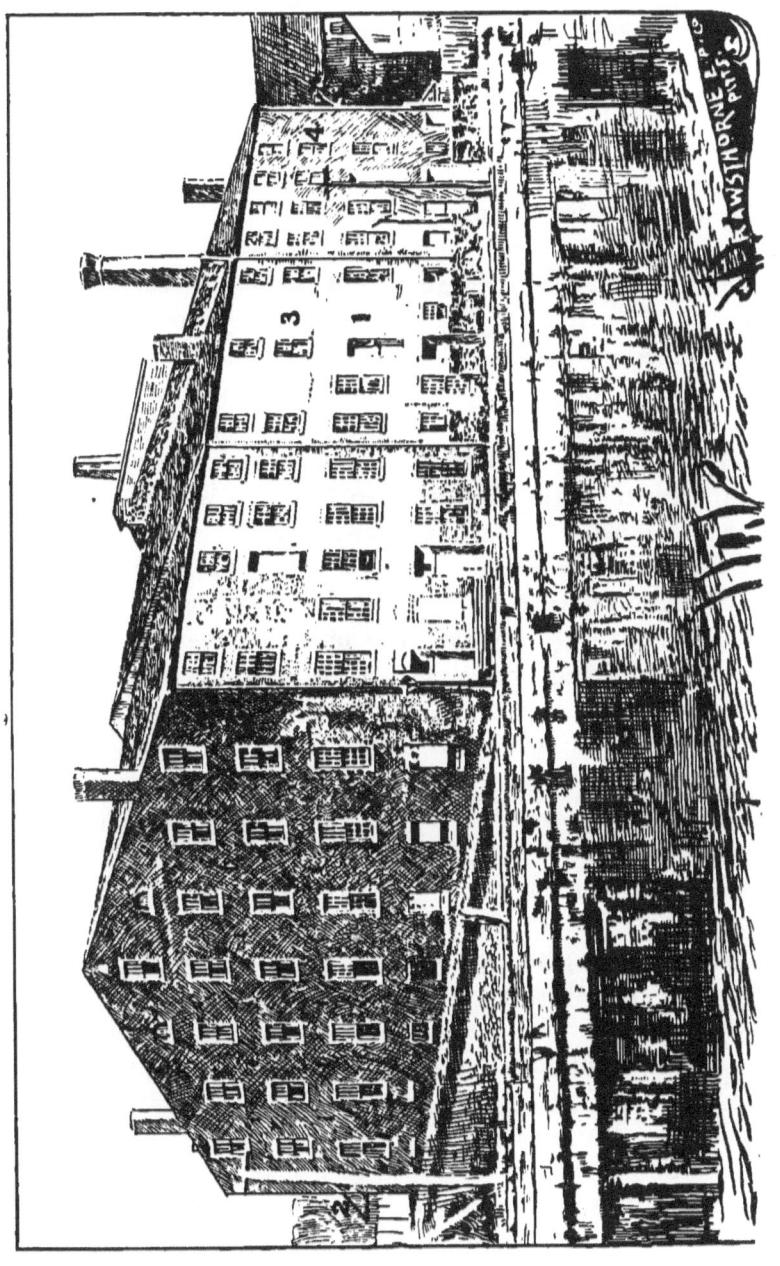

LIBBY PRISON—(AFTER PHOTO.)

now living in Fostoria, O., threw a Spencer rifle cartridge which he wished to be rid of out the window. It struck the pavement and exploded. This occurrence caused a great stir among the Johnnies and they at once rushed a number of soldiers and several officers into the building to punish the Yank who had tried to blow up the guard. The Buck Tail explained that having no further use for the cartridge, he had simply thrown it away ; however, this explanation was not accepted and the man was brutally bucked and gagged. After this incident we were moved across to Libby and confined on the second floor of that infamously historical building, and the notorious Dick Turner, and his pal John Ross, put in an appearance, ostensibly for the purpose of taking charge for safe keeping of the effects of the prisoners of war, but really for the purpose of robbery in a wholesale way. "Now," said Turner to us, "all those of you who voluntarily give up their money and valuables to us, the same will be safely kept and returned to you on your leaving the prison, and the clerk will now take your names, make a schedule, carefully describing everything so left with him, but everybody will be searched, and all property not handed over to the clerk will be immediately confiscated." The first division of Turner's speech was a lie, pure and simple, as that prince of thieves, Dick Turner, and his robber gang, never returned, nor never designed returning anything they had stolen from the prisoners of war. However, the latter portion of the speech of the villain we found to be literally true, for they did search every one of us, and they did confiscate everything that the search developed, lead pencils, combs, pocket knives, jewelry, watches and money ; everything, in fact, but our scant clothing was taken. I happened to have on my person at that time two bank notes, a two dollar greenback and a ten dollar Confederate States note, and when I heard Dick Turner's speech, I at once made up my mind to leave as little property with that clerk of his as I conveniently could ; accordingly I proceeded to cut a small strip of the red leather off of the top of one of my bootlegs, and in this I tightly wrapped my money, and placing it in my mouth I saved it. I also saved my pocket knife, which was a small one, by placing it in the palm of my hand and deftly placing my thumb over it. So I passed the search, and saved my money and pocket knife. This latter article aided me in whiling away many an hour in the prison life which followed, that would otherwise have hung heavy on my hands, for we would sit by hours and whittle and carve, in forming trinkets from bits of wood and bone, some specimens of which I still have in my possession. Shortly after Dick Turner's robbery had been enacted at Libby, we were transferred to Belle Island, which is situated in the James River, above the city of Richmond, Va.

The Tredegar Iron works, now busily at work turning out rebel war material, occupied the upper end of the island while our prison camp, several acres in extent, and surrounded by rifle pits, was located at the lower, or western end of the island. The entrance gate, the cook house and the guards' quarters were on the Richmond side of the island, while an alleyway skirted with tight board fence on either side led to the river on the Manchester side. Through this alley the prisoners passed in getting water from the river. From the alley round to the cook house the river made a sharp bend. In this bend out in the river were several small islands, very small, some of them only a few yards in extent, and the largest of the group was not more than twenty feet distant from the one on which we were imprisoned, but a deep channel flowed between. These isles were thickly covered with a growth of willows and rushes, and were utilized by some of the prisoners in their attempts at escape as will be narrated later on.

Lying between the prison pen and the Tredegar Iron mills, was a hill, upon the brow of which was placed a battery whose guns were trained upon our camp. Then across the river, on the Richmond hills, was another battery, with its guns trained in the same suggestive manner. We were supplied with a few old rotten rags of canvas for shelter, but

were allowed no fire.   And just here I wish to say that in my
humble opinion there existed between the leaders of the Confederate cause, and hell, a league which the Prince of Darkness on the one hand, and Jefferson Davis on the other,
stood mutually pledged to carry out in such a way and manner as should best and most fully employ each and all the hell-
born devices for the affliction and torment of men.   From the
middle of the year 1864 until the collapse of the rebellion, I
say on, and after, the date last named, were the darkest and
most desperate days of the Southern Confederacy.   We
search in vain, the whole category of crime, for one, which
these desperate rebel leaders would for an instant halt, or hes-
itate to commit, to bolster their tottering pillars of state.
They deliberately planned for arson, with all its concomitant
crimes, for the spreading of contagious diseases by means
of infected clothing amongst the people of the North, and
the wholesale murder, by starvation, of the Union soldiers
which the fortunes of war had placed within their power.
For shame !   For shame !   And then to remember that after
all this revelry in crime, after all this hellish refinement of
cruelty toward our brave, but helpless and defenceless boys,
locked as prisoners of war in their dank, reeking prison pens,
to be flayed alive with vermin, and finally starved to death
by a protracted process.   I say then to think that to such
as those was extended the executive clemency, and not a villain of them all received the just recompense of reward for
their crimes.   Oh !   how I thank heaven to-day as I remember and seem to see again, the comrades of my prison life,
with emaciated forms, sunken cheeks and eyes, eyes which
were wont to sparkle and glow with life's loves and ambitions,
now glazing in death's slow oncoming tide, and I seem to
hear again the voice once strong and musical as the spheres,
now weak and sepulchral as though it issued from the tomb,
as its last cadence dies away in a feeble cry for bread.   As I
remember these things my heart swells with gratitude when
I remember also that Jehovah hath said "Vengeance is Mine !
I will repay, saith the Lord !"   It was not until after the

regime of starvation was inaugurated by the rebel government as a course of treatment of the prisoners of war, that the
other barbarities which I have enumerated were put into
practice, so that those of our comrades who were prisoners
during the earlier period of the war scarcely know what
breathing holes of hell these later prisons were. Here it
was that imprisonment for a few months meant death sure
and certain, graduated solely on the power of constitutional
endurance of the individual prisoner. May God forgive
those worse than red-handed murders if he will, but I believe
I never can.

To continue the account and description of our camp
on Belle Isle. The space between the water and the bend
in the river before alluded to, down to the water's edge was
utilized for the purpose of counting the prisoners. We were
turned into this space as often as every other day, and as
we were marched back into camp, we were counted off by
the rebs. This ground was, when first set apart as a corral
for us, well set with grass, but the starving men soon had
pulled the last spear of it, and ate it up, root and branch, until that ground was as bare as the rock of Gibraltar. At all
times save when the counting process was going on, a heavy
guard was maintained along the line of the alley, and also
around the camp, but when we were out for the purpose of
being counted, at such times they only had a light guard
along the river front, as they were well assured that no one
would be likely to attempt swimming the river, at least, in
the daytime, in an effort to escape. One day when they had
turned us out for counting a rebel guard posted at the bend,
in order to mark the end of his beat, laid down his shelter
tent. I had my eye on that tent, and I wanted it, and I concluded to have it, or fail in an attempt to secure it. So I
watched the guard until he rounded the bend on his beat,
then I gobbled the tent and hustled up into the crowd and
gave one-half of it to my comrade, and we made short work
of wrapping that canvas around our bodies, and, sooth to
say, we got safely into camp with it, too. In the course of

the day there were seven brave fellows who had determined
to make a break for freedom, so, watching until the guard
was well around the bend on his beat again, when silently
they dropped into the water, and swimming to the isle
twenty feet away, they drew themselves up amongst the willows without having been discovered by the guard. Their
design was to lie concealed till night came on, then to swim
the river and so make their escape. But the rebs in some
way discovered them, and they were brought back, and made
to ride the wooden horse as a punishment. As some of my
readers may not be familiar with this strain of horses, I will
briefly describe a wooden horse. It is a trestle such as car-
penters use to rest lumber on which they wish to saw, only
that the wooden horse trestle is longer of leg than that used
by the carpenter. Now that is all it takes to make a horse
of the kind under discussion ; but now as to the fellow who
has to ride the horse, I will tell you how they fix him. They
take the offender and set him astride of the trestle, tie his
hands behind his back, a tent pin is driven into the ground
on either side of the horse, a tent rope is fastened to each of
the ankles of the rider, then made fast to the tent pins which
are then tightly driven into the ground, and while the rider's
feet cannot touch the ground, he is stretched down so closely
that he is in no danger of becoming unhorsed, and his hands
being fastened behind him he cannot protect himself from the
swarms of gnats and flies which attack his face and neck ;
and being totally unable to shift his position, the torture becomes unbearable, and the victim often faints away. I saw
two of the recaptured prisoners faint, when I walked away
from the brutal scene, wishing that I had almighty power
for about one minute, and if I could have had it, I am thinking you are making a pretty safe guess as to what use I would
have put it to. The day following the rebels shaved the ver-
dure off those litttle isles until they were as bald as goose
eggs ; there was no more hiding there.

Some days after, when we were turned out for another
count, I observed the imprint of a man in the sand, and like

BELLE ISLE—(AFTER PHOTO.)

Robinson Crusoe on discovering a footprint in the sand, I was startled. It instantly suggested to my mind a method of escape and quickly obliterating the telltale imprint, I walked up to the rear of the cook house, where I had observed an old Sibley tent pole to be lying for a week or more and I had been cudgeling my brain for a chance to secure and use it. Now here was the chance, and the use would come later. I laid hold of it, and after a little struggle I succeeded in wrenching off one of the three iron feet and rolling it up in my shelter tent I carried it into camp. I immediately called a council of war among my messmates, and submitted my plans, which received their approval, and were as follows : The next time we were turned out for count, a compact ring or circle was to be formed by us, so that the guard could not see what was going on within, thus screened we were to dig a cave in the sand, of sufficient size to accommodate two men,(for digging we used the iron foot I had secured from the tent pole). The men were to be covered up in the sand, and to remain until some time the following night, when being outside the guard they could swim the river and make their escape, and at the next count off two more, and so on. On our next outing we dug our hole according to our plans and specifications and selecting Comrades David Richie and Calvin Darnell, they being small men, we buried them up, leaving holes for air which we concealed by placing some dead grass over them. The next time the hole was to be enlarged, and Isaac Moore and myself, two of the larger men in the mess were to have our inning. With what anxiety we watched that spot of ground that afternoon. Imagine our alarm when late in the day we saw some pigs rooting around near where our boys were buried. Those infernal swine, they kept poking around there until one of them stepped into one of the breathing holes. Richie caught him by the foot. I saw the pig jerking to get loose, and as there were two rebels engaged in fishing only a short distance away, I was fearful lest they would observe it, and enter upon an investigation of the cause of the strange action of the hog, but they did not seem to see it at all, and Richie let go of the pig's foot, and he walked off as if nothing had happened. I have often wondered why the rebs kept those pigs in the inclosure about the cook house, but after debating the subject to some extent we reached the conclusion that it was to garnish our soup with a pork flavor, as we have ofttimes detected them with their snouts in our soup buckets before the soup was served to us. However, I never was so fortunate as to find a scrap of meat of any kind in my soup, while in Belle Isle. But I conclude that you also are becoming anxious about the comrades whom we left buried in the sand some hours since. Well as the rebel officer of the guard that evening was making his rounds, a soldier belonging to a New York command called him up to the fence and informed him in regard to Richie and Darnell, and pointed out to him as nearly as he could, where they were in hiding. The officer drew his sword and proceeded to make search after the hiding prisoners. He pierced the ground all about them but failing to find them sent word to Major Turner at Richmond, who had charge of all prisoners of war in and about Richmond. Now, while this Turner was no relation to Dick, of Libby, they were as near of kin in villainies, as two peas in a pod. The major came over to the island armed with an old pepper-box revolver. He had twelve or fifteen soldiers with him. These he set to work jabbing around in the sand, until one of them stuck Richie in the head, which caused him to cry out, then they set about digging them out of their hiding place. As soon as poor Richie was out of the hole the valorless major presented his revolver at his head and endeavored to shoot him but the weapon refused to respond, and after snapping it for awhile, threw it into the river in disgust. He then ordered that the prisoners be kept in the hole where they were found for two days and nights, without food or water, and after placing a guard over them, the chivalrous Southerner returned to his post at Richmond, where he no doubt gave to his associates in crime a glowing account of his deeds of valor done that day against two unarmed

and half starved prisoners of war. On our being turned out
again for count the next day we threw them some small bits
of bread which we had saved for the purpose from our own
meagre rations, but we could not give them any water.
After remaining in the hole for the prescribed length of time,
they were allowed to rejoin the mess. The man who informed the guard of the plot of these boys to escape was
found out by one of our men, and we were about to organize
a court martial for his trial, when we were all shipped to
Salisbury, where I learned he afterward died of starvation.

As food is the all-absorbing thought by day and the
theme of dreams by night to starving men, it is proper to
give a description of the quality and quantity of the grub,
for to call it food would be to misname it, (even if it were designed for hogs). It would be almost impossible to give one
who did not have an opportunity of seeing the rations which
were furnished us, as prisoners of war at our country retreat
on Belle Isle, and at the Hotel de Libby in the city. For
breakfast we had a piece of cornbread about two inches
square, or one slice of wheat bread, (usually sour), and one
pint of coffee, (so-called), made from parched rye. For dinner we had absolutely nothing. For supper we were served
the same amount of bread, and of the same quality, and
either a pint of rye coffee or instead thereof a pint of pea
soup, or one tablespoonful of boiled rice, or two ounces of
rotten bacon or beef. This constituted the entire bill of fare
at the two hostelries named. The variety consisted alone
in the fact that if you got coffee you did not get soup, and
if you got soup you did not get rice, and if you got rice, you
did not get meat. They never made the unpardonable mistake of serving any two of the articles named at any one meal.
The peas used in making soup were of a variety known in the
South as "Nigger peas" and were invariably bug-eaten.
The soup was flavored with a bit of the kind of pork of which
I have spoken ; it was necessary to skim the bugs off before
the soup could be swallowed, as they arose to the surface in
great quantities. In regard to the bacon furnished, if the

human mind can conceive of anything really loathsome, that bacon would stand for its representative ; if a bit of the rind were lifted it would reveal a squirming mass of maggots and worms, or if it were cooked, there they would lie in grim and greasy rows, rigid in death. The beef supply consisted of shin bones and heads from which the tongues were invariably extracted, and the eyes left in, and sometimes the cud would be found sticking between the jaws. When the meat was served an ox eye was a full ration of meat for one prisoner, and the poor starved men would trim and gnaw them until they had the appearance of large glass marbles. On Christmas and New Years, and holidays, we were given nothing whatever to eat. One day when we were to be counted, I saw a rebel give a prisoner a quart of peas, and surmising that they had been given to him as a reward for "informing," I concluded to watch him. I did so. The poor fellow being so near starved gulped them, as a hog might have done, without chewing, but very soon his famished stomach revolted, and he threw them up, when one of his comrades carefully picked them up from the ground where they had fallen and ate them. "Oh, the rarity of Christian charity under the sun !" What a commentary upon Christian progress ! After more than eighteen hundred years of zealous teaching and preaching, here was a Christian man starved by Christian men until he was reduced to the miserable extremity of eating vomit like a dog. This systematic and diabolic plan of starving helpless prisoners by our Christian brethren of the South stands unparalleled even by the annals of the most depraved and barbaric savages of any tribe or nation that was known at any time to have polluted and disgraced God's green earth. The starving of our prisoners by the rebels was not, as some apologists would have us believe, an incident of the war, which was brought about by a chance contingency ; far from it. This method of starvation was deliberately planned and adopted by the authorities of the Southern Confederacy as a means to an end, and that end was the weakening and reducing of the men com-

posing our army, and how well their design succeeded witness the skeletons of nearly seventy thousand men, literally
and absolutely starved to death in the prison hells of the
South.   As a matter of fact, there were about twenty thous-
and more Union soldiers who were starved to death by the
rebels than were slain in battle during the whole course of the
war.   The inexplicable policy of our own government in refusing or neglecting to exchange prisoners of war, or to enforce, by retributive treatment, the proper care of those who
were unfortunate enough to fall into the rebels' hands, was indeed reprehensible, and was only exceeded by the brutality of
the rebs in the execution of their starving policy.   It has often
been said that the rebels really did the best they could to
provide their prisoners with food and care, but that they
could do no better for lack of money.   This is untrue ;   there
never was a time during the whole course of the war that
the rebels could not have fed their prisoners plentifully had
they so desired, statements and affidavits made in Pollard's
"Lost Cause," and the "Life of Jefferson Davis" to the contrary notwithstanding.   Liars and perjurers !   From Jeff
Davis down.   Their ports were blockaded ;   no outlet for
their products ;   their country was literally flooded with rice
and other articles of food, and if there had been nothing but
rice, men would not starve on rice.   There is not a case on
record of a rebel soldier starving to death, and yet these perjurers swear that Union prisoners were fed the same quality
and quantity of food as were their own soldiers.   I call attention to another fact :   Clothing and canned food were sent
in large quantities from the North for our use, and were
stored in a building within sight of Belle Isle, yet none of
these things ever reached us, not a jot or tittle of them.
After the rebels had stolen what they wished of them, the
torch was applied, and the balance of them burned.   This
however was not done until Richmond was evacuated.   This
proves conclusively that the starving of the prisoners was deliberately designed.   It is the settled conviction of all who
were in position to form judgment upon this subject, that had

our government retaliated by feeding the rebel prisoners who fell into our hands in the same manner, as to quality and quantity of food, there never would have been a case of starvation to be reported from any of the prison pens of the South.

This action on the part of General Grant, who had supreme command of all the armies of the United States, preferring to allow our comrades to starve and die by the thousands rather than chance the meeting of the exchanged Confederates in the field, is a sad blot on his otherwise famous record.

CHAPTER XI.

THE FIRST ESCAPE.

On the 6th day of October, 1864, one thousand three hundred prisoners, after being provided with what the rebels informed us were three days' rations, but which by the way were all consumed at one meal by most of the men, and I distinctly remember what an exertion of will power it cost me to even save a small piece of cornbread from my allowance ; we were loaded into box cars and started for another rebel starvation hell, located at Salisbury, N. C.

Sixty-five men were crowded into each car which rendered it impossible for us either to sit or lie down, so we were obliged to stand like cattle in a stock train ; the doors on the right hand side of the cars were locked, while those on the left were open, with two guards stationed in each, and a number of guards also rode on the deck of each car. The cars were old rotten-looking things, and when the train once got under headway it rattled and banged in a way to drown all other sounds, so I set about kicking at the front end of the car in which I was riding, and I soon succeeded in breaking a hole through it large enough to crawl out of if the opportunity came. So giving one-half of my dog tent to my comrade, Isaac Mitchell, I told him that the first stop the train made I proposed to make a break for liberty and he said, "I will follow you." The first stop which the train made was for wood. This was twenty-three miles from Richmond. So out I crawled, onto the bumpers, and down to the ground between the cars and out onto the side where the guards were standing in the doors. I started boldly along side the train toward the engine. One of the guards in the car next to the one I had escaped from as I passed, cried, "Halt, who goes dar ?" Without stopping I turned my head and said, "Who the devil are you talking to !" and

I passed without further challenge, it being so dark they could not distinguish the color of my clothing. Mitchell, who was partly out of the car on hearing them challenge me, drew back, so I was thus left alone. Going up to the engine, where a gang of darkies were throwing wood onto the tank I soon put the woodpile between myself and the cars, and stepping behind a large tree I waited until the train had pulled out and the negroes had gone. At about this stage of the game every white man, woman and child acted as spies for the Southern Confederacy, and whenever a strange face was seen in a community it excited suspicion and the stranger was called to an immediate reckoning. I was fully aware of this fact, and had it confirmed through a bitter experience later on. Being alone, and having no one with whom to counsel, I carefully considered my desperate condition, and pondered upon the best course to pursue in effecting my escape. I was in the enemy's country, South of Richmond, with the rebel army between me and freedom. I was weak from starvation, without food and with insufficient clothing to keep me comfortable during the frosty nights ; no means of lighting a fire and not daring to show myself to ask for food. My case was indeed a desperate one, and I resolved to adopt desperate means in trying to reach the shelter of the old flag once more. I was already twenty miles and more south of Richmond. I planned to go still further south. and thereby either flank the right of the rebel army, or take the desperate chance of running their lines. I resolved to trust no one, not even the negroes, in fear of betrayal. and yet here I was in a country, the topography of which I was in perfect ignorance. I resolved also to travel both by day and night, and thus make the best possible time. and I further resolved to use every means, however desperate, anything short of murder itself, in accomplishing my undertaking to escape. In looking back to these foolish resolves and plans of mine, the things which to me, in my physical weakness seemed so feasible and easy of accomplishment, at this distance assume the aspect of impossibilities ; indeed when thinking of them

in the light of my surroundings, they appear to me like the
vagaries of an idiot.   The gravest of all my mistakes was in
not trusting my case in the hands of the negro, who would
doubtless have guided, fed and concealed me until I reached
the Union lines.   But having resolved my course, I left my
hiding place, returned to the railroad track and started in
the direction which the train from which I had escaped, had
gone.   I soon came to a field of corn, alongside the track,
which I entered and shelling two ears, I ate with great avidity, notwithstanding I had eaten the elaborate three days'
rations with which the rebels had furnished us.   After filling my pockets with corn for future use I continued my
journey until about midnight, when I discovered a fire burning on the bank of a stream, which I rightly guessed to be
the Appomattox River.   The railroad crossed the river at this
point on a trestle bridge, and there was a fort on the farther
bank, and a guard walked back and forth over the bridge,
while the fire which was located between the fort and the
bridge, threw a lurid light for a considerable distance over
all surrounding objects.   Approaching as near as possible
without being observed, I waited until the guard had turned
to walk toward the opposite side, then hurrying to the end
of the bridge, I got onto the trestles underneath without being detected, and crawling from trestle to trestle, while the
guard walked overhead, at length I reached the abutment on
the other side to find to my dismay that it stood in the water
and was about thirty feet high, and that there was no possible
way of getting around it.   If I were to climb to the top of
the bridge I should be in the full glare of the firelight, and
readily seen by the sentinel, so there was nothing left me but
to make my way back to the side whence I had come.   This
I did in safety, and circling to the left I hid myself in a swamp,
designing to swim the river at daylight.   Being tired and
worn out I fell asleep and did not awaken until the sun was
two hours high.   Then after eating some corn I started for
the river but did not reach it until about noon on account of
its being a crooked, winding stream and I had lost the direc-

tion of it. In my tramp from the swamp to the river I found
a persimmon tree loaded with half-ripe fruit. Not being able
to resist the temptation I ate of it until my mouth was puckered so that I could whistle a great deal easier than I could
sing. Reaching the river I stripped, and tying my clothing in a bundle, tied it to my head and swam the river.
While engaged in dressing I heard voices in the distance,
which I located as coming from a plowed field lying in the
direction I wished to go. Observing that a bushy ravine ran
nearly across this field, I entered it and made my way to the
end of it, which brought me opposite to a tobacco barn which
stood at the edge of a woods. The voices I had heard were
those of some negroes who were engaged in sowing wheat
at the upper end of the field which was quite a distance away.
Watching my chance I got into the barn, which was empty,
but I discovered several dinner buckets sitting about and a
rebel jacket was hanging from a peg. I hastily explored the
dinner pails in hope of finding something to eat, but in this
I was disappointed ; they were all empty, but fastening to
that jacket I made off into the woods where I took off my
blue blouse and put on the rebel jacket. I tied my blouse up
in my handkerchief and traveled. Soon after I struck the
railroad track which I followed to the south again, and on
coming to a house I sneaked into the garden nearby and
pulled a number of very small turnips which I found to be
so hot and biting I could not eat them. Resuming my journey I passed through a little hamlet called Amelia Court
House. This was sometime during the night, and going on
a little way I turned into a clump of bushes and slept for a
few hours. But I had made a mistake again. I should have
turned to the north at the court house, but failed to do so.
Keeping to the railroad I came to a ramshackle village of a
few houses and sheds called Jetersville. It was here where
General Lee's wagon train was captured later on. Seeing a
wagon road which ran through the rear portion of the town,
I took it, as I thought that the safer way, and I succeeded in
passing through all right. Immediately beyond the village

the road ascended quite a hill and between this road and the
railroad was an open pine woods through which I designed
to pass and thus reach the railroad track again, but, alas !
an arbiter of my fate was ascending that hill, on the other
side, unbeknown to me.

As I reached the foot of the hill and entered the woods,
I saw two men heave into view on top of the eminence, one of
whom was in a buggy, the other mounted on a horse.   The
horseman dashed down upon me and with drawn revolver
ordered me to surrender, which I did, and he marched me up
to the party in the buggy, who proved to be the sheriff of
Amelia County.   The cavalier was a conscript officer and
they were out for human game, and I was in it.   The sheriff
subjected me to a rigid questioning to which I responded with
a promptitude worthy of a better cause.   I said I belonged to
a North Carolina regiment, that my mother was sick, and
that I had been given a furlough to go to see her, that I had
lost the document, and a whole lot of lies which would have
made the father of lies turn green with envy to have been
able to imitate. But it was no go. That mullet-headed sheriff
would not believe a word of the whole lot.   He said I was
no doubt an escaped Yankee, and he would be obliged to
take me back and place me in jail at Amelia. My corn and persimmon diet had left me in such a famished condition that I
did not care much where he took me so there was something
to eat in it.   I demanded food, and he said he would provide
supper for me at his home, which was on the way to Amelia.
Soon arriving at his house the sheriff ordered supper, which
was shortly on the table and consisted of corn cakes, fried bacon and sorghum molasses, and the facility with which I hid
that "grub" from view, caused the wench who baked the
cakes to hustle, and the sheriff to conclude that he had captured a gormandizer.   While I was at supper, the wife of the
sheriff was busy examining my bundle, which I had left in
another room. I found the contents of my pack very much
disarranged and the sheriff more confirmed in his belief that
I was an escaped Yank.   But he seemed a very humane sort

of a man, and inclined to give me the benefit of any doubts
he might entertain in regard to my loyalty to the South.
But of course I could not prove up on my claim. After supper the buggy was brought out again, and we got in and
drove to Amelia Court House. On arriving there the sheriff
concluded to send me on to Richmond instead of placing me
in jail at the court house, so he took me to the depot, and
while waiting for the train, a number of rebels, both young
and old, fired questions at me, which I answered to the best
of my ability. Finally a man came in and said he was the
major of the First North Carolina Regiment. Now this was
the command I had told the sheriff I was a member of, so you
can guess I felt sort of streaked. Well the major said he had
been desperately wounded, and was home while his wound
was healing, and he proceeded to question me, but I was wary
and cautious, believing all the while that he was a liar, as well
as myself, for I reasoned that if he was a North Carolinian,
how did it come that his home was here in Virginia ? Finally he asked, "Who is colonel of the First North Carolina ?"
"Colonel Anderson," said I. Now by G—d you lie," said the
major, "for Colonel Hawkins commands that regiment, and
you are nothing but a d—m—ed Yankee." "D—n it," said
I, "you have not seen the regiment for over a year and how
do you know what changes have taken place in that time.
And I believe that you lie also, for if you belong to the First
North Carolina, how does it come that I find you living here
in Virginia ?" I knew that the rebels brigaded their men
from the different states by themselves. The sheriff laughed
heartily and this answer shut him up, but another of them
said, "Well I know you are a Yankee anyhow." "And how
do you know it ?" said I. "Why," said he, "you would git as
mad as h—ll when the major called you a Yankee if you had-
n't been one." I answered that fellow with a contemptuous
look, and mentally resolved that the next time I was called
a damned Yankee when I was honestly trying to pose as a
rebel, I would "git as mad as hell." Shortly after this questioning, a train pulled in and I was handed over to the tender

mercies of a sergeant by the sheriff, who told him that I was an escaped Yankee, and that he should hand me over to the proper official at Richmond. The sergeant took me into the forward coach and put me in among a lot of rebel deserters whom he was taking to the city under a strong guard. This car had formerly been used as a baggage car, with a door at either end, and wide side doors in the center, but it had been fitted up with seats and transformed into a sort of a passenger coach. The sergeant appreciating the desperate character of the Yankee whom he had in charge, selected a trustworthy rebel whose special commission was to carefully guard me, and right royally did he attend to his duty. He sat on the same seat with me and acted as my twin automaton ; when I got up, he got up, when I walked the car for exercise, he walked too, when I sat down, he sat down also. Under the seat was the knapsack of my guard, and the car being badly lighted, I took advantage of it to slip my hand down between my knees, and lifting the flap of said knapsack, I "pilfered" therefrom a rebel vest and three pocket handkerchiefs, which I succeeded in placing under the breast of my jacket, unobserved by my attendant who was sitting at my side. The handkerchiefs were marked with the name "Canon," on the corners in indelible ink. I kept one of these for many years as a souvenir of that night's experience, the other two were disposed of as will be related later on ; and now after the lapse of nearly a third of a century, I will say, that if Mr. Canon will make himself known I will cheerfully make him full restitution and apology, and further, in order to emphasize fraternity between the Blue and the Gray, I will set up a supper, a la Hotel de Libby.

On arriving at Richmond, and while the sergeant was marching his deserters out of the left side door onto the platform, at the depot, my guard turned his back to me while buckling on his cartridge box. Instantly jumping from the opposite door, I ran up among the cars in the yard until I reached a street. Here I paused a moment to see whether I was being pursued. I was not followed so I hastily put on the rebel vest and tied my blue one up in my bundle. My uniform was now half reb, and going out onto the street, I hastily decided to try to make my way to Fredericksburg, as I was more familiar with the country about that place. While pondering over the uncertainties of my chances of ultimate escape, I was brought to a sudden halt in seeing Castle Thunder and Libby Prison looming up before me in all their grim majesty. I realized now that I was on Carey street. I hurriedly crossed over by way of a side street to Broad, and boldly started up through the very heart of the city on this street to reach the Fredericksburg depot. On reaching the markethouse I saw a policeman engaged in lighting the gas. I approached him and asked the way to the depot. He answered me that it was three miles directly up Broad street. I then continued my way until I came to the Central depot, and knowing that just twenty-three miles out, at Hanover Junction, this Central railroad crossed the one leading into Fredericksburg, and fearing, should I continue this direct course to that point, that I would be pulled in, I took out along the line of the Central road. After getting out about three miles from the city limits I observed a man who seemed to be drunk staggering along ahead of me, and thinking that I would be able to hold my own with him even should he prove hostile, I quickened my steps and soon overtook him, and as I was passing him he said, "By G—d ole feller, you are going to run the blockade to-night !" This greeting somewhat alarmed me, but I replied, "Oh, I guess not." "Yes you are," said he, and added, "If I only had my shirts here I'd go 'long with you." These words relieved my fears and I admitted that it was my intention to run the lines if I could. We then sat down and talked awhile, and I tried to induce him to go with me, but could not do so. He said everything he possessed in the world was in camp, and he said he would be arrested on his return to camp as he had been on a protracted drunk in Richmond and had overstaid his time. By questioning I received the following information from him. His name was Frank Hardy, and he was

Irish by birth ; that he was sick and tired of the rebellion, and would desert at the first opportunity. He was a member of Company C, Nineteenth Virginia Battalion ; that his captain's name was Hetherington, and his colonel's was Anderson, and that they were in camp at Mechanicsville, engaged in guarding the line of the Chickahominy. He also told me how the guard was posted at the bridge at the crossing of the stream ; and he requested me if I got through to go to a man by the name of Spofford who kept a saloon in Alexandria, and tell him that Hardy was going to run the blockade at the first opportunity. He then gave me his pass, saying that it might be of use to me, and shaking my hand, wished me success in my perilous undertaking, and bade me good-bye.

The pass given me by Hardy was dated Richmond, October 5th, 1864, and read as follows :   "Frank Hardy will immediately rejoin his regiment on the Mechanicsville road." Signed, Brigadier General Gardner, commanding at Richmond, Va.   I have not been in Alexandria since meeting Hardy and so of course I could not deliver his message to Spofford. Neither have I learned whether he rejoined his regiment as he was directed to do in the pass, nor whether the opportunity for running the blockade, as he called it, ever came to him, but of one thing I am sure, that if Frank Hardy is still in the land of the living, even at this late day, I would be glad to hear from or see him.

Soon after parting from Hardy I came to a field of standing sorghum cane.   I cut a stalk of it and chewing it, swallowed the juice and that constituted my supper then taking some more of the cane, I placed it under my arm for future use and proceeded on my way rejoicing.   And reaching the Chickahominy, I crossed it on the railroad bridge without encountering a guard. I found a clump of bushes just beyond which seemed to offer reasonable seclusion.   I crept in and being very weary I soon fell asleep, but on awakening I was chilled to the bone, and was obliged to resume my tramp to get my thinned blood into circulation again, and as I plodded along I was wishing I could get hold of some matches so I could fire the bridges and the wood which were ranked along the railroad on which I was traveling. Not stopping to think for one moment that such a course would result in my certain and speedy capture, and that if captured, with such a charge of vandalism lodging against me, I would have been hung higher than Haman, without judge or jury ; that such an idea should ever have entered the head of a sane person is past all comprehension, and then to think that I was deterred from such a foolhardy enterprise by the merest accident, causes me to shudder. Reference to said accident will be made hereafter.

On Sunday morning, October 9th, and the fourth day after escaping from the box car, at about the noon hour I came to a large clear space, and looking about me, I discerned a fort and I at once concluded that I was in close proximity to the South Ann River. Prudence at once suggested that my safety lay in hiding until night came on, but my famishing condition and my overwhelming desire to reach the Union lines urged me forward and lured me on to my undoing, as the sequel will show.

Leaving the railroad I took across the fields so as to strike the river about a mile below the fort, but as I reached the brink of the stream, two rebels rose from behind the bank and aiming their rifles at me called upon me to surrender, and as there was nothing else to do I responded to the demand with the best grace possible. I had been seen from the fort and these two soldiers had been dispatched to intercept me. I was marched up to the fort and taken before the captain commanding for examination. This officer was a venerable appearing, gray-headed man of about sixty-five summers, I should guess. His company belonged to a reserve corps and was composed largely of old men and young boys. It will be remembered that I still held the pass which had been given me by Hardy. I showed it to the captain and tried to have him think it read Fredericksburg instead of Mechanicsville, but without success. He said his orders were very strict in regard to letting any one pass that point, and that even if my pass had read Fredericksburg he could not honor it, as the time limit named had expired several days ago, so he said he should be obliged to send me on to Richmond.   As I had eaten nothing but raw corn and unripe persimmons since I supped with the sheriff and was famishing for food, I asked the captain for something to eat.   He answered in a surly manner that he had nothing for me, but called up an old man about sixty years of age and a boy of fourteen or fifteen years, and ordered them to take me to a fire which was burning in

"MADDERN HELL."

a corner of the fort, and keep watch over me until the train came along.   In taking me over to where the fire was, the boy, who no doubt had an exalted opinion of his own importance, strutted along close to my side very like a young fighting cock would be expected to do.   I said to him, "You need not be so particular to keep close to me, I'm not going to run away."   Patting the old Harper's Ferry musket with which he was armed, he said, "By G—d, I know you'll not run while I've got this gun, 'case I believe you's a d—m—d Yankee, anyhow."   Now, remembering my promise to get as mad as "Hell" when the next fellow called me a Yankee, I said, "See here, young fellow, if you hadn't that gun I'd smash your nose all over your face. I'd teach you to call me a Yankee." The old man then said to the youngster, "Shut up, G—d d—m you. He might be as good a soldier as you and a d—m sight better, too." This effectually squelched the young warrior and he had nothing more to say to me. I then asked the old man for something to eat, and he answered that they had nothing. I told him I had had nothing to eat for two days, and that I knew they had something that would satisfy hunger, for they could not stay there without food. He then brought me a piece of bacon and two large sweet potatoes, and I soon had those potatoes in the hot ashes and the meat toasting on a stick. About the time I had finished my meal the train came in sight, and the captain sent a man to flag it to stop. I then asked him to return me my pass. He said, "I will send it to Richmond." I said, "You are sending me there and I can take it : it belongs to me and I want it." He then gave me the pass, and put me on the front car of the train, telling the conductor that I was an escaped Yankee. Now in the rear car of this train they had thirty-two enlisted men and two officers who had been captured from some Pennsylvania regiment. They had been taken at Salem, in the valley by Mosby. I think these prisoners belonged to the One Hundred and Sixteenth Pennsylvania Volunteers, and they were being taken to Libby in charge of a rebel captain, and were amply guarded. The conductor took me back through the train, and opening the door of the rear car put me in among the Yankees, and neglected to tell the officer in charge that I was an escaped "Yank." I took a seat beside one of the Yankees without speaking to any one, but I was doing a whole lot of thinking. I had very soon formulated a plan, somewhat desperate and dangerous, I concede, but I had worked myself up to the required pitch for desperate undertakings. And now it became necessary for me to play the role of injured innocence, so I boldly approached the rebel officer and said, "Captain, see here. I'm no Yan-

kee, and I don't want to sit on the same seat with a d—m—d
Yankee. This will tell you who I am," I said, handing him
the pass. He read it, and turning to me said, "Well, sit
down on the seat there with the guard." Observing that the
officer did not seem to question the legality of the pass, I
said, "Captain, I am very anxious to join my company. I
wish you would take me to the provost marshal and have
me sent to the soldiers' retreat, so that I can get back to my
command as soon as possible." He said, "All right, I will fix
it as soon as we get to Richmond." So I sat beside the
guard until Richmond was reached, and on getting off the
train the captain asked me to walk down to Libby with him,
where he was to deliver his prisoners, and then he would go
with me to see the provost marshal. As we walked along
on our way to Libby the captain very kindly pointed out to
me several places of interest, among which, I remember, was
the State House, Jeff Davis' residence, the Spootswood Hotel,
as well as several other places of interest, all of which were
described by him with apparent pleasure. While I was walking on the sidewalk with the captain, and holding this "tete-
a-tete" with him, the poor prisoners of war were being marched down through the middle of the street, followed by a mob
of urchins who were yelling and shouting after them, and calling them "Blue-bellied Yankees," and all sorts of euphonius
names, and throwing mud upon them. We finally reached
the notorious prison and while the newly arrived prisoners
were being counted off I went into the prison office and
warmed myself at the stove. When the poor fellows had
been counted off they were thrust into a living hell ; the
captain took his receipt for them of the prison authorities,
and we started for the provost marshal's office. I was now
about to "beard the lion in his den," but I did this with a settled conviction, that whether I succeeded or failed in passing
examination before the provost it was all one ; I was dead
sure of detection in the end, for if I went to the soldiers' retreat and passed there I would be discovered as a bogus
Frank Hardy on being taken to Company C, Nineteenth

Virginia Battalion, because the officers of that organization would know that I never belonged to them. And the most serious aspect of the whole case lay in this, that if I failed to satisfy the provost that I was a rebel soldier, I would be caught in the very act of masquerading about the streets of Richmond, the capital of the Confederacy, in a rebel uniform. In either case I was sure of imprisonment in Castle Thunder, a trial by court martial, and probably on the charge of being a spy. These desperately hazardous risks had been taken solely that I might obtain food, for I could have easily escaped from the captain at any time after our arrival at Richmond. My previous sufferings from starvation and exposure had been terrible, and only an iron constitution, toughened by the active, outdoor life of a soldier, could have enabled me to endure it as long as I had. And when I considered that both food and assistance could have been secured from the negroes for the asking, and that, too, without risk, I can only wonder at my stupidity. Well, after quite a long walk we brought up at the provost marshal's office and entered. I was, as may easily be imagined, in no happy frame of mind. The captain transacted some business and talked with the provost for a while, and withdrawing left me to the tender mercies of that boss inquisitor of the Southern Confederacy. Calling me up to his desk the following questions were propounded and answered : "What is your name ?" "Frank Hardy." "Where do you belong ?" "Company C, Nineteenth Virginia Battalion," "Who is your colonel ?" "Colonel Anderson." "Who is your captain ?" "Captain Hetherington." "Where are you stationed ?" "At Mechanicsville." "Where were you going ?" "To Hanover Junction." "What were you going there for ?" "To see my wife and children." "How long since you have seen them ?" "I have not seen them for six months." "Well, why did you not rejoin your regiment on this pass ?" "I got on a drunk, sir, and overstaid my time." "That will do," said the provost, and calling a clerk told him to make me an order for the soldiers' retreat, and go show me where it was. The clerk wrote out the order, and calling to a North Carolinian who was sitting in the office, and who was destined for the same place, he started with me for the retreat. In going out the Carolinian tripped over the door sill and fell headlong into the street. The clerk and I laughed heartily at his awkwardness, which seemed to have the effect of putting the clerk into great good humor, and he talked pleasantly as we walked along, and just as we reached the retreat he said, "By G—d, old fellow, I expected to see you go to Castle Thunder, for it is not often that a man gets off as easy as you did." I replied that I considered myself lucky, and was very glad I had gotten off so easily. On arriving at the Richmond Hotel, as rebels who were confined there called the retreat, the Johnnies began calling out, "Fresh fish, fresh fish." "New arrivals at the Richmond Hotel," etc., etc. But without paying any attention to their jeers, I went upstairs and took quarters on the second floor under a gas jet. The Carolinian stopped on the first floor. The retreat was a large three-story building, and like Libby, had formerly been a tobacco store-house. It was closely guarded, the authorities no doubt being suspicious of its inmates. Having arrived too late for supper I lay down under the gas jet and went to sleep. About one o'clock a. m. I was awakened by the shuffling of feet and excited human voices, and was surprised to find a lot of rebels surrounding me. They proved to be North Carolina Tar-heels, just out of the woods, and conscripts from that state. They had never before seen gas burning, and they would blow it out and relight it, and feel the pipe to see if it were hot, and then give expression to their astonishment to each other. As I had put up at this "hotel" for the express purpose of securing grub, I waited until they were all asleep, then I proceeded to search several of their knapsacks and haversacks for food. I found each knapsack contained five or six plugs of tobacco and nothing else, while their haversacks were filled with corn-meal only, so I was balked effectually in my design to steal food from that crowd, and it was evident that they were about as much in need of food as I was. The next morning the Tar-heels wanted hoe-cake, and they wanted it badly, but had no way of baking it. I was the proprietor of a saucer-shaped half of a canteen, which I had concealed inside my pants by suspending it by a string from a suspender button. I was not slow to discover that I was a monopolist. I was sole owner of the only bake-pan in or about that ranch, and I proceeded to work my special privileges for all there was in them. I would rent my bake-pan at a stipulated price, payable only in hoe-cakes. I suspect that the tax I levied upon those Tar-heels for the use of my baker would be classed by latter-day statesmen as high-tariff. Anyhow I did a rattling business for a short time, storing my revenue in my bundle for future exigencies. But after a while breakfast was called, and that burst my short-lived monopoly all to flinders. Our meals at this retreat were served in the following manner : The men to be fed were formed in open rank, and a negro, bearing a tray of bread, would march down the line and as he passed each man would reach in and take a piece ; meat or other food was served in the same way. A half loaf of bread was served to each man, with other food in proportion, every meal. The food was clean and of good quality, and of suf-ficient quantity ; no man would starve or even suffer hunger on such food. There were no beef-heads, nor buggy peas, nor rotten bacon served here, as was the case with the pris-oners of war. With them, as before stated, a loaf was di-vided among four men twice a day, while here a loaf was served to two men three times a day. I had now had practi-cal experience, which proved beyond question that the food served to the rebel soldiers was more than four times as much in quantity and far better in quality than was given to the prisoners. I again positively declare, that all rebel assevera-tions and affidavits contradictory of these statements, by whomsoever made, are wilfull lies and rank perjuries. After I became familiar with the mode of distributing food here I fared sumptuously. I would fall into line at the head of the column at the stair landing. Taking my piece of bread I would frequently run behind the line to the foot of the column, and take another piece, thus securing double rations. By this means I was kept fairly well supplied.

I was here in personal contact with rebels from all portions of the Confederacy, moved among and talked with them, entirely free from any suspicion on their part, and while the great majority of them were densely ignorant, there were some who were intelligent and well posted on the current topics of the day. I learned that it was the universal opinion of the rank and file of the rebel army that should General George B. McClelland be elected President of the United States at the then ensuing election, that England would at once recognize the independence of the Confederacy and the war would be over, but should Lincoln be re-elected it meant a continuation of the struggle, with very little chance for their final success, as they said their resources were about exhausted. They also said that McClelland had been the best quartermaster they had ever had, as he had furnished them with supplies which they could not otherwise have obtained. Amongst the rebels in this room was a young Marylander, a man of fine appearance and seeming intelligence, whom the rebels suspected of being a spy or a Yankee. I was anxious to have a talk with him, but I feared it might excite suspicion against myself, and so refrained. As I had collected enough bread by this time to supply me for several days, and had also completely filled the aching void beneath my jacket, I began considering the situation. I reasoned that I was liable to be sent at any time to the rebel regiment to which I had satisfied the provost marshal I belonged, and in that case I should, when my fraudulent representation was discovered, be sent to Castle Thunder. Hence my only hope of avoiding such a calamity was in escaping from the retreat. I had been thinking of this, but the chance seemed almost overwhelming against succeeding, as the place was so thoroughly guarded, and a sentry always accompanied an inmate when he had occasion to visit the out-house.

I traded my shoes for a pair of rebel shoes, which were

tan colored, and I had exchanged my blue cap for a rebel cap and received a dollar to boot, and I sold the two handkerchiefs that I had stolen from the knapsack of my guard on the train for nine dollars, so I had ten dollars cash capital, beside the several days' rations of bread, so I felt that I was pretty comfortably fixed for almost any kind of an enterprise. Beside I now had a full-fledged rebel uniform, excepting the pants, and as a great many of their soldiers wore blue pants, which they had taken from prisoners, I was easy on that score.

At this time both Lee's and Earley's armies were in desperate need of recruits, and the three hundred North Carolina conscripts, of whom I have spoken, were divided equally between these two armies. Thinking that I saw a glimmer of hope of escape in this allotment of men I just put myself in position to be counted off with the Tar-heels which were assigned to Earley's army, and one morning just about daylight we were marched out of the retreat on to the streets of Richmond. While the Johnnies were busily engaged in frantic efforts to get ignorant Tar-heels into an alignment, I was keeping an eye to the main chance, and seeing a favorable opportunity I quietly dodged out between two of the guards. I slipped up a cross street and escaped them. After walking for awhile I came upon an Irishman who was engaged in taking down the shutters from the windows of a small store. I stepped in and purchased a loaf of wheat bread of about the size of a large rusk, for which I paid one dollar, and a block of matches for half a dollar. I then asked the way to the Fredericksburg railroad station, and being directed I started for that point. I had hastily decided to try the Fredericksburg route again, and on reaching the railroad I started for that city. Two or three miles out this road passed through the outer line of the Richmond fortifications. Here I discovered the works to be so closely guarded that an attempt to get through the lines would be useless. I was obliged to turn back, so returning to Richmond I boldly walked down Broad street until I reached the Central Depot, and started out that line again.

After traveling out for several miles, it being a sunny day, I concluded to skirmish for graybacks, as I had had no opportunity of attending to this highly important operation since leaving Bell Isle. So going into a dense thicket I removed my clothing, and found the enemy in strong force, entrenched along the seams of every garment. Soon the crack, crack, of their plump bodies exploding between my thumb nails, sounded like the pattering fire of a distant skirmish line. I set out to keep count of the number slain, but soon concluded that it would be too great a strain on my mental faculties. When I abandoned the count it had extended way up into the hundreds, but I pressed the fight until every enemy was left cold in death on the field. Then replacing my clothing I resumed my tramp, and soon reached the Chickahominy River and succeeded in crossing that historic stream in safety ; its waters were still as black and turbid as when Mc-Clelland encamped his magnificent army along its swampy banks. The railroad bridge which spanned the river at this point was a wooden structure, and I was considering the advisability of firing it in daylight when I noticed an apple tree growing near, which had several apples hanging from its boughs. I picked up some stones and was throwing to knock the fruit from the trees, when my block of matches went off in my pocket, and the means of starting a fire, either to damage rebel property or for my own convenience or comfort, vanished like a morning dew. The loss of my matches fell upon me like a crushing calamity, especially when I remembered how I had previously suffered in my efforts to escape, without means of starting a fire by which to cook a morsel of food or to warm my frost benumbed limbs, and I just sat down on the end of a tie and cried, as though some great grief had overtaken me. But in looking back over the conditions which at that time surrounded me I can clearly discern the hand of a kind Providence in the loss of that block of matches, for if I had been possessed of the means of so doing I would have doubtless fired that bridge, and later, as the sequel will show, I should have fallen into the hands of the enemy, with the charge of wantonly destroying property standing over against me, and as the rebels executed without mercy any person against whom an act of vandalism was proven, the jig would have been all up with me. And another thing, which after the lapse of time and much cool reflection, I have never been able to fully comprehend, and that is this : How ever I could have hoped to escape from the network of obstacles with which I was surrounded, without information in regard to the topography of the country or the position of the enemy's lines, or in fact anything else which a man lacking a faithful guide could have built the slightest hope upon to aid him in escaping. I have, however, concluded that it must have been the recollection of the ease with which I had fooled the provost and traversed the streets of Richmond in broad daylight unquestioned. I say I am quite sure that these master strokes of diplomacy, as I was pleased to regard them, were the procuring cause of this rash undertaking.

One very important thing in regard to circumstances as they existed in Richmond I had failed to take into account. There the people felt secure, because they were, so to speak, within the walls of their city, where they had no thought of a Yankee spy or any other Yankee being at large. But it was different in the suburbs and outside the lines of the fortifications of the city proper. Here the people stood in momentary fear and expectation of cavalry raids and were suspicious of every one not belonging to their immediate neighborhood. And in regard to my success in imposing upon the provost marshal I do not believe there was an intelligent rebel in all Richmond who for one moment supposed that there was any Yankee so devoid of the proverbial astuteness and caution of the race, as to attempt to pass himself off as a rebel soldier and masquerade through the streets of the city in a uniform, half Reb and half Yank.

After bemoaning for a while the loss of my matches, I resumed my journey, sad and to some extent dispirited, and on arriving in sight of the fort at the South Ann River, where it will be remembered I was captured on the occasion of my former attempt at escape, I turned aside into the bushes and lay concealed until the shades of night had fallen over the scene. I then started out again, making a sweeping detour to the right, thus striking the river below the fort. I stripped off my clothing and swam the stream, and a cold bath it was, I can assure you, for the night was chill and frosty, and on getting out of the water I was seized with a severe rigor, and was scarcely able to dress myself, my teeth rattling like castanets, and I feared lest their chattering should be heard by the rebels in the fort. With great difficulty I made off and soon coming to a field of shocked corn, I crawled under a shock and remained for a time, in hope of getting my chilled blood to circulating more freely, but in this I was disappointed, for the longer I remained the colder I became, and so was obliged to resume my tramp. About daylight I came upon a small hut occupied by a negro family. It was surrounded by woods, near the railroad, and there was standing in the door of the cabin a middle-aged negress, who upon my approach stepped out and asked me if I had any clothing of which I wished to dispose. I replied in the negative and passed on. In this I realized later on I had made a mistake, for here was an opportunity of disposing of my blue vest and blouse, the silent witnesses of my being a Yankee soldier. I should have taken immediate advantage of this chance, and without doubt I could have made myself known with perfect safety and probably assisted through the lines, or at the least have obtained valuable information in regard to the country through which I must pass if I escaped at all, but being fearful of betrayal I passed on to my fate.

It was still early morning when I arrived at Hanover Junction. Our cavalry having recently burned the bridge at that point, all passengers had to be transferred there. The Fredericksburg train was standing there awaiting the arrival of the Richmond train, and as I walked by the engine the engineer eyed me very closely, but said nothing, and I trudged on in the direction of Fredericksburg. Several

miles out from Hanover, as I was passing through a sand
cut on the railroad, I encountered a blowing adder, and it
seemed to dispute my passage, as it was coiled ready for a
spring, while it kept up a hissing which would have done
credit to a full grown "gray gander." He was a large fellow, and as there was neither club or stone to be found in the
cut I skirmished around and finally secured a piece of rotten
tie, which showed its weakness at every blow. But by dint
of perseverance I finally managed to kill the reptile. I was
much surprised to find a snake abroad at that season of the
year, it being well along in the month of October, but he
evidently was out for business, as he made no effort to escape
while I was searching for something with which to slay him.

Shortly after getting through the cut, the train which I
had passed while it was standing at the junction, passed me
on its way to Fredericksburg, and again that engineer eyed
me very suspiciously. About noon, as I sat resting, concealed in some bushes, two men with guns and dogs made their
appearance on the opposite side of the railroad, and it looked for a time as though I should be discovered, but they finally went their way, and I again resumed my line of march.
Toward evening I arrived at Guinea Station, eight miles distant from Fredericksburg. This place was made up of a
water tank on one side of the railroad and three or four houses on the other side, one of which stood near the track.

As I passed the house of which I spoke as standing near
the track, a woman who was sitting in the door with her sew-
ing, asked me for the news of the day and I paused long
enought to tell her about Mosby's capture of the Yankees in
the valley, and then started on, laying to my soul the unction
that I was safely past another bad place in my road. But as
soon as my back was turned a rebel soldier came out of the
house, and stealing softly up behind me ordered me to halt,
and on facing about, I found myself gazing into the muzzle of
a big navy revolver. His questions came thick and fast.
Who are you ? Where do you belong ? And, where are
you going ? And he did not give me time to answer those

questions in the prescribed Yankee fashion either, that would
have been, you know, by asking him question for question.
But I want to remark that a revolver loaded to the muzzle
and in the hands of an enemy, and pointing at you, is a powerful persuader, and has a tendency to sort of make you
answer questions whether you want to or not.   So I said my
name is Frank Hardy, that I belonged to Mosby's command,
that my horse had been killed at Salem in the valley, that I
lived near Fredericksburg, and that I was going home to get
another horse, beside a lot of other stuff I told him, all of
which was manufactured for the occasion, and as I concluded, justified by the end sought to be accomplished.   The
young soldier was favorably impressed by my seemingly
straightforward tale and was inclined to let me go, but by
this time two or three of the shaggy, tobacco-squirting natives had gathered about us and these strenuously objected to
my being released.   They said I might be a spy, or an escaped Yankee prisoner, who might bring the Yankee cavalry
in to "cut hell outen we'uns."   Well, the soldier said he
would have nothing more to do with me, so the natives took
me in charge, and handed me over to the loving care of a
train detective on the arrival of the train from Fredericksburg.   This detective was a stalwart six-footer of a fire-eat-
ing, Don Furioso, bombastic sort of a man, in fact his hide
seemed stuffed with bombast and selfsufficiency, that one observing him would conclude that if the destinies of the rotten
Confederacy did not wholly rest upon his shoulders, that he
at least was the chief corner stone.   He took me into the forward car, where there were sitting three or four brutal appearing fellows. Sallow of complexion, they were with counte-
nances which were as pleasant to look upon as that of a Ben-
gal tiger.   Stripping off my clothing he examined pockets,
linings and seams, also my cap, its rim, my shoes and shoe-
soles, and was rewarded for his trouble by finding nothing, as
I was not so much of a fool as to commit anything to paper.
In answer to his questions I told him that I was unable to
read or write ; I also gave him the Mosby fabrication, but dur-

ing his search of my clothing he unearthed from my vest pocket a printed song which he transferred to his pocket. This particular song was entitled, "The Arms of Abraham." The first verse and chorus were as follows, and will, I think, be recognized by all comrades :

My true love is a soldier in the army now to-day,
T'was this cruel war that made him, he had to go away.
The draft it was that took him, it was a cruel blow,
It took him for a conscript, but he didn't want to go.

CHORUS :

He's gone, he's gone, as meek as any lamb.
They took him, yes, they took him, to the arms of
Abraham.

As soon as I had replaced my garments, the detective turned suddenly and handing me the song said, "Sing that song for us !" "Oh, I can't read," said I, handing it back to him. He was very angry because of his failure to entrap me, and he exclaimed, "You'r a G—d d—m liar ! I never in my life saw a Yankee who couldn't read and write." As I was not in a position to resent this imputation against my veracity, as the boys say, I was obliged to swallow it. This I did with very good grace, for the compliment paid the Yankee intelligence, in his declaration that they could all read and write, had softened the impeachment greatly. I had begun to lay to my heart the unction that I had successfully baffled him, when he reached for my bundle, and untying it he brought out my blue vest and blouse. He was now furious, and drawing his revolver and placing it within a foot of my forehead said, "Yu —— ——— —— of a Yankee. I've a mind to blow yo' brains out, and by G—d I would shoot yo' but I'll have yo' hung for a spy when I get yo' to Richmond." Under these embarrassing circumstances I could say nothing, but I looked him in the eye until he lowered his revolver, then I calmly sat down on a seat next the window

and observed the landscape as we whirled by it. I hoped
to discover some scene of beauty which might serve to divert
my mind from its unpleasant occupation. Those tiger-faced
men, to whom reference has been made, sat there taking no
part in the conversation, but evidently enjoying the act much
as a theater-goer might the tragedy just at the point where
the villain is to be detected and exposed. On arriving at
Hanover Junction, where the train halted for a short time, I
purchased some apples from a lad at the car window, at which
I nonchalantly munched all the way in to Richmond, and

I'LL HAVE YOU HUNG FOR A SPY.

while outwardly I appeared so careless and composed, there
was a tumult transpiring within; indeed I was fearfully
agitated and distressed, for I was now about to be brought
face to face with the same provost marshal as a spy, upon
whom a few days previous I had imposed myself as a rebel
soldier, and I could but think, "Ah, that's the rub." However, I had braced myself for the interview, and by the time
we arrived at the office, I had determined to give my correct
name and a full account of my first escape only, as I thought
this would tally with the register at Libby, and have a tendency to divert suspicion from me as a spy in case they

should accuse me of that offence. But I must admit that the
bearing of my captor, upon arriving at Richmond was anything but reassuring, as my "Furioso" marched me through
the streets, swinging his big revolver like a conquering hero,
his air of importance, and the majesty of his swagger seeming
to indicate that he felt his importance to be great, and he
seemed to expect the populace to turn out enmasse to greet
him with, "Hail to the Chief," or "See the Conquering Hero
Comes." But they did not, and on reaching the provost's
presence, I observed that "Furioso's" airs suddenly collapsed
and I gathered from the marshal's manner toward him, that
he knew him as a chronic blowhard, and a brainless bully.
The marshal asked him where I had been taken, and if I had
been carefully searched, and if so, if any incriminating evidence in the way of papers or any documents had been discovered, and then very curtly dismissed him. I was then
ordered up, and in reply to the questions of the provost I
answered, giving my name, company and regiment, all the
time keeping my face as much in the shade as possible. I
stated that I had escaped from the car on the way to Salisbury, and had been recaptured, and to my great comfort and
delight, neither the marshal nor his clerk recognized me as
the Frank Hardy who had passed as a rebel soldier and been
sent to the soldiers' retreat. Making out a commitment, he
called a guard who conducted me, in company with another
prisoner, down to Castle Thunder. This disheartened me
greatly, as I was aware that only such as were to be arraigned
for some offence against the Confederacy were confined here.
The Castle, to the Yankee, was the veritable "dungeon of despair" to those confined within its gloomy walls ; all hope of
exchange or parole died, and he was released only after trial,
if convicted, to be executed, and to be sent back to Libby if
exonerated. Dante's inscription over the portals of Hades
would have been appropriate above the gates of Castle
Thunder, "Abandon hope, all ye who enter here." But a
mighty burden was rolled off my soul when on reaching the
Castle only the other man, the prisoner of whom I spoke as
accompaning me from the provost's office, was left at that inferno.

CHAPTER XII.

Imprisoned Again in Libby.

I was taken across the street to Dick Turner's office and then confined on the ground floor in the west end of that building. I soon found that my fellow prisoners on that floor were all negro soldiers. I being the only white man in the room and dressed as I was in a rebel uniform, I was at first suspected by them of being a rebel emissary placed among them as a spy for the purpose of watching them. I succeeded in convincing them, however, that I was a Yankee in disguise and then questioned them as to where they had been captured and learned what I could in regard to what had been transpiring outside since I had been a prisoner. These poor fellows seemed to me to be like men who were overworked, and I asked them what they had been doing. They informed me that they had fallen into the rebels' hands at Fort Harrison, and that since their arrival at Libby they had been marched out every day and made to work in constructing rebel fortifications, one of the most flagrant breeches of the usages of civilized warfare. Yet I blush to say that our government made no protest against this great wrong, and, so far as I was ever able to learn, made no effort to prevent it, and to protect these colored soldiers in their rights as prisoners of war. I could not have believed it possible that such treatment would have been imposed upon prisoners of war, and the government to whom they belonged, make no protestation against it. But I saw morning after morning, these soldiers marched out and put to work on the rebel works, where they toiled all day, to be marched back in the evening, so I know there can be no possible doubt in regard to the matter. General B. F. Butler, who about this time was engaged in digging the war exigency device, the Dutch Gap Canal, heard of what the rebels were doing to

our negro soldiers, and that brave and humane man on his
own responsibilty notified General Lee of the Confederate
army that if the practice was not immediately stopped he
would at once put an equal number of rebel officers at work
on the Dutch Gap Canal. General Lee answered, denying
. positively that any United States soldiers were being worked
on their fortifications. General Butler, whose information
must have been of a very reliable nature, refused to accept
Lee's denial, and accordingly put the rebel officers at work on
the canal. This procedure of General Butler put a sudden
stop to the working of the negro troops on rebel fortifications. Meantime I had obtained a copy of the "Richmond
Dispatch," which contained the correspondence which passed
between Butler and Lee upon the subject, and as a consequence I watched closely the result, and I observed that the
colored soldiers were not marched out mornings, and I questioned the negroes after they had been withdrawn from their
labor on the works, therefore I know that this statement is
absolutely true. And yet the highest officer in the rebel
army, the gentlemanly and chivalrous Lee, the pink of per-
fection and the soul of Southern honor, could knowingly and
deliberately lie, just like a common trooper, in the inter-
ests of a traitorous rebellion. And what wonder ? Was not
he a perjured villain the instant he took service under the
Confederacy, and turned his back upon the flag of the
country whose honor he had sworn to uphold and defend ?
All honor, I say, to the name of Ben Butler, who at least to
the full extent of his ability and authority, undertook to protect the poor prisoners of war whom it seems to me the government had wantonly abandoned to death by starvation,
or at most had put forth but feeble and unavailing efforts to
protect and defend from the cruel indignities heaped upon
them by their brutal captors. Hurrah for "Old Spoony !"
he always served an effectual remedy in heroic doses for the
cure of treason, and that fact the rebels duly appreciated, as
was attested by them in the fact that they kept a standing
reward of one hundred thousand dollars in gold on his head,
"dead or alive."

On the two floors above the negro quarters, in Libby, white men were confined and as the prison keepers always took down the communicating stair at night I slept the first night among the negroes. The next morning I chanced to get under the hatchway or opening left for the stairs and I heard some one shout, "By G—d, if here ain't old Father Darby, (father was the nickname by which I was called in my company), and on looking up I beheld the smiling face of David Richie, and others of the comrades of my company. Coming to the opening they let down a blanket which I laid hold of and they soon landed me on a higher plane. On this floor I found as partners in distress the following named members of my company, to-wit : Isaac N. Mitchell, of Uniontown, (he is since deceased) ; Leslie Francis, of Perryopolis ; David Richie, of New Haven ; Calvin Darnell, of Grindstone, and Bartholomew Warman, of Dunbar, all of whom had escaped through the hole I had kicked in the end of the car, but like myself they had been retaken and returned to Libby several days before I was sent back to keep them company. After a hearty greeting, we related to each other our experiences and while they were somewhat varied, they all had the same sad sequence, in that we each and all failed to make good our escape to God's country, as the North was called by the boys in captivity. Darnell and Warman had gotten fifty miles away before being captured. They were sighted by a planter who had a gang of negroes engaged in cutting a field of tobacco. He started the darkies in pursuit of them, armed with their tobacco knives. Warman was taken, but when Darnell's pursuer got close enough, Darnell, without stopping, turned his head and said, "Slack up ! Slack up ! D—n it, what do you want to take me for ?" and the negro pretending to be winded, did slacken pace and allowed Darnell to run away from him. He now made his way to the rebel General Malone's line at Petersburg, and was concealed by a negro for two days at Mahone's headquarters, but was retaken on attempting to run the lines. Mitchell, Richie and Francis had made their way one hundred miles from Richmond and then had been run down by bloodhounds and recaptured. Darnell had been given a silver dollar by a negro, (the only money the poor fellow had). With his dollar he had bought the blanket with which they hoisted me to the second floor on the morning after my arrival at Libby.

On this floor Francis had been placed in command. It was his duty to form the men in double line for the monster, Dick Turner, to count off each morning, and also to report the sick, etc.; for this service he received one exttra ration of bread each day. There were eighty-three of us in this room at the time, and among them were the men who saw me pass myself off as a rebel soldier on the captain in the car as they were being taken to Richmond. These fellows told the other prisoners of the episode in the car, and it created a strong prejudice against me, as being a rebel emissary, who was there for the purpose of watching and reporting them to the rebel authorities, and they probably would have made it very uncomfortable for me had it not been for the assurance given them by my comrades that I was all right, and after I had explained to them how it all came about, I was immediately taken into full communion and goodfellowship.

The nights now were quite cool and we had no fire, and there were no sash or glass in the windows, and in order to keep warm we slept spoon fashion along the walls, and we lay so close that when one fellow wanted to whop over the whole line had to whop. Frequently during the night when some poor starving skeleton, whose sharp hip bones were cutting through to the hard floor, would cry out, "Turn over up there," if anyone neglected or refused to obey the injunction to "turn" the air would be full of imprecations against the tardy one.

Amongst the prisoners was a young cavalryman, I think he hailed from the state of Wisconsin, and he was the fortunate owner of a blanket which he kindly offered to share with me, and as my five comrades were already taxing the ductile qualities of their one blanket to its utmost, I gratefully accepted his offered kindness. After sharing the hospitality of my new found friend for several consecutive nights, I was greatly pained and astonished by being accused by him of having robbed him during the night. I was very indignant at the accusation and felt the hot blood of shame and anger rushing to my cheeks and I could hardly refrain from assaulting him on the spot, but finally I cooled off sufficiently to inquire of him as to whether he had been stirring about any during the night as I had been awakened by his getting up in the night. He answered that he had been to the sink. I told him to go there and find his money, or I should be obliged to wipe up the floors of Libby with his dirty lying body. While he was gone I pulled off my jacket and cleared the deck for action, for really I had no thought of his finding his money where there were so many chances of its having been picked up. But shortly he returned with a fifty-dollar greenback in his hand. It had fallen from his watch-fob pocket, and there it lay just as it had fallen, and to accuse a comrade of stealing it ! I gave him a lecture, couched in language which at this distant day is remembered by me as being more emphatic than elegant. I told my messmates what had occurred and they were angry and wanted to thrash him whether or no, but I finally prevailed on them to allow the matter to drop, which they did. But I foreswore that chap as a bedfellow ever after. But I was most happy in that he found his money as that removed all suspicion of the theft from my skirts.

Francis was taken sick and was sent to the prison hospital, and I was promoted to the position made vacant by his disability and I then had the right by dint of my promotion to sleep under the protecting folds of one-fifth of the blanket which had sheltered him during his tenure of office as commander of that room. At the window, near the stairway, there was a loose brick in the wall, and one of the men took it one night to use as a pillow. On the following morning at the designated hour, I had the alignment made, ready for counting off. Dick Turner, on coming up the stairs, saw that a brick had been displaced from the wall, whereupon he instantly fell into a towering rage, and began raving and cursing all Yankees in general, and the one who took that brick in particular. He swore that not a G—d d—m—d Yankee in that room should have anything either to eat or drink until the son of a b—tch was found who had taken that brick. He then stationed guards at either end of the line with orders to shoot the first d—m—d Yankee that dared to move out of his tracks, and leaving us in this desperate position, he went to the floor above. Now while the loss of one daily meal to a hearty, well man, would be regarded as a hardship, but to men already starving, the loss of one day's food, as can readily be imagined, meant added suffering ; and then the torture of standing in line, not daring to change position under pain of death, I realized that many of the boys in their weakened physical condition must soon succumb, and the older prisoners well knowing the devilish, cruel character of Dick Turner, advised that the man who had taken the brick should confess, and thus save the innocent much needless suffering, and this was done. The man had been a prisoner but a few days, and was entirely innocent of any harmful intention against the rules or discipline of the prison. On the return of Turner to the room, I explained the facts to him and pleaded the inexperience of the offender ; told him the brick had been only and solely for use as a pillow and showed the brick lying against the wall just where the man had left it on getting up from his rest on the floor in the morning. Without making any reply to me he whipped out a large revolver and pointing it at the man, with a horrible oath, exclaimed, "Put that brick back where you got it from, and if you ever touch another brick in this wall I'll blow your brains out, G—d d—n you. He then counted us off, and relieved us of his damnable presence for that occasion.

It seems to me quite proper at this juncture to pause sufficiently long to pay to this "duet" of hell, a passing compliment. Turner, the unmatched villain and miscreant, showed his cowardly, disreputable and brutal character in the

trivial incidents of the brick and cartridge, as narrated in
previous chapters, better than I could hope to paint in a word
picture, in fact the English language fails to furnish words
of the requisite shades of blackness to properly characterize
the infamy of the heart of this miserable abortion of manhood. If God ever created this travesty of man in his own
likeness, some malevolent power succeeded in completely
perverting the work, for he certainly embodied in his vile
makeup all the characteristics of the Prince of Devils. He
was strong, stocky of build, of medium height, swarthy
complexion, and thick, dark curling hair. And I am sure the
declaration of scripture, that "out of the abundance of the
heart the mouth speaketh," found verification in him for he
was possessed of a vocabulary rich in profanity and vile bill-
ingsgate that would have caused the proverbial fish woman
to hide her head in shame. I think that the oft repeated declaration that no bullying, boasting, brutal braggart, ever
made a good soldier is essentially true, and that fact probably
explains why Dick Turner held the position of overseer of
the lousy, dirty, rat-infested, disgusting Libby prison. He
was just simply too great a coward to enter the rebel army
and fight like a man against men for a principle which he professed to hold dear ; he preferred to have the enemy against
whom he was to fight, cooped up and disarmed so that his
dastardly carcass would be in no danger of harm. He was a
lying, hypocritical, ruffianly robber, who would have stolen
the pennies from the eyes of a dead friend, and then malic-
iously mutilated the corpse because they were not quarters.
As often as once a week he would fall into a particularly
cheerful frame of mind and upon such occasions he would tell
us that he had torpedoes so arranged under our prison building that in case the Yankee cavalry reached the fortifications
of Richmond he could, and would, blow every Yankee s——n of
a b——ch to hell, but in spite of this oft repeated piece of cheerful information, the prisoners to a man wished and longed
for the arrival of our cavalry. Pity, generosity or compassion were wholly unknown to his low animal nature, and in

his intercourse with the Yankees he was totally devoid of the finer sensibilities of humanity, therefore an appeal for mercy or compassion made no more impression upon his case hardened soul, than a shotgun loaded with mush would make on the rock of Gibraltar. And now on the banks of the beautiful James River, below Richmond, lives this same Dick Turner, unvexed, unwhipped and unpunished, under the protecting folds of the flag he insulted and under the government he sought to subvert, enjoying the freedom and liberty which he strove so earnestly to deprive others of, while so many of the victims of his relentless cruelty, noble-hearted, brave and loyal men, lie mouldering in the burial trenches of Richmond, "unknown, unhonored and unsung." Let us hope, my surviving comrades, that in the great beyond, when men are arraigned to answer for the deeds done in the body, that Dick Turner will receive the just recompense of reward for his conduct toward the helpless, defenceless prisoners of war ; but I can but think when in the fullness of time Dick Turner knocks at the gate of the portals of the inferno for admission, that the imps of hell should look well to their laurels, and Satan guard well his crown, for lo ! a greater than Satan is here !

And now as to Turner's "running mate." I refer to Lieutenant Boissieux. Nearly all of the indictments charged against the former will lodge against the latter. This detestable, cowardly, low-lived villain, also no doubt held his position at Belle Isle for the same reasons and on account of the same qualifications that Turner did at Libby, to-wit : Villainy and cowardice.

He was French by birth, was of a slight build, much more slender in person than Turner, but he evidently developed about as much depravity to the square inch as did that hellion. I have already told of the punishment through the agency of the wooden horse which Bossieux inflicted on the men who endeavored to escape by swimming to the little isle. I described its severity and the awful suffering it brought to the victims. This showed the innate brutality of the beast

without further comment, but I have somewhat more to offer
concerning this devil incarnate. I know not whether he still
lives in the flesh, or whether he has gone to his reward, and if
he has, may God exercise more mercy toward his soul than
I could do, for I greatly fear if I had to deal with him, his
chances for commutation from severe and eternal punishment
would be slim indeed. I have seen this wretch snatch a musket from the hands of a guard and spring like a she panther
into the midst of a crowd of prisoners, and without cause or
provocation, with the butt of the gun, knock indiscriminately
to the right and left the weak, starved creatures. He also
absolutely made a standing proposition to the rebel prison
guard that whoever of them killed a Yankee prisoner could
have a thirty-day furlough. In consequence of this promise,
whenever one of the guard wished to go home he would
shoot into the camp and kill a Yankee. There were several
who were murdered in this way while I was in that prison,
and what makes the remembrance of these barbarities more
keenly bitter to the survivors of those prison hells, is the fact
that our ungrateful government having adopted its despicable, pusillanimous policy of non-protection and non-ex-
change of prisoners, did not so far as I can learn ever offer
so much as a protest. However, I am aware that some apologists undertake to explain it away by urging that it was because the rebels refused to extend the right of parole or exchange to the negro troops who had fallen into their hands.

There were a couple of incidents which occurred on the
island before my arrival there as a prisoner which I will relate as they were told to me by an eye witness. Bossieux
had a pet black and tan terrier which one day strayed into
camp. A prisoner caught it, cut its throat, skinned and prepared to cook it. Bossieux missing his pet suspected it had
gotten into camp, hurried in, and observing a man in the act
of building a fire of a bit of wood, he had succeeded in col-
lecting for the purpose. The lieutenant approaching discovered his dog ready for toasting. He was furious and drawing his revolver, exclaimed, "Now, you G—d d—n son of a

b—ch,(now this was their pet expression when addressing a
Yankee), eat that dog and eat him raw ! G—d d—n you, or
I'll blow your brains out !" The man who was so near
starved that he could hardly wait to cook it anyhow, went at
it and soon had its bones polished, while Bossieux, who waited to see the last morsel disappear, withdrew. The man
waited until he was out of hearing, shook his fist at him, and
adopting his manner of speech, said, "Oh, you rebel son of a
b—ch, you thought you were punishing me didn't you ?"
Then wiping his mouth on his sleeve said, "I only wish I had
another dog to eat." One day a guard whose beat ran from
the river to the camp on the outside of the fence along the
lane, shot and killed a prisoner as he was returning with a
bucket of water from the river. A Buck Tail, who had seen
the killing, armed himself with a shin bone and slipping down
along the fence reached over and striking him a fearful blow
on the head, killed him, whereupon Bossieux shut off the rations of the camp and swore he would starve every d—m—d
Yankee to death unless the man who killed the guard was
found ; but the men toward evening became desperate and
threatening, and Bossieuxs', cowardly heart failed him and
fearing a revolt he rushed the grub into camp. Leaving these
two worthies to the infamy of the damned and consigning
them to the abode of the imps infernal, I will resume the
thread of the narrative where it was dropped to indulge in
this digression.

Being, as I said in a previous chapter, in the western
end of the prison Libby, we commanded a good view of the
wharf, where we used to stand behind the bars and watch the
rebels land from the exchange boat. Fat, hearty, saucy
and happy, they would run down the gangplank onto the
wharf shouting and hurrahing for Jeff Davis and the
Southern Confederacy, kicking up their heels like a lot of
colts on being turned into a field of fresh clover. After a
little a miserable, melancholy procession of Yankees from
the hospitals, to be exchanged for these hearty, well-fed
rebels, would appear slowly and painfully staggering toward

the boat, a great number of whom would be unable to walk
at all, having to be carried aboard the boat on stretchers.
Now just here I am reminded was another reason assigned
by our government for stopping the exchange of prisoners
(and the rebs taunted us with the fact upon every occasion).
It was this : The rebels, on being released from our northern prisons, were ready to enter immediately into their
armies for service ; while the Yankee soldiers, if they were
fortunate to survive at all, were so reduced by starvation
that it would be months before they were ready for field service.   Very manifestly the proper way to have corrected this
evil would have been to have furnished the rebel prisoners
with the same kind and quality of food, shelter and clothing
that was furnished us by the rebels.   Any other course than
the one suggested placed the Union prisoner of war at a
disadvantage, and was unjust to him ; but I imagine I hear
you saying that would have been inhuman.   War is inhuman, cruel and unjust at best.   Right is eternally right, and
wrong is just as eternally wrong, and no war ever waged
ever yet settled the right or the wrong of the question at
issue.   Therefore the golden rule of warfare is, "What so-
ver the enemy doeth unto you, do ye also unto the
enemy." If one of the belligerents wages a war of humanity,
and the other a war of brutal savagery, the humane party
will be the sufferer every time, as they are unable to restrain
the acts of savagery on the part of the enemy, and also fail
to inflict a corresponding loss upon him by the practice of
the same kind of tactics.   The treatment of Union prisoners
of war is a forceful illustration of this fact, as seventy-one
thousand men died as a result of the cruel savagery practiced upon them by the rebels, in whose hands they were as
prisoners of war ; while no corresponding loss was inflicted
upon them by the Federal government.   I hold it to be true
that it would have been quite as humane to have starved to
death rebels who were in armed rebellion, as to starve to
death Union men who were heroically striving to maintain
the government and preserve the national life.   Any coun-

try engaged in a war, and refusing or neglecting to protect
its soldiery by a just and equitable system of reprisal and retaliation, is unworthy the support of loyal and courageous
subjects. But I find I have been indulging in another digression, but when I arrive at a point where the spirit moves me
to make a comment, I hope the reader will indulge me, while
I will leave you to accept or reject my conclusions as the
proof may sustain or fail to sustain the positions it may lead
the reader to take.

The views obtained from the windows of Libby were
necessarily distant ones, as we were forbidden on penalty of
being instantly shot down, from approaching nearer than
several feet to the sills of the windows, and the guards would
shoot any going near enough to the bars to be seen by them
from the street below. One of our rooms was ornamented
with a stove of the common variety, but the rebels would allow us no fire. There were several boxes of sawdust in the
room which were used as spittoons, and were as a rule in a
very filthy condition, yet I have seen starving men pick bones
out of this mass of filth and corruption and gnaw at them
most ravenously.

One day about the 1st of November, 1864, Dick Turner
accompanied by several other rebels came into the prison
room and selected me for the position of hospital wardmaster
to serve in a hospital which they were about to establish for
the care, (or perhaps, more properly speaking for the slow
death), of a number of sick and wounded Yankees who had
been taken in one of our hospitals at or near Fort Harrison.
They accorded to me as wardmaster the privilege of selecting four men to act as nurses, and one to serve as hospital
steward, from among my fellow prisoners. I selected
Mitchell, Darnell, Richie and Warman for nurses, and a
man by the name of Fogle for steward. Fogle was one of
the men taken by Mosby, and was on the train at the time I
passed myself off on the captain as a rebel soldier. Fogle
assured me that he was well posted upon the subject of medicines, having, as he said, served as prescription clerk in a

drug store ; however, when he undertook to fill prescriptions I found him to be an unmitigated liar, as he knew absolutely nothing about medicines, not so much as a mule might be expected to know of mathematics. I however did not blame him particularly, as he took this plan to get out of the living hell Libby. On the contrary I assisted him all I could, and as our materia medica was not elaborate it required no proficient Latin to handle it successfully, and we got along fairly well after all. If Fogle is still in the land of the living I should be pleased to meet him and take a pill with him for the sake of "Auld Lang Syne." We were inducted into our new-found field of usefulness in a large three-story brick tobacco house which fronted on Broad street ; the building and grounds were inclosed with a high board fence. There was a two-story frame addition to the brick building which also fronted on Broad street, the upper story of which was used as a sleeping room in common by the attendants of the three wards composing the hospital. The lower floor of this building was partially filled with stems and refuse tobacco, covering the floor to the depth of several feet, and to this room we had free access. Now directly across from the main or brick portion of the building was a small brick structure which was used as a gangrene ward.

Myself and comrades were assigned to duty on the upper floor which was furnished with cots for about fifty patients. We drew soup, which was very thin, its chief ingredients being rice and potatoes, skins and all, but as our patients did not arrive until long after the dinner hour, Mr. Woodward, the steward in charge, allowed us to eat as much of the soup as we desired, and I am here to say that my five assistants and myself got away with it slick and clean, thus taking a fairly good fill up on the ration which would have had to answer for the fifty men had they arrived in time for dinner. Darnell, although a small man, managed to eat an ordinary wooden bucket full of the soup, which so distended his proportions that it was impossible for him to flex his body, and in consequence he was obliged to sit upright as stiff as a ramrod.

This hospital was really but an annex to General Hospital No. 21 from which our food and medicine were obtained and to which our dead were carried. This general hospital, if my memory serves me correctly, was located at the corner of Cary and a cross street, one square distant from ours, and when any of us Yankees had occasion for any purpose to go there, we were attended by rebel guards. In cases of emergency, where a doctor or remedies were needed promptly, this awaiting the motion of the guard caused a delay which in numerous instances proved fatal to the patient, whereas prompt action would have saved the life of the sufferer.

Toward evening of our initial day at the hospital annex our expected patients arrived and were promptly installed upon their respective cots, many, alas, of whom were never to leave them in life. I had but one case of amputation in my department, and that was performed upon a cavalryman by the name of O'Brine. He was a member of a New York regiment the number of which has escaped me. The leg was amputated below the knee. I had numerous cases of gunshot wounds, some of which were very severe ones. The other patients were sufferers mainly from desperate attacks of pneumonia, chronic diarrhoea, scurvey, diphtheria, pleurisy, typhoid and remittent fevers. Our ward was fumigated daily by a negro attendant who walked silently up one aisle and down another bearing in his hands a shovel of coals upon which was burning coal tar or pitch. This operation was performed in the mornings before the arrival of the doctor on his daily rounds. Our materia medica embraced the following named, well recognized drugs and remedies, to-wit : Aqua pura, sheep's tallow for dressing amputations, Spanish fly and mustard for blisters or counter irritants, flaxseed for poultices, nitrate of silver as a caustic, opium and corn whisky as stimulants, tincture and iodide of iron, and perhaps a few other drugs of like character. We had no quinine or chincona, nothing whatever of that kind.

I shall probably have occasion in the course of this narrative to refer personally to some of my patients ; meantime I will introduce to my readers the supervisors of this hospital. I mean those who were conducting its affairs under the rebel authorities.

CHAPTER XIII.

WOODWARD.

First in order I beg leave to introduce to you Mr. Woodward. He was a citizen of Richmond, Va., a merchant by avocation, whom I strongly suspect of occupying his present position of hospital superintendent only to avoid service in the rebel army. Mr. Woodward was a genial, pleasant-faced, mild-mannered man, a little above medium height : and good humor seemed to be his ruling characteristic. He was so striking an exception to the average rebel official that I cannot pass him by without a kindly word. In all the time of my association with him I never knew him to be guilty of applying an abusive or profane epithet to a Yankee, nor did I ever see him display an angry mood. His good humor bubbled up from the midst of his vile environments and sparkled forth like an oasis, from a Sahara of disgusting obscenity, vituperation and profane abuse. His business requiring most of his time, his visits to the institution resembled the proverbial angel visits, they were "few and far between," usually not oftener than once or twice per week. He however had an assistant in the person of one, Charles Walters, who occupied a room on the second floor of the annex, where a space had been partitioned off for the purpose. Mr. Woodward was in general good favor with the prisoners, as a matter of fact he was well liked by them, and I have no doubt but at heart he was really a Union man, in fact he more than intimated as much to me upon several occasions. He told me that it was the universal belief in Richmond, at that time, that if General George B. McClelland were to be elected president at the North, that the Confederacy would instantly become an assured success, and this view of the situation was also held by his assistant, Charles Walters, who by the way, was a rampant rebel in his views

and sympathies, and I had heard rebel officers at Libby repeatedly make the same assertion ; so also I heard the same
declaration from officers at the prison at Belle Isle. The
opinions of the rank and file of the rebel army upon this subject have already been stated in a preceding chapter of this
work. It would therefore be quite in order to seek a motive
for this generally prevailing rebel belief both of the rebel
civilian and soldier as to the success of the cause of the Confederacy depending upon the election of McClelland to the
presidency of the Northern states.

In searching for the causes of the rebel faith in McClelland's desire and ability to save them, it will be necessary to
review the Peninsular and Antietam campaigns, or at least
such portions of them as may testify to his incompetent and
treasonable acts. To begin with, it could not be reasonably
supposed, that in the absence of any evidence or knowledge of his being favorable to the success of their cause, that
the rebels would have developed such a liking for McClelland that would cause them to become so solicitous for his
election to the presidency, as to cause them to cheer repeatedly from their breastworks for him, as many a comrade still
living can testify to having heard them do. It was the col-
lecting of immense numbers of small arms and large quantities of munitions which he failed to have issued to his own
troops, notwithstanding that thousands of his soldiers were
armed with the old Harper's Ferry muskets, an arm which
was almost entirely worthless ; it was, I say, the fact of his
leaving thousands upon thousands of stands of those new
Springfield rifles, together with numberless munitions which
he left to fall into their hands as narrated in a previous chapter, which had rendered McClelland to the rebel heart so
dear. Of the millions of dollars worth of military stores collected at White House Landing and Savage Station, a small
fraction only was destroyed, just enough to cover
his treasonable design, the balance of which was purposely
left for the rebel army, and this explains why the Johnnies

referred to him as being the best quartermaster they ever had.

The Fifth Army Corps occupied the north side of the Chickahominy, and the balance of the army was on the south or Richmond side of the river, with three bridges connecting them ; one at Deep Bottom, the railroad bridge at Dispatch Station, and one still lower down the stream. General Lee, leaving Magruder in the defenses of Richmond with twenty-five thousand troops, crossed the Chickahominy at Hanover Junction, twenty-three miles from Richmond, and being re-enforced by Jackson, attacked the right of the Fifth Corps at Mechanicsville. The Union line at this point was held by the division of the Pennsylvania Reserves under General Mc-Call and the Reserves fought the battle on that part of the line without assistance from the rest of the corps. The rebels were badly defeated and suffered a severe loss in killed and wounded, while our loss was trifling. The next day oc-curred the battle of Gaines' Mill, where the loss was about evenly divided. At Mechanicsville the Confederate loss was six thousand, so in the two battles the results, in so far as loss of men was concerned, was largely in favor of the Union army. The Fifth Corps was now withdrawn to the Rich-mond side of the river and the bridges were destroyed. Now to an ordinary high private serving in the ranks it appears that now would have been the moment to hurl the victorious Army of the Potomac upon Magruder in Rich-mond. Can there be a reasonable doubt of the ability of the noble Army of the Potomac taking both Richmond and Ma-gruder's army if this course had been pursued, and especially as Jackson had left the valley and gone to Lee's assistance ? Fremont's army was free to go to the defenses of Washing-ton and thus secure the safety of the Capital City. Lee would have been obliged to rebuild the bridges over the Chickahominy or to have taken a circuitous route via Han-over Junction, and in either case would have been delayed from thirty-six to forty-eight hours in reaching Richmond, and before the lapse of that time the Army of the Potomac could have engulfed Richmond and its little army of defenders.

McClelland was not lacking in confidence in the bravery of his men or in the devotion of his army, but on the contrary feared the intensity of their courage and patriotism lest it should inflict irreparable injury upon the enemy with whom he was in undoubted sympathy. This solves the mystery why he never fought a battle unless compelled so to do, and then fought them only in detail. His unexplained and inexcusable delays are easily accounted for when we consider that time, with the rebels, was the great desideratum ; it was time they needed, time to fortify, time to recruit and replenish, in fact, time was their only hope of salvation. Richmond at that moment was in a state of complete panic, and "Little Mac," the ever unready, lavishly granted them time galore. General Heintzelman said after the battle of Fair Oaks, "I have no doubt but that we might have gone right into Richmond," and Heintzelman's opinion was shared by almost every officer in that army whose knowledge of the situation entitled them to consideration. And if this could have been done after the Battle of Fair Oaks, against the whole rebel army, how much more easily could it have been accomplished after the battle of Gaines' Mill, when only Magruder and his twenty-five thousand men were within the defenses. Now the losses of the two armies in killed and wounded in the series of battles which culminated in the Battle of Malvern Hill, were about equal, if we except Mechanicsville and Malvern, where the rebel losses far exceeded those of the Union army. And it is a matter of history that at Malvern Hill General McClelland abandoned his army and took refuge on a gunboat six miles distant from the field, and was not on the ground at any time during the progress of the fight and in fact during all my term of service in the Army of the Potomac I never saw him under fire in any battle during all these campaigns. Now, my comrades and countrymen, I appeal to you, was this the part of a brave, loyal-hearted general, one who was true to his country and her cause ? Was it not rather the act of a cowardly, incompetent and traitorous commander, who did not desire the success of the cause he affected to espouse, and cared not for the disgrace and defeat of his devoted army ? In fact does it not conclusively argue that he wished, and anticipated the defeat of his army, and consequently made sure of his own safety ?

At the opening of the Battle of Malvern the corps commanders formed in line in an open field without defenses or protection of any kind. The combined forces of Lee and Jackson had been augmented by Magruder and his twenty-five thousand troops from the defenses of Richmond, and their lines were well protected by dense woods. The army of the Potomac up to this time had lost about fifteen thousand men. Allowing the rebel loss to have been equal to our own, by the addition of Magruder's army they outnumbered us by at least ten thousand men at this, the last of the seven days battle, in excess of what they did at the opening of the fight at Mechanicsville. And yet this superb Army of the Potomac, notwithstanding the hardships and losses of six successive hard-fought battles, met the increased forces of the rebels in the open field and crushingly defeated them at every point, and that too while their cowardly commander was ingloriously skulking on board a gunboat six miles away. Oh, for a Phil Sheridan at this supreme moment ! There would have been a total rout of the rebel army, and the spoils of victory would have been gathered in, and the utter destruction of the army of the insurgents accomplished. Now I claim that if it were possible under the circumstances as above stated, for the Army of the Potomac to thoroughly beat the rebel army in the open field as they did do, then there never was a time from the opening of the Peninsular campaign when they could not have done it if it had been competently and ably commanded. But McClelland, upon hearing of this complete and gloriously decisive victory, instead of marching over the shattered rebel army in triumph into Richmond, ordered an inglorious retreat, thus allowing the chaplet of victory, so heroically earned by his gallant army, to be borne off by their defeated foemen.

I cannot close this article on Malvern without quoting the appropriate and burning words of the lamented General Phil Kearny upon receipt of McClelland's traitorous order for the retreat : "I, Philip Kearny, an old soldier, do most solemnly enter my protest against this order for a retreat. We ought instead of retreating to follow up the enemy and take Richmond, and in full view of all the responsibilities of such a declaration I say to you all, such an order can only be prompted by cowardice or treason !" Surely those are strong words for a general to use against his commanding officer. But the best evidence of their being truthful is the fact that the cowardly and treacherous McClelland never called Kearny to an account for their utterance.

I will now take up the flag of truce incident at Antietam, and I am safe in saying that history fails of a parallel in audacious criminality and treachery, followed not only by the escape of the traitor from all punishment for his crime, but instead thereof being honored by a great number of prominent citizens of the commonwealth which he had essayed to ruin ; and what seems still more singular is the fact that he retained the sympathy and devotion of a large number of the soldiers of the army he had so basely betrayed, even after he had been relieved of his command.

A flag of truce suspending hostilities for the space of twenty-four hours was granted Lee by McClelland while a decisive battle was rapidly being decided in favor of the Union cause. Such a procedure in the whole course of the war up to that time had never been thought of, neither was such an action taken by a commander of either army during the remainder of the war, and I feel safe in saying that history fails to furnish a parallel to this audacious criminality, at least where the traitor escaped punishment by the country betrayed. Why then was this truce granted ? There can be but one answer to this question, viz.:   It was the only possible way of saving the rebel army from utter annihilation. Lee's army had been defeated at every point along the whole line, and was now penned in a bend of the Potomac River, with no bridge over which to escape, and his destruction was assured if the battle continued, hence McClelland ordered a cessation of hostilities for twenty-four hours to enable Lee to make good his escape with his army to the Virginia shore, and well did he improve the time granted him.   Every dead soldier on the battle field of Antietam was a wilful sacrificial offering to the Moloch of rebellion, and the villainous traitor who was responsible for this useless sacrifice of human life went scot free of all punishment ; even in his book, entitled "McClelland's Own Story," he does not mention, or in any way refer to this traitorous event which caused such a wanton and appalling waste of precious lives, neither does he refer to or offer any excuse for his cowardly desertion of the army at the Battle of Malvern Hill.   Now some of my comrades may take exceptions to this arraignment of McClelland, but the evidence, to my mind, is conclusive and must be disproved before I can change my opinion, and this I feel cannot be done by any dissenting comrade.   Hence I again denounce General Geo. B. McClelland as the champion traitor of the Nineteenth Century, and it is high time that he be shorn of the glamour which has surrounded him, as the outgrowth of a false sentiment, and blind devotion on the part of his misguided followers, and he should be relegated to that niche in truthful history to which his traitorous deeds and perfidious acts justly consign him, in order that future generations may execrate him as the Benedict Arnold of the Great Rebellion.

Having, as I think, shown sufficient cause for the friendliness and solicitude manifested by the rebels for McClelland, I will resume the narrative by introducing to the reader a hybrid individual who was second in command at the hospital, of which I have previously spoken, in which I was appointed to serve as wardmaster. This person bore the name of Charles Walters. He was a berouged, bepainted, effeminate weakly, dried up individual with an angular face almost sharp enough to shoot fish with ; this apology of a man was most heartily detested by the Yankees and was always spoken of by them as belonging to the female sex. She was supposed to be, and no doubt was, a played-out member of the Richmond demi monde, dressed in mail attire. She always made her appearance in the morning freshly rouged and painted and with a dudish and dandified air illy befitting her threadbare and over-worn garments. Her sharp cheek bones protruded from her withered and painted face like bumps on a peeled log. She would select a young and good looking Yankee for a patient and pet, much as an old maid would be expected to select a kitten or poodle, and I have often seen her and her favorite having a jolly time in her room where she would serve oysters and other luxuries. The fortunate Yankee who secured Charlie's favor was quite sure to get a parole at an early date, whereupon she would select another upon which to lavish her maudlin affection. When Woodward, the superintendent paid his visits, "Charlie" always had a long string of complaints and charges to pour into his ears against the horrible Yankees, but Woodward, upon such occasions, would chuck her affectionately under the chin and laugh and joke and make light of her complainings, and this would sometimes put her in a very angry mood. I never knew him to take action on her complaints, evidently considering them but the vaporings of an ill-humored and antiquated old maid. She railed out upon Richie and Warman one day until those gentlemen became very angry and threatened to boost her out of a window ; for this she promptly reported them to the higher rebel authorities, and as a consequence they were promptly sent over to Libby and confined in what was known as the retaliation room, where they were kept for some time as a punishment for their offense against "her highness." I supposed they had been paroled, and I did not learn of their incarceration in the penal room until we had returned from the war.

CHAPTER XIV.

DISCIPLES OF ESCULAPIUS.

Our hospitals afforded to the fledglings of Esculapius and the nonentities styling themselves physicians, an elegant opportunity, which by the way they were not slow to avail themselves of, to practice their art, or rather to demonstrate their ignorance of the principles of the science which they affected to be masters of. And as the prisoners had no friends to protest against their being subjects for the experiments of harlequins and their unskilled and senseless treatment, the consequence was that changes in surgeons (falsely called) were frequent.

Among the patients in my department was a vigorous, hearty German who had been hit high up on the forehead by a bullet, causing a depression of the skull at that point, resulting in compression of the brain and causing the most excruciating pain. Obviously, relieving the pressure was the thing needed, which could have been readily accomplished by trepanning, and such a course would doubtless have saved the life of the sufferer. But on the contrary, one morning a blear-eyed, stupid-looking individual, announcing himself as a doctor, came in, and after walking through the aisles of the ward, prescribed either a flaxseed poultice or a mustard plaster for every patient in the place, excepting only a man who had suffered an amputation of a leg. A poultice was accordingly applied to the poor German's head. The result of this process was of course to still further tax the already overcharged brain with blood, in response to the irritant, and as a consequence the patient died on the following morning. I have mentioned this case in order to show the reader to what danger to life and limb the soldier is subject, even though he succeed in escaping death on the battlefield. And it is a fact beyond controversy that there were exhibits of fortitude and bravery in our hospitals which equaled, if they did not excel, any displayed on the field of battle.

I must be excused for mentioning a case of extraordinary nerve as displayed by a man of my department upon the occasion of the poultice doctor's visit above referred to. The name of this hero was Albert Morse. He was a native of the State of Massachusetts and a sailor on the gunboat Underwriter. He had received a gunshot wound in the shin ; he was captured by the rebels at Plymouth and confined for sometime at Charleston. S. C. His wound had proven very obstinate and the government having abrogated all exchange of prisoners, Morse was sent with many others to Richmond, and when the doctor proposed poulticing his wound, he was given to understand in language more expressive than elegant, that he would submit to no such nonsense. Reduced in flesh to a mere skeleton and consequently very weak, the wound on the leg was a desperate one. The bone for the space of five inches in length, was bare of flesh, and to add to his discomfort, he had three frightful bed sores, one on each hip and one on the back, either of which was at least six inches in diameter. Yet notwithstanding his sufferings, this man exhibited the most determined resolution and courage ; indeed it would seem impossible, under the surroundings, and in the midst of such sufferings, for any human being to have maintained such pluck and nerve ; and by the way, he was in no way chary of his language when making known to the doctors his disapprobation of their methods. He would roundly curse and damn them daily for refusing to amputate his leg. Gangrene finally set in and he was transferred to the gangrene ward and there submitted to the painful operation of having the affected flesh burned out with nitrate of silver. On being returned to my ward he said to the rebel doctor, "G—d d—n you, why don't you cut that leg off ? You think I'll die ! But I'll show you that I'll never die in your damned old Southern Conthieveracy. I'm

going to live to get home." The doctors still refused to take
the limb off, and in spite of all our efforts to prevent it gangrene again set in.

Then the doctors concluded to amputate, and did so.
Morse stood the operation like the hero he was, and we gave
him the best care possible under the circumstances. Nevertheless, thirty days later the flesh had receded three inches
from the end of the bone, leaving it protruding from the
stump. This condition was due largely of course to the
careless and bungling manner in which the operation had
been performed. Sloughing of the parts ensued, a piece of
flesh as large as the palm of my hand dropping out from
alongside the bone, and at the same time an artery gave way.
Chancing to be near him at the time, I at once seized the
artery and held it until the doctor, who was summoned, arrived. But for the timely discovery poor Morse's life would
surely have gone out in a few seconds. Upon the arrival of
the doctor he ordered that the wound be syringed with tincture of iron and a tourniquet applied, but it was found that
the patient was too far reduced in strength to endure the
tourniquet, so for three days and nights we, by alternate re-
liefs, held the artery. By this time the process of coagula-
tion had put him beyond danger from hemorrhages, and in
a short time he had so far recovered as to be paroled, and the
last I ever saw of the courageous-hearted Morse he was being borne upon a stretcher to the wharf to take passage on a
vessel bound for God's country, and now after the lapse of
nearly thirty-five years, it would be a source of the greatest
gratification to me to know that this lion-hearted man lived
to reach his home in safety ; but that he did verify his prediction that he would not die in the Southern "Conthieveracy." I am well assured that his indomitable pluck and will
would sustain him until he was safely within our lines again.

I observed in my intercourse with my prison associates
that the brave-hearted, determined fellows were the ones who
stood the ravages of starvation and exposure much more suc-

cessfully than those of a softer, gentler disposition. When one was seen to be despondent and homesick, we at once concluded that the chances were against him, and as a matter of fact, such were the first to succumb to the effects of the terrible regime ; and knowing this, we made all sorts of efforts to cheer each other up by song singing and story telling, and when these diversions failed to arouse a dispondent comrade we generally looked upon his case as hopeless, and as a rule we were quite correct in our judgment, for after losing heart the individual usually lived but a brief time. So to prevent as much as possible any of the boys falling into homesickness, we used to keep up the singing in our frame building, which we occupied as a sleeping room, until late at night. One of our best and happiest singers as I remember them, was a comrade by the name of Paul Graham, who was a resident of Ligonier Valley, and I think he was a member of the Fourth Pennsylvania Cavalry. I never had the pleasure of seeing Graham after the war, but sometime since I learned through the postmaster of Ligonier that he died some years ago.

There were many instances of suffering in that hospital which might have been relieved, if not entirely obviated, if the doctors in charge had been humane and skillful as they ought to have been. To illustrate, one of my patients, a large, robust man, whose name escapes me, was attacked with diphtheria, and was desperately sick, but having great vigor of constitution, we saw no reason why he might not pull through it all right if the proper treatment was given, but one evening shortly after the doctor had made his usual rounds and left the building, the patient was taken worse, whereupon I immediately sent for the doctor, but as was usual a vast amount of circumlocution had to be enacted before a response to the call could be made, so before the doctor arrived the man was dead. He died in great agony ; in fact of all the deaths which I was called upon while there to witness, his, I think, was the most horrific. Then the doctor had the assurance to tell me that he could have saved the man's life by an operation. Well knowing the patient's condition, and seeing that an operation would save his life, why did he not perform it at the proper time ? There can be but one reason assigned for his failure to do so, and that is this, it meant death to one more Yankee and as a sequence one less loyal-hearted foeman to oppose the hell-hounds of red-handed rebellion. There were quite a number of deaths oc-curring in my ward, the names of the persons escaping me, but I remember quite well that among those who died there were Charles Robinson, ot Wisconsin, and Hiram Hornbeck, of New York.

I had one case of scurvy which terminated fatally, the patient being one mass of putrefying sores from the crown of his head to the soles of his feet. This foul disease results from want of proper vegetable food.

About this time the rebels began to fill the places made vacant by death in my ward, by bringing in from Libby enough to fill the cots with her lousy, ragged inmates, who from the treatment they had received, were more dead than alive. Our first care was to free them from the myriads of vermin that infested their meager clothing and preyed upon their poor, emaciated bodies. As soon as we received a re-cruit from Libby he was stripped naked, washed and put to bed, and his clothes were hung out of a window in order that the lice might suffer death from freezing. After a week or two of exposure to the frost, the lice would disappear, and then the clothing would be tied into a bundle and placed under the head of the patient's couch in case the owner of the clothes still tarried in the flesh when the louse kill-ing process was ended; if not,, which was often the case, some other poor suffering soul got them. It is, I am well aware, a difficult thing for persons who have had no opportunities of observing with what rapidity "body vermin" will multi-ply, to conceive of the condition a person will find himself in in a short space of time after being infected with those little brutes. Verily ! they "grow and flourish like a green bay tree," especially if one is hampered in his facilities for fighting them, as all prisoners in Southern prisons were.

I am inclined to pass over this in silence on account of its repulsiveness, but for the horribly miserable condition of the poor Union prisoners as they came to us at the hospital from Libby. As one object of this publication is to inform the people as to the sufferings of our soldiers while confined in the prison pens of the South, I shall offer no further apology for the following narration, every word of which I assure the reader is true. I frequently received men into the ward whose bodies were literally eaten full of holes by these parasites, as though it was not enough that their poor bodies, weakened by starvation, had scarcely vitality sufficient to sustain the spark of life within them, but they also were obliged to furnish sustenance to the multitudinous insect life which swarmed and preyed unhindered upon their emaciated frames. Our conflicts with the "graybacks," or body lice, thanks to the freezing process, were not so long drawn or desperate, but when we came to deal with the head lice we were never quite sure when the conflict would end. Our weapons, both of offense and defense, against this enemy were crude and consisted only of a comb with teeth something after the order of those of a garden rake, which a Yankee prisoner had made from a piece of bone with a pocket knife. Then we had a bit of an old gum-blanket which we utilized as a receptacle for the fallen foe, and in addition, an old iron kettle, and with this armament we waged a war of extermination against these pestiferous parasites. The "modus operandi" resorted to in the case of a man having a heavy head of hair and an unusually thick beard will suffice to give the reader an idea of the process in a general way.

As I say, when this man was brought in from Libby, Richie and I took charge of the patient and after divesting him of his garments, put him to bed. We then, after allowing him to rest a little, propped him up on his couch and spreading the rubber blanket over his lap, commenced the raking process, and at every passage of the rude comb through the hair, the lice would rattle down upon the blanket like falling rain.   The poor man himself was greatly astonished at the magnitude of the catch, and as he looked upon the constantly increasing pile of live animals, his exclamations of surprise were both pathetic and amusing ; and no marvel, for we actually secured in this particular case about one pint of lice from his head and beard.   Our next move was to fill our kettle with tobacco stems from which we ma.le a strong decoction with which we bathed his head, and with cloths soaked in the same, bound up his head and luxuriant beard.   In following this process for a time we succeeded in ridding our patient of his tormentors, but the operation was prolonged from the fact that every hair in the man's head was covered for at least one inch from the scalp with nits, and these continued to hatch out, so we were obliged to repeat the bathing with the infusion of tobacco for several days.

The first day of January, 1865, was a day long to be remembered on account of its being so intensely cold at Richmond.   The James River froze over its entire width that night, a thing which rarely occurred ; "Indeed," said Superintendent Woodward, "it had not happened for twenty years before."   A large number of the prisoners in Libby were cruelly frozen during that night, and no marvel : the wonder being that they did not all perish of the cold, as they were allowed no fire at all, and the windows were entirely open.   On the day following I received a contingent of the victims of the frost from Libby and a sorry lot they were, I assure you.   Some of the number had had their feet so badly frozen that their toes actually dropped from their feet. This hellish act on the part of the rebels, for a wonder, called out uncomplimentary comments from their own people which resulted in their boarding up the windows, thus leaving the prisoners in perpetual darkness, subjected to a combination of the plagues of intense cold, darkness and lice, and I firmly believe that if the hellish rebel authorities could have devised any other plagues they would have been added to those above enumerated. The tomahawk and scalping knife of the savage, the rack and thumb-screw of the Holy Inquisition, or the nameless barbarities of the "Unspeakable Turk" are all mild and merciful in comparison with the tortures heaped upon the inmates of the Southern prison hells. How could human beings become so heartless and cruel as to let their fellow creatures suffer and die of cold and hunger? The question has been so often asked I beg leave just here to say that the people of the South generally, if they had been left to follow their own inclinations and desires, would have made the prisoners comfortable ; but the rebel authorities were maddened by their failure to accomplish, by arms in the field, their scheme of secession, and having lost all hope of successfully coping with the Yankees in the field, they deliberately devised and put into operation that damnable regime of starvation with all its concomitant horrors. Why such brutalities were allowed by our government to be practiced upon our soldiers, whom the fate of war had thrown into the enemy's hands, as I have before stated in this work, I cannot understand, for the reader will remember that it is stated in a previous chapter that the government had stopped the exchange of prisoners of war, thus enabling the rebels to starve many thousands of our soldiers who otherwise would have been restored to usefulness in our ranks through exchange. The war, it must be remembered, was not waged on the part of the North, for the purpose of abolishing slavery, but it was fought with the sole object of suppressing the rebellion of the slave-holding oligarchy of the South against the government of the United States, and instead of going at the traitors "hammer and tongs," as any other government on earth would probably have done, our authorities truckled, with honeyed words, hoping to win the recalcitrant states back to their allegiance to the Union at any cost short of its own existence ; and all this time the uncompromising rebels were scorning every offer of reconciliation, and were practicing all the hellish arts of a refined barbarism to win their cause.

Under the so-called Proclamation of Emancipation, if
the rebellious states had laid down their arms prior to January 1st, 1864, they could have resumed their standing in the
Union and retained their property in human souls, and the
"sum of all villainies" would probably exist to-day in the
"land of the free, and the home of the brave," as in the ante-
bellum days.   There evidently should have been issued, on
the day Fort Sumter was fired upon, a proclamation containing just four words, to-wit :   "Unconditional surrender,
or death !" and the war should have been fought on that
line, "an eye for an eye, and a tooth for a tooth."   In that
case I grant you it would not have dragged its weary length
through four dreary years and more.

It seems so strange to us now, standing as we do a
whole generatiton this side of the momentous transactions
crowded into the years between April 12th, 1861, and April
13th, 1865 ;   it seems so strange I say, that even our most
brilliant statesmen and wisest philosophers failed to recognize the fact that the cup of iniquity of the slave-holding
South was filled to repletion, and that we of the North, who
were not wholly guiltless for its continuance, were the chos-
en instruments of Providence for the wiping from our nation's fair escutcheon the foul blot of human thraldom.
Had this underlying fact been recognized from the first, and
the war prosecuted with the vigor that would naturally grow
out of such a heaven-imposed task, it doubtless would have
reached a speedy termination, for our army was composed
of as courageous a body of men as ever caused old earth to
tremble to their martial tread.

However, toward the latter part of January that year,
an exchange of prisoners was arranged for, and our patients
were being sent north.   Finally my comrades were all taken
away and my ward was closed, and I was sent to the floor
below for a few days.   While here I formed the acquaintance of a patient whose name was John Swihart, and whose
home was at Massillon, Ohio, and of all the poor, lean men

I had ever seen, John was the thinnest. I think his weight
would have fallen under fifty pounds. I used my own person as a standard of measure in such cases, as I had, while in
perfect health, been reduced from one hundred and seventy
pounds normal weight, until I tipped the beam of the rebel
scales upon which our rations were weighed to us, at just
one hundred pounds. So thin was John that I often thought
that if his stomach itched he was just as likely to scratch his
back bone through it as not.

His condition proved a great puzzle to the rebel doctors
who were unable to determine the nature of his malady, as
he became thinner and weaker day by day, and yet showed
no symptoms of organic disease. His lung power was un-
impaired and remained remarkably strong, for one so emaciated as he, and when he took a notion to "yell," as he frequently did, his stentorian voice would wake the echoes
throughout the entire building. John would be talking with
some comrade or attendant in an ordinary tone of voice, and
as intelligently as anyone, when perhaps in the midst of a
sentence he would break off and give vent to the most un-
earthly yells, screaming, "Ouch ! Ouch ! Oh, Lord ! Oh !
Oh !" and then, resuming the conversation where he had
left off, he would talk on as if nothing had happened. John
was cared for by a stalwart Michigan cavalryman by the
name of King, who nursed him tenderly, and handled him as
easily as an ordinary man could have handled a baby. Finally the annex to General Hospital No. 21 was closed, and the
patients and attendants, with the exception of a New Yorker
by the name of Sawyer, and myself, were all paroled, and the
last I ever saw of poor John Swihart he was being carried on
a stretcher toward the boat that was to speed him away in
the direction of his home in the Northland, but whether he
died or still lives, I know not.

Sawyer and myself were now transferred to Hospital
No. 21 where I had the distinguished honor of being in-
stalled wardmaster over a small room on the first floor, with
Sawyer as a nurse. This room contained only twenty-eight

cots and was reserved for the most desperate cases only. At about eight o'clock in the morning the rebels brought in to my ward a patient for each cot in my room, and they were the toughest, most miserable an pitiful specimens of humanity I ever cast my eyes upon during all my terrible experience with destitution, disease and starvation. None of these patients had received a bath for a month or more and they were smoked until their skins were the color of a smoked ham. Clothed in filthy rags and with their skeleton frames and gaunt faces, they were indeed pitiful and distressing objects to behold. We proceeded at once to make the poor creatures as comfortable as was possible under the circumstances.

While we were in the midst of our efforts to make our patients more comfortable and presentable, the rebel doctor came in. He was a gray haired man of some sixty years, I should say ; his name, if my memory serves me, was Rathburn. I shall never forget the expression of horror which overspread the old doctor's face as he looked upon the desperate condition in which these poor wretches were. "My God !" he exclaimed, "we can do nothing for these men. They will all die. All I can hope to do for them is to make it as easy for them as possible ;" and he prescribed ten drops of laudanum in a gill of whisky, three times per day, to each and every patient. Eight of these men expired within four hours after being brought in. Among these men was one, John Barman, with whom I had been well acquainted, he having belonged to Company F, Eighth Pennsylvania Reserves, my own regiment. I had failed to recognize him owing to his blackened and terrible condition, but while I was fixing him up as comfortably as I could, he called my name and told me who he was. Grasping his wasted hand I sat down by him on the cot, while in the weak and trembling voice of a dying man, he told me of the horrible deaths of many of my comrades, as they had met their fate in the prison hell at Salisbury ; and as he mentioned the names of long-loved schoolfellows, messmates and fellow soldiers, who had been swallowed up in that hellish maelstrom of rebel malignity, it seemed to me my heart must break, and I gave way to a flood of tears. But they were not tears of unmingled grief, for indignation claimed her rights. Alas! my comrades, though I. Alas! brave heroes of many a hard fought field; and is this then thy inglorious end? For shame! ungrateful Republic! thus to abandon thy gallant sons to the ignominy of death by starvation, when one act of justifiable retaliation would have saved their valuable lives for the service of their country. Why could not those in authority in our government see, and understand, that it was better and more just that a thousand rebels who were fighting to destroy our government should die, than that one loyal, patriotic man, who had undertaken to defend the nation's life, should suffer even the loss of a single cracker which might be necessary for his subsistence while he stood guard over his country's honor and integrity? And it stands to reason that if the rebels had the food supplies which were requisite to sustain their traitorous armies in the field, then surely they also had the food necessary to keep their prisoners of war from starvation. I never have been able to see any possible excuse for our authorities failing to demand of the rebels proper treatment of our prisoners of war.

· This news imparted to me by Barman, concerning the fate of my poor comrades at Salisbury, was the first tidings I had received of them since my escape from the box car, and so depressed was I by his narration of the sad and melancholy facts concerning them, that I was greatly dejected for several days after; but poor Barman soon after responded to the last roll call, and was mustered out of the earthly ranks to join the great majority of our comrades on the eternal camping grounds above.

As no clothing was allowed to remain on a corpse, Sawyer removed the ragged habiliments from Barman's body, and covering it with a sheet, he and I carried it to a building across the way used as a dead house. Oh, my God! what a horrible sight was here presented to our view. I cannot think of it even to this day without a thrill of horror, for there on the floor lay sixteen corpses, perfect skeletons, stark naked, with eyes, noses and mouths all eaten away by the rats. The eyeless sockets, missing nose and grinning teeth of these poor bodies made such a scene of gruesome, horrible reality as was never conceived of even by the morbid imagination of a Dante. No picture of the deepest inferno could equal it. Summon, Oh, Satan, from the remotest regions of gloomy hades and expend thy hellish vocabulary of hate in showering the imprecations of deep damnation on the heads of those who planned and perpetrated this fiendish mutilation upon these brave and noble dead !

DEAD HOUSE OF GENERAL HOSPITAL NO. 21.

The dead-cart was purposely allowed to make but one trip each twenty-four hours, so that those dying after the cart-man had made his round could be left in the dead house to fatten the rats until the next day. These rats, like the vultures on the towers of silence among the Parsees of India, from long usage had become adepts in their gastly work, and attacked only the eyes, nose and lips of their victims until these had been exhausted, and as the supply of new corpses was always equal to the demand, they fed on these dainties constantly. Now this hideous mutilation could have been prevented by having the cart conveying the dead make two trips daily, and allowing the bodies of those dying after the last trip to lie on the cots until the following morning or until the cart came around again ; but this you see would not have so fully gratified the rebel desire to heap indignities upon the Yankee dead. The rat-eaten dead were thrown indiscriminately into the cart, like so many logs of wood, a tarpaulin was stretched over them and they were hauled out through the streets of Christian Richmond and consigned to a ditch and slightly covered with earth, and left there unrecorded and unknown, to molder back to dust ; and thus was their identity effectually obliterated.

This was the fate of every Union soldier who died at General Hospital No. 21 at Richmond, Va., during my sojourn there, which covered a period of several months. Brave defenders of an ungrateful Republic ! Thou hast sealed thy devotion to thy country's cause by a martyr's death ! and thy name hast been stricken from the annals of earth as though thou hadst never been, but thy memory shall remain green in the hearts of thy surviving comrades until the grim reaper shall summon us also to the eternal shore !

CHAPTER XV.

Among my patients was one, Patrick Kane, who, as his name would imply, was an Irishman. He was a member of the Seventh Regulars. He was suffering from dropsy and although too much reduced from the combined effects of disease and starvation to stand upon his feet, or even to sit up, he was very pugnacious and was ever ready to fight everybody and everything in sight. Pat's cot was located about the center of the ward, and if Sawyer, the nurse, did not give him the first slice of corn bread cut from the loaf when he distributed rations, he would fire his piece at his head as soon as he got it into his hand. He finally made his mind up that he would take no more medicine, or if he did pretend to take it, he would, after holding it in his mouth for awhile, squirt it over the other patients. The doctor one day told me to hold Pat's nose and make him swallow his medicine. I did so, and when he found I was also determined to make him behave himself, he became despondent, and although his condition seemed much improved and he seemed to be gathering strength, he continued his growling. One morning soon after making him take his remedies, I said to him, "Well, Pat, how are you this morning?" "Oh, Jasus," says he, "I'm going to die to-night!" "Oh, you are all right," I said, "You are getting stronger every day." On the following morning I said to him, "Well, Pat, I see you did not die last night after all," whereupon he smote his breast with his fist, and said, "Be Jasus, if I don't die to-night, divil a bit will I die at all, at all," and he did not and it was not long after until Pat was paroled, and I have every reason to believe he lived to reach God's country once more.

There was partitioned off of the end of my ward a little

room which Sawyer and myself used as a sort of storeroom
for medicines and any extra rations which might chance to
fall into our hands. It was fitted with a bench which extended
across one end of it, and underneath it was boxed off into
small compartments, and as the majority of my patients were
in such a physical condition as to be unable to eat the rough
food supplied by the rebels, I sometimes had an accumula-
tion of rations from this source, to which I was able to add,
from time to time, a little from my own allowance, as I drew
as wardmaster full allowance. So from this surplus under the
bench I was often enabled to carry and distribute food to the
men in the other wards who were in a condition to eat. But
I was very careful not to let the rebels catch me at it for if
I had been detected in sharing my rations with the poor
starving prisoners, I probably would have been hustled off
to Libby as a punishment.

The building in which our hospital was located, had,
prior to the war, been used as a tobacco manufactory and the
brand of their output was known as "The Conqueror," and
there were strewn about the place numbers of their circulars,
upon which was printed the picture of an armored knight
with plumed helmet and a drawn sword standing over his
supposedly fallen foe. Some Yank having secured two of
these circulars cut from them the pictures and printed under
them the following apt quotations : "He that taketh sword
shall perish by the sword," and "The sword is my inheri-
tance, let tyrants tremble," and had pasted them on the wall,
and strange to say, they were left undisturbed by the Johnnies ; and as the collapse of the Confederacy followed so
soon after, it almost seems as if those quotations were pro-
phetic of the just doom which was so soon to fall upon this
traitorous conspiracy. Despondency seemed to settle, like a
thick pall, over the hopes of the rebels from the moment
they learned of the overwhelming defeat of Geo. B. McClelland for the presidency ; and although rapidly tottering to
its fall, the agents of the Confederate States (so-called) abat-
ed no jot or tittle of their malignancy, their desire and effort

to kill and destroy seemed rather to intensify in hellishness, as their hopes of success grew less, until finally she lay prone and helpless, like a huge serpent, in impotent rage, and for want of power to do further damage to the cause of humanity, turned and rent its own body, for it is a fact that an effort was made by the rebs to destroy their own city of Richmond.

The following are some of the prices of articles of necessity prevailing at the capital of the Confederacy just prior to its fall, in Confederate money. One thousand dollars for a suit of very ordinary ready-made clothing. Five hundred dollars for a barrel of flour. One hundred dollars for a cord of wood. One dollar for a loaf of bread weighing not to exceed five ounces. One dollar for a clay pipe, and fifty cents for a block of matches. Onions could be had for one dollar each, and a dollar in greenbacks would purchase forty dollars in Confederate currency, and it was amusing to observe with what avidity the Johnnies would gobble up the few greenbacks which came in their way even at the disparity of forty to one, thus showing their lack of confidence in their government to ever redeem its pledges to the holders of its bank notes.

I have seen Mr. Woodward, the superintendent of the hospital, of whom I have before spoken, twist up a twenty dollar blueback and use it to light his cigar.

It was now about the middle of March, 1865, and General Hospital No. 21 was about to pass out of existence with the ebbing tide of the rebellion. The greater number of the patients had already been paroled, and none were being received, and as you may safely conclude Sawyer and myself were anxiously awaiting our turn for release to come. I had been suffering for some six weeks from a peculiar and distressing disease called by the doctors, the Confederate itch, and this circumstance added greatly to my desire to get home, as I well knew I could never recover from my malady under the rebel regime, and besides my comrades had all been released and the loss of their companionship worried **me** greatly. The itch above referred to was a skin disease which made its appearance in the form of small watery pimples no larger than a pin-head, confining its attack to breast, hands and the insides of the arms and legs. The pimples came out in myriads, close together, and were so excruciatingly itchy, especially when the sufferer would approach the fire, as to become unendurable, and if scratched it served only to exaggerate the suffering, and to forbear to scratch I believe was impossible, as with me it was "scratch Yank or die." Finally when the disease had expended its force on one particular spot, the rheum would dry up, the skin become indurated, and scale off in flakes. It was several years before I was rid of this disease ; even after the lapse of twenty years it would occasionally make its appearance upon my person.

On the 23d of March, 1865, the auspicious moment came and Sawyer and myself were, with the few others remaining, paroled and I think we were the last squad of Federal prisoners to be exchanged. About ten days later Richmond was captured. Words are inadequate to express the happiness and joy we experienced when at last we turned our backs upon that detestable city of misery, starvation and death, or with what glad exultation we marched down to the wharf and boarded the rebel flag-of-truce boat which was to bear us back to the sheltering folds of "Old Glory" once more. Farewell my dead comrades ! A long farewell ! Peacefully sleep, quietly rest ; though it be in the unhallowed soil of traitorous Virginia. No more shall war's rude alarms burst upon your devoted ears ; no more shall an ungrateful country call you as a bootless sacrifice to the unholy ambitions of false and incompetent chieftains. Sleep. Requiescat in Pace !

Our boat backed away from her moorings, and we steamed away down the James to the outpost of the rebel lines, where we were met by a Union vessel to which we were transferred, and so at last were beneath the starry folds of the banner of the free. Out of the depths of perdition. Out of the prison cell. "Out of the jaws of death ; out of the mouth of hell."

It was indeed a pathetic spectacle to see those poor, miserable starved men, clothed in filthy rags, with their weak voices cheering at the sight of the old flag, with tears of joy and gratitude streaming down their cheeks. We were soon on our way to Fortress Monroe, which point we reached in the evening, and after a short stay proceeded to cross the bay to Annapolis, Md. This was on the night of the 23d of March, and the day had been cold and raw. As the night came on it was frosty on the Chesapeake, and as the boat could furnish neither blankets nor overcoats to the men, they were obliged to lie out on deck in the open frost-laden air, without covering of any sort. As a conseqeunce, in the morning there were several of the poor fellows lying dead on the deck, with their glassy eyes staring up at the masthead, where floated the flag they loved so well. And thus, on the very threshold of freedom, and so near to friends and home, they perished, victims to somebody's carelessness in not supplying the boat which was designed to transport these starvelings to their homes, with a few blankets.

In due course of time we arrived at Annapolis and were quartered in the barracks designed for the use of returned prisoners. On arrival each prisoner was stripped to the buff, given a bath and furnished with a new and complete outfit of clothing, and given two months' pay. As I had received no pay for almost two years, this money was highly acceptable to me and I was enabled to purchase a few dainties and nicknacks of which I had long been deprived. Sawyer's solicitude also seemed largely centered in his stomach, and on receiving his money, said he would have one full meal anyhow. A peddler coming along at this juncture enabled him to put his desire for a fill-up into practical form and illustrated his capabilities as a gastronomic expert. The peddler's wares consisted of hard boiled eggs with salt and pepper for dressing, and Sawyer proceeded to put himself outside of twenty-six of those eggs, which astonishing feat he accomplished in a very short space of time. The peddler's 'eyes were distended in surprise, especially after the disappearance of the

first dozen, but as he had evidently struck a bonanza in Sawyer's unappeasable appetite, for his stock in trade, he offered
no objection to its reduction. I, however, was alarmed for
his safety, but I remonstrated and pleaded in vain. I told
him such a gorge would surely kill him. His reply was, that
if it did, he would have the satisfaction of dying on a full .
stomach anyhow ; but strange to say he suffered no seeming inconvenience from his reckless indulgence in hard boi'ed
eggs. A few days after this episode Sawyer and I par'ed
company, probably never to meet again on the shores of time,
as I have had no tidings of him since I bade him god-bye
that March day in parole camp at Annapolis.

This camp was rather an uninviting spot, especially to
the returned prisoner, as he was invariably anxious to get
home to loving friends after his long absence and terrible
sufferings in Southern prisons. The immense heaps of cast-
off shoes and clothing, crawling with graybacks,, which ac-
cumulated there, was a constant reminder of his late prison
life, and he could scarcely realize that he was indeed once
more a free man.

I had the good fortune to meet here my old comrade,
James W. Eberhart. We had not met each other since the
day upon which we left the inferno at Belle Isle to be transferred to the hell at Salisbury. Eberhart was terribly reduced in flesh, was sick and weak and had entirely lost his
voice. It is needless to say that our comradeship was resumed. We ate and slept in the same barrack. He had
been paroled from Salisbury a month before I was at Richmond, but the rebels had sent him by the way of Raleigh,
causing many delays, so that he was nearly a month in reaching Annapolis. He occupied a bunk directly over mine in
the barracks and one night while in a trance, he fell out of
bed and was stunned by the fall, and on being carried out
into the air and revived his voice suddenly returned to him
as good as ever.

Among the rank and file composing a company of
American volunteers may be found men of such sterling

qualities of both head and heart as to command the respect and admiration of the entire company. Such a man was Sergeant James W. Eberhart, of Company G. Generous, kind-hearted and uncomplaining, he cheerfully performed any duty assigned him, however arduous or dangerous it may have been. Brave and courageous at all times, yet so gentle and kind to all that he never aroused the ire of any-one. His grandfather was a patriotic soldier during the "Times that tried men's souls" at Valley Forge, and the grandson was not a whit behind the grandsire in soldierly qualities during the war of the Great Rebellion.

Like all members of the company he was nicknamed. He was dubbed "Pedee" and as Pedee he was universally known throughout the war.

To show his equanimity and self-control under aggra-vating circumstances, I will relate an incident of camp life which occurred at Alexandria. Pedee, who was a member of my mess, was an inveterate smoker, and after taking his noonday smoke would always lie down for a nap when off duty. We had been supplied with waterproof cartridges which were inclosed in a glazed film. These films were highly explosive and one day while Pedee was sleeping, I emptied his half-smoked, short-stemmed pipe of its contents and in-serting one of these films in the bottom, replaced the to-bacco on top of it. After his nap was over Pedee reached for his pipe and, lighting it, sat himself down for a nice quiet smoke. Suddenly there was a swish, and the pipe dropped to the floor, while the contents went sailing up his nose, which immediately overhung it. Did he sneeze ? Well, you would have thought he would sneeze his head off. His snorting, sneezing and coughing drew forth shouts of laughter from the boys at first, as they all expected him to get furious with rage, tear around and threaten to wipe up the ground with the noodle-headed imbecile who had served him such a measly trick. But he did nothing of the kind. After the paroxysm of sneezing was over, without saying a word, he picked up his old dudeen, loaded it to the brim with fresh tobacco, lighted it, and sat down for a smoke as calmly and placidly as if nothing unusual had occurred. Ninety-nine out of a hundred would have been fighting mad upon being served such a trick, but Pedee had such complete control of his feelings. I never saw him show excitement under the most dangerous or aggravating circusmstances.

In that hell-hole of misery, starvation and death, Salisbury, Pedee was the Good Samaritan, visiting the hospital, cheering the despondent and despairing and relieving the misery of the sick and dying comrades. Although starving, with a devotion sublime, a self-abnegation unequalled, he deprived himself of his rations of bread that he might make poultices for those whose desperate sufferings were greater even than his own.

He was attacked by the scurvy and his teeth one by one dropped from his jaws. He lost all power of speech, which, however, was miraculously recovered after his release from prison, as related elsewhere, but under all trying conditions whatsoever he remained the same kind, congenial and uncomplaining Pedee.

My messmates were all good men and true, but the qualities of Sturgiss and Eberhart seemed to have a more lasting impression on me than the others.

The three left flank companies of the regiment, K, G and B, naturally became friendly and social, entering into each other's sports and becoming acquainted with the individual characteristics of its members. Company K had two unique members, of whom one was called "Groundhog" and the other "Pig-Tracks." The former was a singular looking man with a heavy reddish beard and derived his name from the fact that he endeavored to burrow into the ground for protection in our first battle, and it would make him very wrathy to shout "Groundhog" at him. It is safe to say we all became groundhogs and gophers before the war was ended. The other man received his euphonious title from the fact that whenever he got filled up on commissary whisky, he would go about shouting "Pig-Tracks" in the most unaccountable manner. Like "Groundhog," he re-sented the name, and for this reason they stuck to them throughout their service, but what their ultimate fate was I do not now recollect.

Eberhart left for home several days before I did and after he had gone and I had started I was taken violently ill on the train with bronchitis, and on arrival at Harrisburg I was so weak I could not sit up and had to lie on the station platform until the train arrived for Pittsburg. I finally reached my home in Uniontown and after being confined to my bed for about three weeks I recovered sufficiently to re-join my command at Arlington Heights after they had re-turned from Richmond. After completing our muster out rolls here we were moved to Harrisburg and I was there dis-charged after four years, two months and eleven days of con-stant and active service. The slaveholders' rebellion was crushed ; the Union was saved ;

And the Star Spangled Banner in triumph shall wave
O'er the land of the free and the home of the brave.

CHAPTER XVI.

SALISBURY.

Below will be found a cut of the prison which became so notorious on account of the diabolical tortures which were there perpetrated upon the prisoners of war who were unfortunate enough to fall into the rebel hands during the years of strife from 1861 to 1865. It is really and truly humiliating to me, as a soldier of the Republic of the great United States of America, to be obliged to record that here at this Salisbury prison, prisoners of war, brave, patriotic men, who while fighting in defense of their government, were by the fortunes of war, thrown into the hands of those who were in rebellion against that government ; that they should have been subjected to such barbarous and inhuman treatment by those who had been born, reared and fostered under the same beneficent institutions as themselves, and who up to the breaking out of the rebellion had been accounted as worthy citizens of one of the most highly enlightened and thoroughly Christian nations on the face of the earth ; I blush, I say, with shame for my countrymen, when for truth and history's sake, I am obliged to record the diabolical treatment which was accorded the Union prisoners at the hands of those who were at the time in armed rebellion against our government. I fain would frame some excuse, some extenuating circumstances or pretexts, if I could, but I cannot, and none exist. The bald fact alone remains, that the sufferings to which we, as prisoners of war, were subjected were inflicted coolly, deliberately, and with malice aforethought, with a view to either compass our death outright, or to render us hors de combat by reason of the wrecked physical condition in which their cruel regime would naturally leave us. This and this alone must have been the deliberate design, for they had no score of retaliation to

settle, for their men who had fallen as prisoners of war into
the hands of the government had been and continued to be,
treated with the utmost kindness and consideration.   Everything was done by our government to render their captivity
as little galling to them as possible.   They were provided
with clean, comfortable quarters, where sanitary conditions
were the best obtainable ; they were provided with comfortable clothing and supplied with abundance of wholesome
food, and particular care was always exercised by our government to locate their camps of detention where abundant
supplies of pure water was obtainable, and in addition to all
these primal arrangements and conditions for the health and
comfort of the rebel prisoners, there were always in attend-
ance upon their wounded and sick, the best of medical and
surgical skill, which was employed for the relief of their sufferings with as great care and tenderness as would have been
shown them had they been members of our own legions, instead of our foemen.

I thus particularize in regard to the treatment, at the
hands of our government, of its prisoners of war for the reason that so many attempts have been made by rebel apologists to create a diversion, from the fact that the Confederate
or rebel authorities did treat prisoners of war with hellish
cruelty, by asserting that their soldiers, held as prisoners at
the North, were also treated with barbarity ; but in clear
and complete refutation of this charge of the rebels, is the
historic fact that the rate of mortality among the rebel prisoners confined in Northern prisons, was more than fifty per
cent. less than among the Union prisoners confined in Southern prisons, and this great disparity in the death rate between the prisoners dying in the hands of the North, and
of the South, is explainable wholly and solely by the fact that
the great majority of those dying in Southern prisons were
actually starved to death, or were so far reduced in strength
by starvation, purposely inflicted for the securing of that
end, that they fell an easy prey to diseases which swept
them off in great numbers.   I realize how hard it is for the

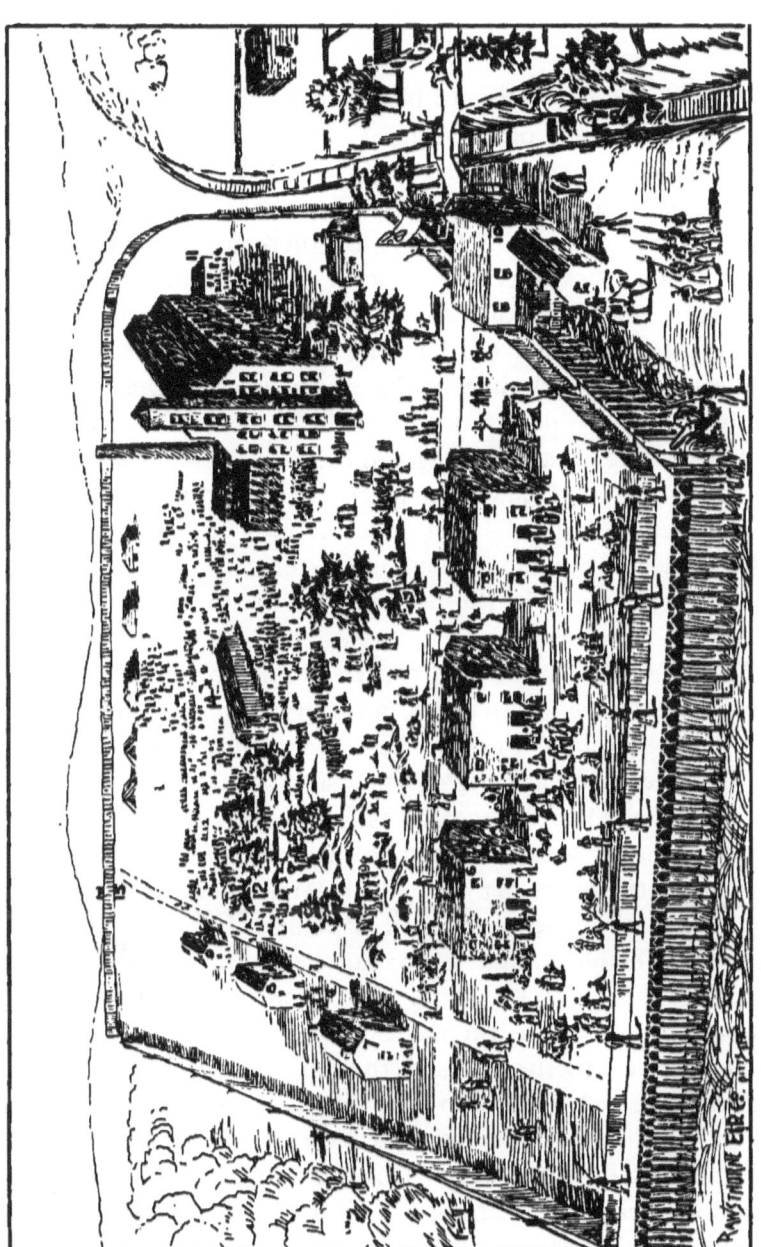

SALISBURY—(AFTER PHOTO.)

average American citizen to believe it possible that one portion of the people of this great and enlightened country
could have been so incensed at the other that they would
have resorted to such means to satisfy their spleen ; but that
they did is as true as the Gospel, for there are living to-day,
thirty-three years after the close of the war, strange as it
may seem, hundreds of men who attest to the truth of the
statements made in regard to the treatment of the Union
soldiers who passed time in the prison pens of the South,
and the universal declaration made by these men is that the
half has not been told, neither can be, for with me, they fully
agree that human language utterly fails to furnish words
with which to faithfully paint the pictures of suffering and
distress which our brave boys were called to pass through
as prisoners of war in the pens of the South, and more especially at Salisbury, N. C.

As we have before said earlier in this volume, the first
thing that happened to a prisoner upon falling into the
hands of the rebels, was that he was carefully robbed of all
his valuables, such as watch, money and pocket knife ; then
he was stripped of hat, coat, vest and shoes, and indeed in
many instances I have seen men made by rebel officers to
give up their pants, leaving them bareheaded, barefooted,
and with nothing to cover their nakedness but their under-
garments, blankets and overcoats being the first things
usually to be grabbed from the prisoners by the greedy,
brutal rebels, and thus the men were left to shiver and suffer
from exposure to the frosts of the fall and winter nights of
that latitude.   And then to supplement the sufferings caused by nakedness, the regime of starvation was at once commenced and I assure, you, that it was carried on to comple-
tion, for I think if the arch fiend himself had been set to de-
vise ways and means to make the process of starvation completely torturous and horrible, he could not have improved
upon the methods adopted by those who were intrusted
with the care of the prisoners by the rebel authorities, for
without question it would have been more merciful to

withhold food entirely and allow the victims to die in a relatively short space of time, than to have pursued the course they did, subjecting their victims to the pangs of slow, but no less sure, death by starvation.

To prove these facts I wish to say a word here in regard to the bread made from the cob meal. The rebel authorities well knew that there was not a particle of nutriment in a corn cob, and they also knew that a human being could only live at most for a few months if fed upon bread made from corn, ground cob and all. Therefore for the purpose of killing off the prisoners more rapidly this corn cob bread was invented and introduced through their hellish ingenuity. The poor, weak, half-starved creatures compelled to eat this bread would be attacked by a violent diarrhoea which in their weakened condition would soon become acute ; then chronic and in a short time end in a lingering death. This was surely an effectual means of converting live Yankees into dead ones.

Captain Davis of a New York regiment was shot by a guard when he was not near the dead line. This was another of their favorite methods of making dead Yankees and many innocent, inoffensive prisoners were thus brutally murdered, the rebel authorities urging and inciting the practice by giving a thirty-day furlough to the murderer as a reward.

As enough has been said of the brutal rebel regime in this prelude to Salisbury, I submit, by the kind permission of Comrade C. H. Golden, of Jacksonville, Greene County, Pa., an account of his miserable and fearful suffering in that hell-hole of despair and death.Comrade Golden was a member of my company, and his account, in connection with my own, gives complete and truthful history of the sufferings of the company in the prisons of the South.

CHAPTER XVII.

COMRADE GOLDEN'S EXPERIENCE.

".\ realistic story
Without any gush or glory :
With no sentimentl limelight,
And no fire work display."

I was a private soldier during the civil war. I enlisted as a recruit in the Eighth Regiment, P. R. V. C., and was taken to Camp Copeland, near Pittsburg. (Braddock's field) January, 1864. I was here detailed as second clerk in the quartermaster's office, Joseph R. Harrah being first clerk, who was also here and was a sergeant from One Hundred and Fortieth Regiment Pennsylvania Volunteers. The last day of May I requested the post commandant and quarter-master to relieve me from duty, and return me to my regi-ment. The commander of the post refused to grant my re-quest. I then and there resolved to go to my regiment without their permission, and did make my way from Camp Copeland, Pa., to near Petersburg, Va., and there found my coveted prize, Company H, One Hundred and Ninety-First Regiment. At this time, about the first of June, all the vet-erans and recruits of the Reserve regiments were consolidat-ed into two regiments, known as the One Hundred and Nine-tieth and One Hundred and Ninety-First Regiments, Penn-sylvania Volunteer Infantry. The two regiments at this time formed the Third Brigade, in the Third Division, Fifth Army Corps, G. R. Warren commanding. As I commenced to narrate my prison life and countermarches during the summer, in front of a vigilant enemy about Petesburg, I will confine myself to that subject.

On the 14th of August, the Fifth Corps marched out from the front line, before Lee's army, and about noon we struck the Weldon railroad at Ream's Station. Our regiment did not tear up the track, but we did the fighting while others of our corps destroyed the railroad for several miles, and as we held on to the road, we pushed on toward the south and rear of Petersburg. But the Confederates saw the danger and were at their old flank movement. Taking a road unknown to our commander they came suddenly upon us, taking a Maryland brigade in the flank and hurling it back. We arrested the charge, however, repelled the Confederates, and fortifying our position, held the Weldon railroad at last. But the usual slow movements nearly proved disastrous to Warren. He was without support, and at a distance from the rest of the army. The space between should have been filled by General Bragg, whom our corps commander again ordered to occupy it. Before it was done, Hill charged according to the uniform Confederate plan, striking our brigade on the flank and rear, capturing twenty-five hundred men, including about one regiment of the Second Brigade—all of the Third Division, (Crawford's). We were hurried from the field into the south side of Petersburg, but a few of our men or officers made their escape. We were rolled up as it were, doubled back, which crushed the two brigades. A sadder looking lot of men never entered the Confederacy than we looked and felt. As the rebel guards marched us through the streets of Petersburg, we were cursed and abused to such an extent that we could hardly stand it. The women and little boys ran along and threw stones at us. It had been raining and the streets were full of muddy water. The boys threw muddy water in our faces, and the women from fine houses ran at us with fiendish faces and demoniacal yells, and would say "Grant is taking Petersburg. The old butcher." A rebel officer on horseback dashed up to me, grabbed by hat, without even having an introduction to me, and threw back to me his old lousy linsey one in its place.

We were marched over a small bridge to an island in the Appomattox River. We were ordered to remain, while a heavy guard was placed over us during the night. This

being the 16th day of August. As soon as I discovered
that all hope of escape during the night had been cut off, A.
J. Bissett, my messmate, and myself lay down to sleep. It
would have been pleasant indeed to lose ourselves in grate-
ful unconsciousness of our unfortunate condition for a short
time, but I found it impossible to do so. Although weary
in body my mind was in such a disturbed condition that I
found it impossible to fall asleep.

After darkness enveloped the camp, we found to our
sorrow that the camp was not only guarded by thieves but
was alive with them. We used every precaution in hiding
all our belongings under our bodies, for the rebels had then
taken our blankets and overcoats. After tying our shoe
strings in hard knots. It was well for us that we had made
so secure our precious traps before we lay down to rest, and
at last tired nature overcame us and we fell into a deep
sleep. The thieves had found us, and they were at work on
our shoes, but only succeeded in making off with my most
valuable utensil, a quart tin cup, which I grieved so much
over the loss of such an indespensable article in my long imprisonment. August 17th, Saturday. After the beautiful
orb of day had risen above the earth, all was astir in this
camp, and without apology to us for not giving the
Yankees something to eat, marched us to the cars, and
secured every mothers' son of us free transportation to Richmond, the capital of the so-called Confederacy. We arrived
late in the evening. We were hurried from the cars and into
the Pemberton building and as we were fully accounted for
by the proprietor for one night's lodging, we lay ourselves
down to sleep ; but as our stomachs were empty and had
been for forty-eight hours, we could not sleep, but only talk
of Greene County and its good things. The morning
dawned again and found us without anything to eat. This
was our first Sunday in the Confederacy. We were soon
called out into the street of the city, and marched up along
the canal to a building which was in appearance like a state
penitentiary, and as we were halted in front of this mam-

moth building, the terrible wail came from our ranks and from the throat of one who had seen this building before, the plain word "Libby." We were ordered in two ranks, file left, march ; and as no one preceded us we ran up against the brick walls in the historic prison. This day was called Jewish Sabbath, and many of us who were there that day will never forget it. In this place we were called up in line, and searched the second time for valuables and money. The two men who entered the room were rebel officers and said to be of Hinglish origin, don't you know. At any rate they were expert thieves. The rebels with a malignity that would disgrace a South Sea heathen, dropped on the floor pictures of our dear ones, and stamped them to pieces. The men's faces were livid with rage and indignation, but we were powerless to prevent it, although these South Sea islanders got all we had, only the clothes on our backs. Near noon we received our first ration since our capture ; we ate it all at one meal. If my readers would not say it was a lie, I would describe my first ration in this, I must say, infamous prison. At this time the rebels issued, and did on this day, as my ration, a loaf of bread as large as a man's fist, made of cornmeal. It weighed perhaps four ounces, and with it was given a piece of meat weighing two ounces. The sergeant over the division divided the ration for the prisoners, as we always selected one of our non-commissioned officers to draw and divide the ration. The sergeant would say to the man who would call aloud, "Who's this ?" Caller would answer, "Jack Bissett ;" and "Who's this ?" "Golden," etc. At this first ration of meat my lot was an eyeball of a beef's head. As I was forty-eight hours without eating solid food since being captured, the physical man overcame the intellectual.

The number of prisoners confined in Libby prison at any one time was never very large, but this was owing solely to the fact that its capacity was limited. "Standing room only." Large numbers were confined there temporarily and transferred to the worse holes further south. The total number of the unwilling guests did reach far up into the thous-

ands. Notwithstanding the discomforts and deprivations of
the prisoners, and the almost total lack of hospital service,
the death rate, although large, never approached that of many
of the other prison pens, notably Belle Isle, Millen, Salisbury
and Andersonville. Hundreds of brave men died there in ab-
ject squalor and wretchedness. Hundreds died after their
release from the effects of rebel brutality, while a few of us
survive, living witnesses to the martyrdom which well nigh
wrecked our tortured bodies. We remained but a few days
in this prison, for Libby was overflowing with prisoners.
Many more were arriving from beyond the Weldon railroad,
and from the Second Corps. In a few days we were all
called out of the Libby prison and formed in four ranks.
Many of the boys sang "Tramp ! Tramp !" and "John
Brown's body lies moldering in the ground," thinking we
were going home. But alas ! we were marched off and over
and through the Tredegar Iron Works to Belle Isle.

Its very name now sends a thrill of horror through my
very being, as well as to thousands of hearts. Those who
suppose that Libby prison witnessed all the horrors of the
Southern captivity must learn that a still lower depth of suffering is yet to be exposed.

Belle Isle is a small island in the James River, which, as
viewed from a little distance, has enough pretentions of
beauty to justify its name. A portion of the island consists
of a bluff covered with trees ; but the part used as a prison
pen was low, sandy and barren, without a tree to protect it
from the rays of the sun. The Belle Isle prison pen was an
inclosure of some four or five acres, surrounded by an earth-
work several feet high, with a ditch on either side. On the
edge of the outer ditch guards were stationed all around the
enclosure at intervals of forty feet. The interior of the enclosure had some resemblance at a distance to an encamp-
ment, a number of low tents being set in regular rows. Close
inspection revealed the fact that the tents were old, rotten
and torn and at best could have sheltered only a small per-
centage of the prisoners. Within these low tents were hud-

dled from fourteen to sixteen thousand men at one time, (September), not housed up in walls nor buried in dungeons, but simply turned into the field like so many animals, to find shelter when and how they might. So crowded were they that if each man had lain down on the ground, occupying the generous allotment of a "hospital grave," say seven feet by two, the whole area of the enclosure would have been covered. Here thousands of us lay from the 18th of August, 1864, until the 8th of October, with naught but the sky for a covering and sand for a bed. When the hot glare of the summer sun fell upon the oozing morasses of the James, covering its stagnant pools with green slime, we prayed in vain for some shelter from the sickening heat of day, and torrents of rain at night, that our fevered bodies might be dipped in the stream beyond. But no, we were forced to broil and bake under the tropical rays of a mid-day sun, or huddled together like cattle throughout the livelong night in the pourdown storm. Some of us burrowed in the sand, while others scooped out a shallow ditch long enough and wide enough to receive their bodies, and covering it with brush, made a temporary refuge. When the rain descended they were forced to abandon this haven of rest.

What can I say of the food ? It was worse than that at Libby prison and less of it. No man in God's country ever fed his swine on such swill. A fragment of cornbread, perhaps half ground, containing cob, husk and all ; meat, often tainted, very mule-like, and only a mouthful at that ; a tablespoonful of rotten beans ; soup thin and briny, and worms floating on top. Not all these luxuries at once, only one at a time, and that in quantity insufficient to support a child of four years. As the weary days and nights dragged on, hunger told its inevitable tale on all ; diarrhoea, scruvy, low malarial fevers and lung diseases set in. We poor captives became weak and emaciated. Many could not walk ; when they attempted it, giddiness and blindness came on and they fell in their tracks. I shall never forget, during the month of September, I had become so weak from the exposure and eating unwholesome food that for three weeks I could not straighten myself. The prisoners were turned out every day on the other part of the island, and guarded while the enclosure was being cleaned up, after which we would be marched back in four ranks, and counted into the enclosure. I was one of the prisoners in the rear of the column. I was too weak to keep up. A rebel sergeant of the guards became infuriated at me, and grabbing a musket out of a guard's hand, struck and felled me to the ground. Some of my comrades tenderly carried me into the enclosure and restored me to consciousness.

To add to all this misery there came unavoidable consequences of being herded and crowded together. Lice were in all quarters. The bodies of prisoners were encrusted with dirt and vermin. They were sore from lying in the sand and some were lice-eaten to such an extent that hardly a healthy patch of skin was visible. All manner of rumors would originate from the rebels who had charge of us, especially the officers. We did not think it could be possible that our enemies could find a more terrible place than the one we were leaving, but then we did not know anything of the horrors of Salisbury, and it was fortunate for us we did not, and that that terrible future was hidden from us, for could we have foreseen the horror and misery of the prison that was to receive us, we would have given up in utter despair. It was only the continuous hope of a speedy release that enabled us to live through it.

On the 8th of October we were marched from Belle Isle prison out through the Tredegar Iron Works and on over into Manchester, a town directly opposite Richmond where we were loaded on the cars as so much inanimate freight, and at seven o'clock p. m., we started on our long journey for Salisbury, N. C. We did not know at the time where we were going, but from what we learned from the guards, we supposed our next prison would be somewhere in the far south. We were placed in and on top of freight cars. The first night, between Richmond and Danville, Va., the suffering was more than I had ever witnessed, suffering from diarrhoea, cramp in the stomach and unquenchable thirst. At last morning came. We had reached the city of Danville, about one hundred and forty miles from Richmond. We changed cars at this place, and comrade James M. Seals, of my company, begged a large ear of corn, and burned it at the fire where the railroad men were drying sand. I ate this burnt corn during the day and felt much better. We were ordered aboard the cars. Again A. J. Bissett and I were on top of a box car with other prisoners. We remained there all day, and oh, how cold that wind was upon us, without blanket or overcoat, only thin cotton pants, short coat, and those in rags and desperately lousy. As the darkness of night was closing above us the train stopped. We had reached a place called Salisbury, in North Carolina, and this was to be, will say, home or hell.

I was so very cold and stiff I had to be helped from the train and into the prison. We had by this time found out that Salisbury was to be our place of imprisonment, and various were the conjectures as to what kind of a place it was, and what kind of treatment we would receive from our jailors. Surely in our case, "ignorance was bliss." We were informed by some of the guards that it was a camp in the woods, and that alone made the impression that it would be a better place than prison life in a building like Libby or Belle Isle. The description we received of the place was not unfavorable, and the rebels assured us that the treatment we would receive would be much better than that which we received in Richmond. Whether they did this from ignorance, or from a desire to keep the truth from us until they had us safely enclosed in the pen, or from a fiendish desire to increase our torture by disappointment, we could not find out ; but we did discover that they were liars or ignorant of what they were talking about, and that all our former experiences and suffering in rebel prisons were but an intimation of what was still in store for us.

"But that I am forbid
To tell the secrets of my prison-house,
I could a tale unfold, whose lightest word
Would harrow up thy soul ; freeze thy young
blood,
Make thy two eyes like stars start from their
spheres :
And each particular hair to stand on end
Like quills upon the fretful porcupine."

In writing the following description of Salisbury, or what I have already said of Libby and Belle Isle, I do not intend to describe the horrors of the places more than is absolutely necessary to set forth the scenes enacted ; and in writing this short account of my prison life in the South, I do not expect to produce much of a literary work, but merely a simple, truthful story of life in Southern prisons. I claim but one merit for this narration—truth—and I shall not relate anything but what I know to be the truth, and that I will be willing to answer for on the great day of final account. If things should appear that may seem incredible to you, dear reader, please remember that comparatively little is known of the sufferings of our soldiers in the South ; if much has been said, much more has been left unsaid, and a great deal will remain "with the secrets of unwritten history." No tongue can express, no pen can describe the sufferings of the inmates of the prisons of the South ; and it is only through the experience given to the public by the survivors that this thrilling part of the history of the war can become known. No chapter in the Civil War is so imperfectly understood as the one relating to the military prisons of the South. This part of the history of our country can only be given by those who endured its horrors, and tasted of its bitterness ; survivors of these stockades and most terrible dens will tell the story of their sufferings to friends until the last of them have passed away ; but much will remain with the unwritten history of the war.

It must, however, be remembered that the stern reality of our prison life, the horrible scenes there enacted, are not brilliant romances or stories of fiction, and, if things should appear that seem incredible to you, remember that in reality comparatively little is known of the suffering of the inmates of these Southern hell-holes ; and from all you may glean from those who endured their horrors, and relate their sufferings, yet will it be far short of the whole truth—for no human pen or tongue can describe the agony, wretchedness and misery the poor soldiers endured who fell into the hands of the rebels.

In Salisbury alone, over twelve thousand Union prisoners, who were in the prime of life—strong, robust and healthy —perished. And in all the Southern prisons, as near as could be ascertained, about seventy thousand men fell victims to rebel brutality.

To Jefferson Davis, his cabinet, advisers, and to the demons whom they sent to the prisons to carry out their devilish plans, and who appear to have been well adapted to that kind of work, belongs the infamy of perpetrating one of the most horrible crimes known in the history of the world, and one that will forever remain a blot and stigma on that page of our country's history.

The prison at Salisbury was for some time a palace as compared to other pens, but ere long it degenerated into one of the worst. The prison yard covered some four acres, and it was surrounded by a high board fence. A few tents were set up in the yard, but when the number of prisoners increased to thousands there was not shelter enough for one-half of them. Thousands were exposed to the weather, day and night, throughout the entire winter, and in a majority of the cases the men possessed neither overcoat nor blanket, not even a blouse nor a pair of shoes. In this condition of semi-nudity we burrowed in the earth, crept under buildings or worried through the chill December nights in the open air, lying unsheltered upon the muddy, frozen or snowy ground. To see these brave sufferers, coatless, hatless and shoeless, shivering around the yard, was a sight piteous beyond description.

The rations were one pint of cornmeal, cob included, and one pint called rice or bean soup, once a day, without salt, perhaps even more scanty. The men were organized into divisions of one thousand each, and the divisions were sub-divided into squads of one hundred. It was a daily occurrence that one or more divisions were kept without a mouthful of food for twenty-four hours, and in some cases as long as forty-eight hours. The prisoners sold every scrap of their personal belongings, often down to the shirts on their backs, to obtain money to buy bread, and it took from five to twenty dollars of Confederate money to buy one small loaf. At this very time the commissary warehouse in Salisbury was packed to the roof with corn and pork, and this starvation of the prisoners was a deliberate and willful piece of cruelty on the part of Major John H. Gee, the post-commandant. When a subordinate, who knew of the plenty which existed, asked Gee for permission to give the prisoners full rations, this chivalrous product of Southern civilization replied, "No —— them, give them quarter rations !"

To call the filthy pens where the sick soldiers were confined, "hospitals," is a strange perversion of the English language. A better term would be "slaughter-houses"—and in fact that was the term applied to them by the inmates of the Salisbury prison. Long, low structures, averaging twenty-five by seventy feet, some of brick and others of logs, they were unattractive without and unspeakably horrible within. The sick and dying prisoners lay in rows on the rough, cold floors ; no beds or bedding—rows of ghastly, starving faces —skeletons in rags. To see that spectacle once was to see it forever. The wasted forms, the sad, pleading eyes of those sufferers, the sobs of sorrow and the wails of despair, the awful hack ! hack ! hack !—such scenes and sounds can never be forgotten. The nurses could not even procure water enough to wash the hands and faces of those sick and dying men, and there they lay in the filth that proceeded from their own bodies. The air in these enclosures was stifling, and one would have thought would be sufficient to poison all sources of life within.

The last scene was the dead wagon with its ghastly load of stiffening corpses piled in like cord wood, the arms and legs swaying with the motion of the cart, the pitiful white faces staring, with dropped jaw and stony eyes, rattling along to the trenches outside, where its precious burden was hastily dumped and covered over with a few inches of dirt. Suffering everywhere ! Not a face relaxing into a smile, every eye dull with despondency, every cheek sunken with want, every lip trembling with unuttered pain. From every tent and hut, from every hole in the ground, came forth gaunt and ghastly men perishing by inches, naked, hungry, ravenous, wild with pain and suffering. Imagine a raw December day. The air is raw and penetrating, the ground is half covered with slush and snow, and a chilly rain is falling. Of the twelve thousand poor wretches within the prison walls, less than one-half can find shelter in the buildings, tents and mud huts ; the rest are striving as they may to escape the blighting blasts this dreary afternoon. Hundreds are shoeless, with no clothing save a light blouse or shirt, with, perhaps, a pair of thin cotton trousers, never strong and now tattered and torn. Starved and hollow-eyed creatures everywhere. We huddle over a fire of green and smoky wood in a crowded tent ; the very atmosphere is suffocating. We cling shiveringly to the outside chimneys of the squalid hospitals, hoping to extract a little warmth from the half-heated bricks. We curl ourselves up in the narrow caves while the burning pine fills our eyes with smoke without warming our benumbed bodies. We stand with pallid cheeks and wistful eyes, begging for admission even into those "slaughter pens" where our sick comrades are lying in dirt, distress and despair. Night comes, but with it no relief. The darkness shadows the misery, but intensifies it. The men lie down wherever the chance affords, huddling together for mutual warmth. A dozen of us fill a trench. At sunrise some of us arise and resume our weary tramp and some are frozen stiff.

CHAPTER XVIII.

THE MASSACRE AT SALISBURY.

One cold November day the crisis came. A handful of men resolved to break from our captivity or perish in the attempt. Without deliberation or concert, but acting solely upon a momentary impulse, a portion of the prisoners made a desperate, ill-advised and futile effort to escape from bondage. Forty-eight hours we had been without food, even the scanty prison fare being denied us. We were weak and faint, but desperation gave us superhuman strength. "We may as well perish by the swift bullet of the guard as by the systematic starvation of the authorities," we said. A rebel relief of sixteen men entered the prison yard at noon. The stoutest and most desperate prisoners, armed with clubs, sprang upon them. The rebel soldiers, surprised by the onset, were quickly disarmed. One guard resisted, but a quick bayonet thrust let out his life-blood. The rest rushed back to the camp outside and gave the alarm. The prisoners all rushed to one part of the enclosure, hoping to make a break in the walls. Axes we had none, not even a pick or crowbar. The clubbed musket was insufficient ; not a man escaped from the yard. Had we divided our forces into small squads, some might have escaped in the confusion of the guards. As it was we were massed in one spot and in less than three minutes from the outbreak, every musket in the garrison was turned upon us, and two or three field pieces were hurling grape and canister into the struggling throng. Not a man was freed, but one hundred and fifty lay stretched upon the ground, not one of whom, in all probability had anything to do with the insurrection. After the occurrence cold blooded murders were frequent. Guards would deliberately shoot and kill prisoners at will, without the slightest rebuke from the authorities. The negro prisoners were the chief objects of this murderous practice, but black and white fared alike. The excuse and opportunity for wholesale slaughter was too good to be neglected.

Some of the men in Salisbury prison died in lingering agony, and others passed away instantly as though their spirits had suddenly given up the unequal struggle, and had parted from the pain-racked bodies. Many died from actual starvation, their stomachs being unable longer to digest the food. For a man to find, on awakening in the morning, that the comrade by his side was cold in death was an occurrence too common to be noted.

I have had men, since the war, to say they would not be taken prisoners, and if they had, would have made their escape, etc. On second thought a true and brave soldier would say, such a man would never be close enough to be taken prisoner. I want my readers to understand that we had all opportunity, during the months of January and February, to leave Salisbury prison. Once a week or oftener they would offer us liberty if we would take the oath to the so-called Confederacy, telling us that all they would require of the galvanized Yankees was to guard forts and build fortifications. This Captain Wirz No. 2, of Salisbury, would mount the stockade, or fence, along side of the guards and call the prisoners close up to the fence. The poor creatures, with sunken eyes, skinny and ghastly looking faces, would stagger up to hear what this babbler had to say.

"All you Yankee prisoners who want to take the oath to the Confederate States of America will please come up close to the small gate here, and go out into a good clean camp, and have plenty to eat." Although food, clothing and life were offered them to betray their country, less than five per cent. accepted the offers ; and it is but justice to them to say that some of these fled to the Union lines at the first opportunity that presented itself.

This noble son of southern chivalry, by using every vile epithet against our men and officers at the head of the general government, calling us Lincoln hirelings, and Grant, the old butcher, would not exchange us man for man.   We could not help contrasting the generosity of our government toward their captives,. with our miserable condition ; and is it strange that we sometimes felt embittered against the government for not making a greater effort to release us.   But as true as the needle to the pole so were most of the Union prisoners confined in the Southern prisons to the government they had sworn to defend.   They might feel themselves slighted, neglected or even deserted by the government, and among themselves be tempted to say some bitter things ; but a word or insinuation to that effect from their enemies would excite their ire and indignation to the utmost, and they were always ready to defend the government from the charge that it was not doing all it could to release them.   It was, however, a sad fact that hundreds died with the fear haunting them that it was so.   Men who had cheerfully faced death on many a battlefield, lay down and died broken-hearted, as the terrible suspicion forced itself into their minds that the government they loved so well and had fought so hard to save, was indifferent to their sad fate.   That fifteen thousand men had suffered all the horrors of a living death, and that more than twelve thousand died from exposure and starvation rather than betray their country, established the fact that there is no spot on the face of the earth where greater heroism or loyalty was displayed than in this horrid prison pen.

These men, exposed to the cold winds by day, and to rain and snow and sleet by night, suffering from maddening thirst and gnawing hunger, consumed by lice and maggots, suffering from scurvy till their teeth dropped from their gums enduring all the pain, agony and misery that could be inflicted on them, and dying at the rate of more than fifty a day, unflinchingly remained faithful to their flag.   A great army of these, and many of them our near and dear friends, passed away to the great beyond.   We left their frail bodies and they were buried in a strange land.   They quietly sleep where the woodbine twineth and the weary are at rest.   I have but one tribute to offer, prayers for the living, tears for the dead.

I have already given a partial description of the hospital at Salisbury, although I am fully aware that almost a third of a century has passed, and a new generation has come upon the stage, and they perhaps will require more testimony that is impartial. I do not consider it necessary, however, to give a long description of the hospital, but to give the reader a proper conception of the place, I will give an extract from the testimony of Dr. Bates, a physician from the state of Georgia, and employed by the rebel government at the hospital. He said : "I saw a number of men and was shocked. Many of them were lying partially naked, dirty and lousy, in the sand ; others crowded together in small buildings, unserviceable at the best. I felt disposed to do my duty, and aid the sufferers all I could, but knowing it was against orders to take anything to the men, I was obliged to slip whatever I took to them very slyly in my pockets. They frequently asked me for a teaspoonful of salt, or for orders of siftings of meal, that they might make a little bread. Again they have gathered around me and asked for a bone. I found persons lying dead among the living, and thinking they merely slept I have tried to wake them up and found they were taking their everlasting sleep. This was in the hospital, but I judge it was the same all through the stockade."

In Salisbury prison, besides buildings called hospitals, was a brick building about forty feet long by twenty feet wide, with a fire place in it and a dirt floor. This was called the dead house, where all the dead were deposited during the day and night. The men who had charge of the dead house lived well, and they both belonged to my company and were from Greene county. I say the men lived sumptuously every day, although some of our most unfortunate Greene countians begged of them even the crumbs that fell from their haversacks and they would not give them a single one. As I may create a desire on the part of my readers to know how men could live well having charge of the morgue or dead house, I will say the dead were taken to the dead house with their clothes they had on, and many of them had money sewed up in those old clothes or rags ; sometimes jewelry and other valuables were found. The clothing was removed except the drawers, if they had any, and these poor bodies of our once near and dear comrades were handled in their nude state and loaded into an old fashioned wagon and hauled outside to be placed in the trenches by our other dead. "What is man that thou are mindful of him ? And the son of man that thou visited him ?" Man is a thinking, reflecting being, intellectually speaking, but physically speaking man is an animal of the higher order. I was fully convinced by my long imprisonment, by not having proper food for mind or body, the mind became enfeebled to a greater extent than the body, and the finer feelings of the intellectual man had left. Only the animal part predominated. Some of the prisoners died so suddenly that we could hardly realize that they had passed away. On one occasion a mere boy belonging to my company, Perry Hickman, whose home was in Newtown, Whiteley Township, Greene County, died. As gently and quietly as falls the autumn leaf, his pure spirit left his tortured body and winged its way to a better and more blissful land.

"Matted and damp are the curls of gold
　　Kissing the snow of the fair young brow.
Pale are the lips of delicate mould,—
　　Somebody's darling is dying now.
Back from the beautiful blue veined brow,
　　Brush all the wandering waves of gold ;
Cross his hands on his bosom now.
　　Somebody's darling is still and cold."

At Salisbury the following members of my company whose homes were in Greene County, all passed away as if they were sleeping :　Clark Burk, William Watson, William Funk, Marian Morris, David Keys. They were loyal to their country, and died that the nation might live, and may the principles of true fidelity be a living monument to their memory. A great many more died who were from Greene and Washington counties that have passed from my memory as to name. The death rate in Salisbury during December and January was from fifty to seventy-five each day. I would often go to the dead house, usually in the morning, until I became so weak and almost broken-hearted. During the twenty days of February that we remained in this prison I seldom visited the place of the dead. My object in going when I was able to go was to see if any of my friends had died during the night, as Bissett and I were separated and at some distance from our friends. The dead were placed in two rows, usually their feet toward the middle of the room, with a small aisle between the two rows. I would pass up the row and look at the upturned faces of these ghastly creatures, and down the other side, and very often did not recognize my nearest and dearest friend. My own mother would not have known her own son from a South Sea islander if she had met me at the gate of the prison. Scurvy, the most destructive disease that afflicted us, had become fearfully prevalent, and more than one-half of the prisoners were more or less afflicted with it. More than one-half the number that died perished of this terrible disease. This disease is the result of impure air, bad water, and improper food, and as we had the two first named articles in abundance, and what we did have of the third was of the improper kind, the result was, of course, scurvy. I shall not enter into a full or detailed description of the symptoms or approach of this dreaded disease. My left hip and my lower limbs became full of holes, until any one could see the bones in my hip, and in my feet, ulcerated sores left large scars upon my limbs which medical boards in their examinations have persisted were gunshot wounds. During almost all my suffering and terrible affliction not a murmur escaped my lips against the government and the dear old flag that I loved so well. But like Job of old, I was firm in the full assurance that my Redeemer lived ; although they (the rebels) might afflict, deface and almost dethrone reason, yet would I remain loyal. Many a poor soul found relief from their tormentors by the swift bullet from the guards. My own life was in jeapordy five times by these prison guards. Once in a box car from Petersburg to Richmond, while in transit, I got into an argument on the state of the Union with one of the guards.   I told him it was a mistake about one southern whipper-snapper of a Johnnie reb whipping five Yankees.   He flew into a southern rage, and would have bayoneted me had not my comrades formed a circle about me. Twice by the bullet while in Richmond and once by the butt of a musket.   A rebel guard at Salisbury, as I was lying down one night in the tent, having only a brick for a pillow, fired into the stockade, the bullet entering just under my head.

Captain Wirz and Lieutenant Davis paid the penalty of their crimes on the scaffold, but John H. Gee, of Salisbury, went scot free.   On what principles of justice the government hung the old Dutch captain and his lieutenant, and let this man go unpunished is past finding out.

More than one civilian has listened to the pitiful tale of a returned prisoner, and afterwards remarked : "Well, no doubt it was a rather tough place, but that fellow was probably stretching it a little."   And this in all sincerity, for we doubt if any man who never saw Salisbury, Belle Isle or Andersonville, ever had a full realization of its horrors.

On February 21st a rebel officer entered the stockade and ordered all the sick in the hospitals to be put in readiness and be taken to the cars.   All prisoners who were not able to march would get ready to be shipped with the sick from the hospitals by way of Richmond.   At noon all of the sick were taken out of the stockade and tenderly placed in box cars. After the sick came all the men who were just able to walk to the train were called out and placed in charge of the sick, and soon the long train of cars left the prison.   Many of us that were left behind in this miserable place looked upon our most fortunate comrades with jealousy.   We had often been deceived by just such promises of release, by having been taken from prison to prison.   But by this time we had become more jubiliant, as we received encouragement from the new arrivals from Grant's and Sherman's armies.   We were

now confident, from the information we had received, that
the Confederacy was about petered out.

What joy in that faraway camp or valley of death, as our
poor sick comrades were carried and led along to the cars.
How the tears trickled down our sallow smoked cheeks as we
clasped each other by the hand and gave thanks to the Father
of all mercies.

A small army was yet left within the gates, and as we
gazed out through the open gates at our companions or skeletons in rags, we could hear some comrade say the last farewell, and another one would say, "Good-bye, John, until we
meet again. Tell my mother I am still living, and hope to
be at home soon." At last the gates of Salisbury prison
were closed upon the prisoners who had wished to remain
and march out on the morrow. In all my change from
prison to prison I never had been separated from my army
messmate, Sergeant Bissett. We were at this time separated,
as he chose to go with the sick by way of Richmond. I had
always said I would walk out of Salisbury and if there was a
living man in this prison in the spring I would be one of them,
and I kept my word. On the evening of the 21st of February
we were given three days' rations, consisting of one loaf of
bread and one pound of pork. After the shadows had spread
her darkness over the land and prison, we scarcely closed our
eyes all that long night. I had eaten my last rations ere
morning came. We had spent the night talking of home,
our comrades who had left us and those we were compelled to
leave behind. I was now in the old shelter tent we were placed in in November, 1864. We then numbered fifty men. During this night of sleeplessness, Sergeant Mart Hazen, of this
squad, called the roll ; of the original fifty, only ten answered. Only one of our fifty joined the rebels and one went out
with the sick and thirty-eight had died. They quietly sleep.

At daylight on Washington's birthday a rebel officer
walked into the prison, while the drum beat for the assembly
of the prisoners for perhaps the last time. We were ordered
to fall in in two ranks and take the parole, not to straggle or

try to make our escape until we were regularly paroled, which would be at Goldsboro. The gates of the prison were opened and all the Yankees that had remained from the day before marched out into the free open air. I became impatient and felt as though I could fly, if they would only let me out. When I stepped out of this prison into the open country, I was sadly disappointed, I found I was very weak. It was imposible for me to walk without the aid of two canes and I was very frail and tottering. Imagine, reader, a man just from a long spell of typhoid fever, you then can form an idea of my frailty.

At last night came of the first day's march from Salisbury toward Greensboro, N. C., and a hard tramp it was to me. I was scarcely two miles from the prison I had left with such a light heart in the morning. I was without food, blanket or shelter. I dropped upon the cold, damp ground beside my more fortunate comrades of the old Libby tent of the past winter. Morning came and the second day out from Salisbury, and this day I had nothing to eat but a few wild onions that grew sparsely in the old field on either side of the railroad. When we left the prison we were ordered to follow the railroad and I tramped on toward Greensboro, which was about fifty miles distant. The second night I came up with three of my regiment and tentmates at Salisbury and Belle Isle. They had been foraging on either side of the road during the day. These comrades had not made much progress in making a zig-zag march after raw material. They had found, or begged, some food, and they gave me of such as they had. My Good Samaritans got permission from an old tar-heel for several of us prisoners to sleep in his stable loft on the bare floor. In this stable loft I almost lost my life, or what little there was left in me. When I climbed up in the stable it was dark. My friend James Eberhart procured me as comfortable a place as he could. During the night one of our prison thugs wished my place ; he fell upon me and almost beat out the little spark of life that remained in me. I am indebted to comrade Eberhart for saving my life at this time.

At sunrise the prisoners all left the barn and left me in my sad condition and reflection. On looking over the Carolina barn, I espied a large pile of corn in the ear. I would say two hundred bushels. I procured several ears of this corn and parched it at a camp about one mile from the barn. I came up with the camp fires of the rebel guards and some of our own men's camp. They had stayed here during the night and had left good fires, and I parched all the corn I had confiscated. My skillet was the one-half of a tin canteen and in trying to parch the corn I burnt it, and I discovered it afforded me temporary relief in checking the chronic diarrhoea.

The greatest trouble with my decrepit condition was, first, the scurvy sores ; second, the chronic diarrhoea. Both were fast telling on me. I filled my pockets with the parched corn, which was all I had to eat until I arrived at Greensboro, about the 9th of March, 1865. I was permitted to ride on the cars for about twelve miles. We were driven out of Greensboro into the wood about a mile from the town, and told to remain there until called, which would be by the army bugle. The first night in the woods the rebels gave us soured flour. We mixed it with water and baked it on a stone by setting it before the fire like our mothers did with the old time tin reflector. I was permitted to lie down on the ground in this woods. It rained all night and in the morning half my body was under water.

At dark of this day, which was the 11th of March, the bugle sounded and as many of the prisoners as could filled a long train of cars which came into the depot and the train was made ready to start. The doors of the cars were closed. The rain was coming down in torrents, and when I appeared on the platform at the depot no one could be seen without but I could hear the voices of my comrades inside the cars. I approached the train and tapped on the door of one of the cars. No one answered. A rebel lieutenant, with his sabre dangling on the platform, came tripping along looking after his guards and trainmen. He approached me in the darkness. Calling to me he said, "What are you here for and what are you doing here at this time ?" I informed him I was so weak I could not get here any sooner, that I started with my comrades and my wish was to go with my messmates but I could not reach the train sooner. My plaintiff appeal softened his heart. He told me to follow him. He stopped in front of a car door, and pounding with his sabre on the door, called to those within to open. The men at first refused to open the door, but afterwards repented and opened it ; the lieutenant helped me into the car and when inside I discovered that all my tentmates with whom I had spent a long prison life were in this car. It was remarkably strange, and yet it is true, that in all my long tramp from Salisbury to Greensboro, Goldsburg, and to the sea, I slept every night with these three comrades of my regiment who had been with me in all the prisons, Hazen, Vaughn and Eberhart. During the afterpart of the night we arrived at Goldsboro. We were unloaded at the depot and the guards drove us out into the open country at the point of the bayonet. In getting to this camp in the woods, I thought my time had surely come. I would sometimes drop into a North Carolina sink-hole up to my hips, and at another time first one leg and then the other. In the darkness I would catch my sore and bleeding feet in large, thorny green brier. At last I fell against a stump, it striking me in the pit of the stomach. I became unconscious and remained in this conditioin for some time. When consciousness returned I thought, will I get up and try to reach home or will I die ? I then resolved I would live. I got upon my feet again and steadied myself by a fallen tree. After standing here a few minutes I discovered four men preparing to lay down for the night, only a few feet from me. One of them spoke my name. I then approached them, and speaking to Sergeant Hazen, he turned around and looked at me, and placing me between him and the light, he exclamed at the same time, "Good, he still lives." When all was in readiness for the night, the sergeant called me up and placed me in the middle.

Although it was a down-pour I was informed that I slept soundly, and I dreamed of eating good things at home, among kind friends.

When morning came the rebel officers called us up into a camp and we signed the regular parole. This was the 12th day of March. The rebel officers thought strange that so many of the Yankee prisoners could write their names. In the evening of this day we were called up and marched into the city of Goldsboro and ordered to lie down in the dusty streets until the railroad men could get up a train large enough to haul all the Yankee prisoners out of this place into our lines near Wilmington. At midnight the train started with all of us on board for our lines. At ten o'clock a. m., the 13th day of March, we were run into General Terry's lines, near Wilmington, N. C. After remaining in this city for one day we boarded a fine ocean steamer for Annapolis, Md. We arrived at the city of Annapolis, college yard, on the 16th, which was Sunday evening. When we stepped upon the gangplank at the wharf, hundreds of men and women, old and young, from all parts of the United States, were there looking for some dear husband, father or son, and with tears in their eyes would ask us if we knew John Jones, of Company C, or William Smith of Company E, etc. We could only shake our heads. Many of them wept and were almost broken-hearted. We could hear the wail of some tender-hearted mother or father say, "Can it be possible that men of this so-called Confederacy would be so brutal ?"

We were washed in the bath house at the capital city of "My Maryland," and clean clothes put on us, and giving us two months extra pay and fifty dollars commutation money gave us a thirty-day furlough.

All I have written in regard to my life in the Southern prison pens and my journey home is the truth. On the 18th of March I left Annapolis and arrived at my sister's home in Blacksville, W. Va. After months of suffering with typhoid

pneumonia, between life and death, I have been permitted
to drag along these years with a broken constitution.   I
hope to give you facts of how our Christianized government
treated prisoners of war, that you may draw the line.

CHAPTER XIX.

Treatment of Rebel Prisoners at the North.

I see in the *National Tribune* of May 7th, 1896, an account of the famous outbreak at that place of suffering, (Salisbury), the only open insurrection of prisoners during the war, by comrade Henry Mann, Fifty-Ninth New York Regiment, almost identical with my account of the outbreak and suffering. There is no blacker page in the world's history than that on which is recorded the atrocious cruelties practiced upon the Union prisoners of war by the officials of the so-called military prisons. I say this in full consideration of the fact that a lapse of thirty-one years has softened the realities to such an extent that some tender-hearted apologists fear to speak of the matter, save with bated breath, while others affect to believe that the horrors of the rebel dungeons never existed except in the distorted minds of the unfortunate captives. There have been not a few persons, otherwise apparently sane, who have asserted that all this talk about suffering, starvation and cruelty is not only untrue, but that it is merely a string of falsehoods gotten up in sympathy for the soldiers and to further political schemes. Strange as it may seem, there are scores of such apologists in the North ; but it is safe to say that every one of them was in the North all through the war, or else have been born since the struggle ; unless, indeed, he be a foreign exotic or a member of the noble band who found Canada a convenient abiding place during the early sixties. I have interviewed scores of ex-prisoners, and many of them have long since buried the hatchet and extended the olive branch of peace to their old enemies, and without a single exception, the records and statements as set forth by me, have and will meet with a complete endorsement. If there is one Union ex-prisoner of war in this or any other county who

was confined in other prisons of the South. I call on him to
rise and call me to an account.

I willingly grant that this black stain will forever mar
the history of that country which is conceded to be highest
in the world's civilization, although it would be fortunate
indeed for all concerned if it could be blotted out and entirely obliterated. But this would not be just to the memory of the heroic thousands whose gallant deeds in the forefront of battle were eclipsed only by their heroic fortitude
in the presence of untold tortures compared to which the
whistle of the bullet and the shriek of the shell were as the
sweetest music. In ancient times and among barbarous nations it was the custom to subject captives of war to gross
indignities and tortures, but the laws of all civilized nations
prescribed for the captives taken in honorable warfare, treatment as humane and comforts as great as those enjoyed by
the rank and file of the conquering army. To treat prisoners of war, captured in battle, with neglect and cruelty far
greater than the most inhuman master could inflict upon
the most worthless of his brutes, is a distinction which was
reserved for the chivalrous and highly civilized rulers of the
late Southern Confederacy. It has been claimed that
Southern leaders were not responsible for the horrible condition which existed in the Southern military prisons ; and
it is a matter of fact that many of the worst atrocities were
directly chargeable to the malignity of the brutal under-
strappers who had immediate charge of the prisoners, such
as Winder, Turner, Wirz, Gee, and others of that ilk. But,
nevertheless, the ultimate responsibility rests and must ever
rest upon the shoulders of those high in authority, who permitted these things to exist and continue—not one week,
or one month, but for years, without so much as entering a
protest or raising a hand to stop the wholesale murders.

The utmost exercise of Christian charity will not prevent the friends and comrades of the slaughtered victims
from cherishing the devout hope that when Gabriel sounds
his trumpet on that great day, these monsters of cruelty will

be incontinently hurled to the depths of the Bottomless Pit, a fate to which their deeds done in the body most justly entitles them. It has been claimed, as an offset to the complaints of the Union prisoners, that the Federal government treated its Confederate prisoners with equal severity. Fortunately for the good name of our common country the charge is false, as will be shown hereafter. And it is also claimed that the rebels were unable, from scarcity of provisions and fuel, to provide for the comforts of the captives, and that therefore they were morally blameless. This also has been proven to be false, or generally so, although all christendom would be glad to know that it were true. Any unconscious or unintentional form of crime is less reprehensible than that which is knowingly or deliberately committed, but the established facts point to a deliberate design on the part not only of the prison-keepers and the superiors, but of the Southern people as a whole. The idea seems almost too revolting to be entertained, but no other theory will cover the immensity and variety of that system of abuse to which we soldiers were subjected.

It was a well known fact that certain rooms in Libby prison were packed with stores of eatables, while the prisoners were actually starving within the walls. The storehouses in and about Salisbury were overflowing with grain and provisions, while the Union captives, within a stone's throw, were hungrily gnawing at old bones plucked from the miry filth ; in many places the captives were freezing by inches within full view of swamps and hillsides burdened with timber. Again, one prison pen was like another, one hospital like another hospital. Salisbury was Belle Isle over again, five times enlarged and two times intensified. A remote prison at Tyler, Tex., sent out a report on a par with Libby and Salisbury.

No supposition of negligence, or accident, or destitution, or necessity, or inefficieny can account for all this. The similarity of conditions at all the Southern military prisons forbid the idea of accident or unfavorable location. So many and surely positive forms of abuse could never have come from merely negative causes.

Figures are stubborn things, and the official reports of the United States government show figures that must forever extinguish the idea that rebel prisoners confined in the United States military prisons were treated with undue severity, or with disregard of the established laws of civilized warfare. Take Fort Delaware for example. The official records show that the daily rations received by each military prisoner at Fort Delaware, up to June 1st, 1864, were three pounds of solid food, besides coffee, sugar, molasses and other luxuries. After June 1st, 1864, this was reduced to about thirty-four and a half ounces per day, which reduction was made according to the report of Quartermaster General Meigs (July 6th, 1864), "for the purpose of bringing it, (the ration), nearer to what the rebel authorities profess to allow their soldiers," and no complaint has been heard of its insufficiency. This ration was issued all through the war and was generally composed of bread, (made of four parts flour and one part Indian meal), fresh meat or bacon, and vegetables according to season. The ration was practically the same at all the United States military prisons, including that at Johnson's Island, Lake Erie, of which so much complaint was made. At the same time the Union prisoners at Libby, Salisbury, etc., were receiving a maximum ration averaging eight ounces of solid food, and this frequently dropped off to a minimum ration of only five ounces, of which four ounces were musty corn bread, and one ounce was "salt-horse." Take the matter of clothing and personal care. At Fort Delaware the prisoners, some eight or nine thousand, were kept in well built and ventilated barracks, and had free access to adjoining enclosures for air and exercise. There was abundance of water, so that if any man choose, he could bathe every day. Each man had a commodious bunk to himself, the head properly elevated above the foot in striking contrast to the Confederate prisons, where the inmates slept on bare flat floors or on the cold and frozen earth, without so much as a wisp of straw between them and the ground.

Thirty thousand gallons of drinking water were brought daily from the sparkling Brandywine Creek across the channel. This was done to prevent the prisoners from drinking from shallow dug wells producing brackish water. Each prisoner was inspected when received. If dirty he was washed, his clothes burned and new ones supplied : if sick he was sent to the spacious and airy hospital, placed in a clean bed and given every attention. Each man was furnished with blanket, overcoat, etc., if needed. Some idea of the amount of clothing furnished by the United States government may be gained from the official statement of the quartermaster, which shows that from September 1st, 1863, to May 1st, 1864; thirty-five thousand eight hundred and eighty-four articles of clothing were issued to the prisoners, (about eight thousand), at Fort Delaware. The chief items were : seven thousand one hundred and seventy-four pairs of drawers, six thousand two hundred and sixty flannel shirts, eight thousand eight hundred and seven pairs of woolen socks, four thousand three hundred and seventy-eight woolen blankets and two thousand six hundred and eighty woolen overcoats ; the remainder being largely made up of boots, coats, jackets and trousers. Every prisoner who had not a blanket or overcoat of his own was provided with one, and all that were in want of clothing received it. Some thirteen hundred tons of coal were used each winter to keep the barracks warm and comfortable. As a natural result, the average condition of health among the prisoners was good, and the death rate very low except during July, August, October and November, 1863, when smallpox carried off several hundred victims. A majority of the prisoners had never been vaccinated, for vaccination appears to have been almost unknown among the poor classes of the South, and the attempts of the prisoners to vaccinate each other only led to a variety of more serious disorders, from the bad quality of the virus employed. After this disease was conquered the death rate steadily decreased, until in May, 1864, but sixty-two died, out of eight thousand one hundred and twenty-six confined on the island, or less than ten per cent. per year. The entire year, including the small-pox epidemic, showed a death rate of less than twenty-nine per cent., and this includes death from wounds and exposure occurring previous to capture.

Compare this with the average death rate at Salisbury of over four hundred per cent per. year, and the death rate of Andersonville, which cannot be accurately computed, but which was greater than any one prison in the South.

By such contrast of mortality at United States stations and at rebel stations, argument and comment are struck dumb. Referring again to the rations we find it officially recorded that considerable quantities of surplus food were found concealed beneath the bunks of the rebel prisoners at Fort Deleware and elsewhere. Imagine the possibility of a Union prisoner having any surplus to conceal.

The DeCamp General Hospital, David's Island, N. Y., was on a par with that at Fort Delaware. Many of the prisoners arrived in a horrible condition—ragged, barefooted, wounded and covered with vermin. Their clothing being removed and burned, they were washed, furnished with clean linen, and placed in clean and well-aired beds, and full suits of clothes issued to them. This government did everything but place a ring on their fingers. They were allowed during convalescence, the freedom of the whole island, inside of a line of sentries. None of them were ever shot at, none were ever frost-bitten. Ice-water was furnished in profusion ; soap, combs and towels were distributed for private use ; and there was one trained nurse for every ten prisoners. A library of two thousand volumes was at their disposal.

Johnson's Island, Ohio, has been a special subject of misstatements. This island, of about three hundred acres, is located at Sandusky Bay, close to Kelley's Island, which is a favorite place of summer resort. It is one of the most salubrious and delightful spots in the United States. True, it is cold in the winter, but the barracks were new, well built and well warmed, and there was not an instance of suffering from exposure, except in the case of a few prisoners who attempted to escape. The stories of ill treatment and exposure are effectually exploded by the official figures, showing that in twenty-one months, out of an aggregate of six thousand four hundred and ten prisoners, there were only one hundred and thirty-four deaths. In the months of May and June, 1864, there were about two thousand three hundred prisoners. In May five died and in June only one.

Contrast that with the death rate the same months at Andersonville. A similar beneficent state of affairs is revealed by an examination of the records of all the other United States stations and hospitals ; and the public sentiment of the North, outraged though it was by the harrowing tales that came from her imprisoned heroes in the deadly Southern prison pens, would never have permitted any other than this magnanimous and Christian course of "heaping coals of fire" upon our enemies' heads.

The reader cannot have failed to be struck by the contrast that has been shown between the military stations for prisoners North and South. But the contrast was overwhelmingly great when the exchange of prisoners was made in March, 1865, when the flag-of-truce boat landed within the rebel lines and the two systems confronted each other.

On one side were hundreds of feeble, emaciated men, ragged, hungry, filthy, diseased and dying—wrecks from the Southern slaughter pens. On the other side an equal number of strong and hearty men, well clad in the army clothing of the government they had fought to destroy, having been humanely sheltered, fed, cleansed of dirt, cured of wounds and diseases, and now honorably returned in prime condition to fight that government again.

From this preamble, in which I have aimed to give a true idea of the treatment accorded rebel prisoners at the hands of the Federal government, we must turn with sadness to the portrayal of our own suffering. I can but justly say by my own experience, after thirty-one years, that individuals, parties and the Republic have been ungrateful to me.   C. H. GOLDEN.

RETROSPECTIVE.

Cavilers. falsifiers and perjurers have for many years since the war resorted to every dishonorable, false and despicable means, (even criminal perjury as per "The Lost Cause" and "The Life of Jefferson Davis"), to explain, excuse and deny the horrible and deliberate starvation of Union prisoners of war. The facts and figures presented by Comrade Golden are true and unanswerable, and from my own experience as a rebel soldier in the Soldiers' Retreat at Richmond, I positively know they had good and sufficient food. And the truth of this statement is amply proven by the fact that no rebel soldier was ever known to starve to death, and yet according to these liars and perjurers the Yankee prisoners of war were being fed the same quantity and quality of food as were the rank and file in the rebel army. And this same rebel army although fed upon the same kind of food upon which many thousands of Union prisoners starved to death, were capable of prosecuting and conducting active and vigorous campaigns throughout the entire war. Moreover, to prove that the starvation of Union prisoners was deliberately planned and executed, is the fact that of all the food and clothing sent to the prisoners from the North none of it was ever issued to them and they were allowed to die in agony, with their starved eyes resting upon the very building containing this food. In the two hundred and thirty-two battles of the Civil War, over forty-nine thousand Federals were killed upon the field in action. In the prison-hells of the South over seventy-one thousand brave, patriotic martyrs suffered a lingering death in their country's cause.

Sleep on, brave heroes, neither 'storied urn or animated bust" may ever mark the unknown, unhonored ditch which swallowed up your fleeting clay, but, forgotten never shall be your suffering and heroism by your surviving comrades.

"Cease guns, be still ; one day is set
  Which strife nor battle mars,
For souls that in their cloudy tents
  Are camping near the stars.

"Some forms on lofty hilltops rest,
  Some in the valleys lie ;
The tropic grasses wave o'er some,
  O'er some the waters sigh.

"Rank, line and file forever more
  Shall dream of glory proud,
While floats the flag they carried far,
  And gathered for a shroud."

About the time of our capture by the enemy General
Grant, with the approval of Secretary Stanton and President
Lincoln, issued an order stopping the exchange of all prisoners of war. The stated reason for this order was that
the healthy, fat and well-fed rebel soldier on being released
was immediately capable of active service in the rebel ranks,
while the starved, diseased and dying Union soldier received
in exchange for him, had to be sent to the hospital either to
die or to recover only after months of careful nursing and
treatment.

This heartless and cruel order consigned the thousands
of brave defenders of the Union, who had been captured in
the forefront of battle, to a lingering and ignominious death.
The rebel authorities, through malignity and revenge, and
for the purpose of weakening the Union army, instantly redoubled their infamous efforts at starvation, especially as the
United States government, having seemingly abandoned
its captive soldiers to their fate, neither protested nor retaliated upon the enemy in an effort to protect its hapless defenders in the just rights accorded prisoners of war under
the international law. In so far as making no effort by a
just and lawful retaliation upon the enemy to enforce the
proper treatment of prisoners of war, the United States
authorities were particeps criminis in the most inhumane,

terrible and barbarous act that ever disgraced the pages of ancient or modern history.

As the admitted treacherous acts of General McClelland, as discussed by the rebels in my presence in the Soldiers' Retreat at Richmond, while I was a supposed comrade, are amply borne out by the facts of truthful, unprejudiced history. I firmly believe them to be true and reliable. Therefore, "I have written the things I see, the things that have been and always shall be true, conscious of right, nor fearing wrong."

www.ingramcontent.com/pod-product-compliance
Lightning Source LLC
Chambersburg PA
CBHW030115030726
47498CB00007B/2392